To Jill an

with happy memories
of Carisbrooke.

Deadly Nevergreen

L. J. Clayton

L. J. Clayton

Prosochi

First Edition Published 2012 by Prosochi,
an imprint of Endaxi Press, Unit 11, Concord House, Main Avenue,
Bridgend, CF31 2AG

www.endaxipress.com

ISBN 978-1-907375-77-4

1 3 5 7 9 10 8 6 4 2

British Library Cataloguing in Publication Data.
A catalogue record for this book is available from the British Library

Typeset by ReallyLoveYourBook Bridgend, South Wales.

Printed by Lightning Source, Milton Keynes.

Foreword

by Jake Barton, best selling crime & thriller author.

This is one of those rare books that starts off like a house on fire and the pace never slackens.

Set in the close communities of the Isle of Wight the book is often gruesome and almost all the people the reader meets are representative of a world most of us would rather not talk about: sink estate dwellers with questionable morality and poverty of outlook.

Deadly Nevergreen is a brave book; an honest book, and the author's ability is evident at every stage: drawing together the strands of plot and a host of, mainly unlikeable, characters. Don't read this and expect to be uplifted. It has a visceral quality about it that guarantees fascination even for those to whom the content is an alien landscape. I've met enough characters depicted in the pages to vouch for the writer's skill at bringing them so vividly to the page.

I devoured this beautifully composed peek into the

sordid mindset of the underclass at a sitting. There's a morality here, amongst the murder and mayhem, along with humour, vivid imagery and damn fine storytelling.

I strongly recommend this book. Congratulations – this is a hugely impressive debut.

I dedicate this book to my mother

One

If you're ever on the Isle of Wight and find yourself in the village of Wilfridstone, have a look at the ship's figurehead over the door of the museum, because it's the double of Naomi Long. That rough-hewn quality of nose and cheeks, the jutting neck, the hair in a stiff little pigtail – they're all Naomi to the life. Give the figurehead legs and it could do no other but walk like her – a long stride causing a slight stoop. And with that bold look into the future it would be completely at home at Naomi's spiritualist sessions, which was where she was driving to now.

Along the lane where a bunch of flowers was always tied to the same tree; over the downs as the sun sank behind the white cliffs and turned them black; then through the village where the sign *Twenty's Plenty!* made her put her foot down and do seventy all the way to Ryde. Here she parked her Morris Minor in a back street of shabby Victorian houses and knocked on the door of the shabbiest of the lot. It was opened by a little hunchbacked man.

"Good evening, Miss Long. You're a bit late

tonight."

"Evening, Mr MacArthur. Yes, I'm one of the last, I expect?"

"No rush, no rush, my sister won't start without you. Straight up at the top of the stairs, as usual."

With agility belying her age, sixty-five in a few days' time, Naomi galloped up several flights of dusty staircase till she came to what had once been a bedroom and was now the Spiritualist Chapel of the Anointed.

It didn't look much like a chapel. True, there was a wooden cross on the mantelpiece, and an upright chair on a small dais somehow suggesting the prospect of sermons. But with its pink velvet curtains and cabbage rose wallpaper the chapel could have become a bedroom again at a moment's notice. And unlike more conventional places of worship, it was packed with people. Row after row of them, mostly elderly and mostly female, sat on an assortment of old dining chairs and amid desultory chat, stared with a mixture of impatience and longing at the empty seat on the dais.

With her figurehead's eyes Naomi had no choice but to stare too, glossy brown irises swivelling like coloured swirls in marbles as she searched for Dougie Benson's fat face. There he was, on the back row, and taking up with his great behind what Naomi considered more than his fair share of room. He ran the newsagent's shop in her village, and along with an extensive choice of pornography offered a sideline of fairy weathervanes he made in his garden shed. But it wasn't the thought of these, or even the pornography, that made Naomi fizz with excitement.

"Saw your wife and her boyfriend slinking down to

the beach last night," she whispered as she squeezed herself in beside him. "A bit chilly for dropping your panties but she did it in a trice. Mind you, the ends of her tits were puckered and that's often a sign of feeling cold, isn't it? Standing right out they were, like stalks on the ends of marrows."

Though Dougie was flabby, he had namby-pamby hands and Naomi knew he'd heard her when they twitched. Itching to get hold of his wife, no doubt. What a beating he'd give that wife tonight! She hoped she'd be awake to hear it. She was thinking about opening her bedroom window as soon as she got home to let the sound carry better, when the tap of a walking stick on the wooden floorboards made her sit up and look as blameless as she knew how. The medium, Emily MacArthur, had entered the room.

There was no getting away from it – in Naomi's eyes Emily would have cut a more impressive figure if she'd worn big earrings and a kaftan instead of slippers and a peach twinset. And how could you feel you were getting your money's worth when the old dear hadn't even the sense to charge for her services? Still, Naomi waved and beamed encouragement to her as she hobbled in and tottered to her seat. But when the medium sprang up suddenly in the manner of someone who's sat on a drawing pin (making several other people jump too from surprise), Naomi had to suck in her cheeks to avoid giggling out loud.

Craning forward as if listening for mice in the skirting board Emily demanded, "Who's Brenda? Come on, speak up now dears. I've a Brenda, or is it a Glenda, with me? In the spirit. Used to complain of a pain here."

In apparent agony she clutched and struck at her head while gazing blandly at the opposite wall.

"It's my sister," said a woman, her lower lip quivering. "Our Glenda. She died of a brain tumour."

"Careful of the steps, she says. Danger. Are there stairs where you live now? No? Then it's the house that's to come. Watch those stairs, Glenda says, and go in peace. Who's Jeff?" Listening for mice again. "In the spirit ... liked doing jigsaw puzzles."

Other people's messages bored Naomi almost as much as their fucking jigsaws. To divert herself she was staring at Dougie and smirking every time he twitched, when the sound of crying made her lunge forward and peer between the heads in front of her. No mistaking that long blonde hair – it was that snooty ballet teacher, Verity Shaw.

"You recognise the Ellen I have with me in the spirit?" asked Emily as she scrutinised the pelmet.

"Yes," cried Verity. "It's Mummy. Mummy."

"She passed over very recently, didn't she?"

"Three months ago."

"She wants you to know she's happy. Were you on the stage? Yes, it made her proud. Never do wrong, she says. Do you understand? Speak up, if you will, pet."

"Yes. I understand."

"Talk to her. When you find yourself losing strength, talk to her and she will guide you. No more weakness. Go in peace."

Naomi found this very weird. She worked in the post office at Newport and only last Thursday Verity Shaw had been in to cash her mother's pension. Yet tonight she claimed her mother had been dead for three months. Naomi thought about it. She thought so hard she almost missed her own message.

"Don't go to town? Don't go to Down? Are you planning a trip to Ireland?"

Annoyed at the distraction, Naomi said she wasn't.

"Yes, Down. It's definitely Down. They want you to avoid the place. Not alone, they say. Goodness, they're most clamorous about it. All right," flapping a hand to swat away the dead, "don't all speak at once. Never go to Down alone, they say. Respect the spirit world's wisdom and go in peace."

Bollocks, thought Naomi. *County Down, of all places, full of IRA dickheads.* She had no intention of setting foot in it in her entire life. But she intended without delay to delve into the affairs of Verity Shaw. At the end of the service she got up, managing as she did so to thump the back of Dougie's neck with her bag, and forced her way through the chairs to the front row.

"Verity, petal." She bent down and brought her face so close that Verity became a Cyclops with one big blue eye. "Are you all right, sugar plum? I've got my car here. Would you like a lift home, sweetheart?"

Verity covered her nose with her hanky and blew it like a trumpet. "It's, er, Ruth, isn't it? Oh, no – Naomi – that's right. It's very kind of you, but I live in Maryford. Too far out of your way. Please don't worry, I'm used to the bus journey."

"Rubbish." Naomi grasped hold of her arm and half-pulled her from her chair. "I enjoy driving at night. Are you ready? Shall we get going?"

Verity glanced round with as much desperation as a kidnap victim. "Actually, I was hoping to have a few words with that wonderful woman. Thank her, you know."

"What wonderful woman? Oh, Emily, you mean, too late for that, cherub, she's out of it, look. Be out of it for hours. Come on."

With a waggling of the fingers she chivvied Verity to the door and drove her downstairs like a collie driving sheep, the clatter of her feet and the bark of her voice spilling into the street and evaporating into the night.

A rattle of teacups came up from the kitchen. A kettle whistled and was silenced. Mr MacArthur put his head round the chapel door.

"Supper's ready, Emily."

Emily opened her eyes and blinked. She fumbled for her stick and forced herself to her feet. Then she stood rigid as if playing a game of statues.

"Those two women who've just gone, Bert – were they the last to leave?"

"Naomi and her pretty friend, you mean?" Mr MacArthur straightened the chairs Naomi had pushed awry. "Yes, they were the last."

"Are you certain? You saw no one behind them?"

"No one, my dear. All the others had gone."

"Then it's as I thought." She grasped Bert's hand and limped from the dais. "Death's travelling with them. I didn't recognise him at first. I saw him catch them up at the head of the stairs."

"Oh, Death, yes." Mr MacArthur switched off the lights. "He was in quite a hurry. I had to stand aside and let him pass."

Two

The night was black as only a country night can be. Stars forever hidden to town dwellers crowded the sky and the moon, a pearl in a mourning brooch, cast its gleam on the weatherboarded tower of a solitary church as if it were the ghost it grieved for. The car headlights shone on a few feet of hedgerow, at one point catching a hare in their beam, its hind legs like elbows and its ears flattened as it ran along the edge of a ditch.

But Verity, dreaming of a past in which the dead lived, saw none of it. Like Lady Macbeth, she looked with eyes whose sense was shut. So when Naomi leant towards her and yelled, "Boo!" two inches from her ear, she came back to the present with such a jolt she almost hit her head on the roof.

Naomi hooted with laughter. "Miles away, weren't you? Thinking about that meeting, I bet. First time, was it? Well, don't you worry. We'll go together from now on. In fact, we'll make a night of it. Yes, why not?" she demanded as though an imaginary presence had contradicted her. "Meeting first and a few drinkies after at my cottage. Quite a few drinkies. Lots of drinkies. Oh, I really like the sound of that."

With a whoop that made the car reverberate she reached out and gave Verity's knee a bruising squeeze. "Mind you, I've got to sort out an itsy-bitsy problem first. Wouldn't be fair if I didn't."

"Problem?" Verity swallowed to try to get rid of the *Boo!* which still rang in her ears. "What problem is that?"

"The problem of the pension, sweetheart."

Nothing like a shock for getting rid of the ringing. Except it sounded like a curse. The pension, her mother's pension – she'd forgotten that last week this dreadful woman had cashed it for her. And now Naomi knew her mother was dead. She felt something sink inside her as something else rose up and hammered in her throat to be free.

"Oh, what's the matter, petal? Feeling a bit unwell?" Naomi peered into her face while the car, as though seeing its chance, made a desperate lunge for the dead drop of the valley. "I tell you what, let's stop for a while, eh?"

She turned down a gravelled track. It might have been the entrance to a farm though there was no sign of one, only the silhouette of the earth crouched against the sky. The car crunched to a halt.

"Open your window and get some air. No, hang on, let Auntie Naomi do it."

She leaned across Verity and gave her a whiff of unwashed clothes. "There, that's better, isn't it? Soon be okey doke. Now what are you hiding that lovely face for?"

Verity could hardly confess it was the smell that made her turn to the open window. "I feel utterly ashamed.

"Little silly, let me give you a nice cuddle."

It was like falling into in a doss-house laundry basket. The smell pumped out as from a bellows whenever Naomi lifted a hand to stroke her hair.

"You don't think you're the first to have cashed a pension when you shouldn't, do you? Come across it hundreds of times, I have. And some of the people…well, you'd never fucking – oops – flipping believe it of them. But I bet you were driven to it, weren't you? Yes, I thought so. What's that saying – something like find the cause before you throw the first stone? Well, that's Auntie Naomi's motto."

In disbelief Verity felt the stroking slip to her breast. It was as alarming as waking up and seeing a stranger standing over you. Was she imagining it? She didn't want to imply Naomi was a lesbian if she wasn't in case she was the type to be offended by the suggestion. And if she was a lesbian, she didn't want to over-react because if you thought about it, there was no other way for the older woman to make her feelings known – a bit like the Masons with their secret handshake. But if you didn't return the handshake it meant you weren't one. So she'd ignore the fondling and hope it gave the right signals.

"Let him who is without sin amongst you cast the first stone," Verity quoted and as if inspired by religious fervour drew away; nothing like the Bible for raising the tone. "It's a wonderful motto, Naomi, and it does you credit. But it also tells us to sin no more. And I shan't. I promise you, I'll never cash the pension again." She gave what she hoped was a conciliatory smile and glanced at her watch. "Goodness, is that the time? Would you mind if we set off now? I'm feeling much better and my daughter will be wondering what's happened to me."

"Yes, it's never too late to mend, as they say. Tempted beyond endurance you were, I expect." She eyed Verity's breasts as if she herself were tempted beyond endurance and considered it part of Verity's penance to yield. "Come on, tell Auntie Naomi all about it. Get it off your chest."

If a man had refused to take her home, Verity would have been terrified. She wasn't that, exactly, but she felt increasingly uneasy. She knew she ought to tell Naomi to mind her own business and start the car immediately. But there was no doubt about it – years of domestic abuse had made her a thoroughgoing coward. She could no more stand up to a confrontation with Naomi if it came to one than she had stood up to Ophelia. But at least she could run away from Naomi. Except that at the moment the dark frightened her even more. She looked out at it. Not a light anywhere. To make matters worse, she had a feeling they were close to Michael Morey's tump – an old burial mound that used to be the site of a gibbet. Things would need to get very unpleasant with Naomi for that to be preferable. The key was not to antagonize her. If you found yourself with a rapist (not that Naomi was one), you didn't tell him to keep his hands to himself, you tried to distract him through talk. A bit like Scheherazade. So she must seem to confide in Naomi, win her sympathy. Surely as an actress she could do that. *So, speak, and get it over with.*

"To begin with, I must stress that I never planned to steal the pension. The first time was an innocent mistake."

"A mistake?" *Bad start.* Naomi's coarse laugh, in spite of her motto, gave a glimpse of something far from forgiving. "If you knew the number of times I've been told that…"

"But it *was* a mistake." Infuriating to have one's honesty doubted in the sole instance where it was genuine. "Mummy had been dead only two days. I was so demented with grief I didn't know what I was doing. I cashed the pension automatically, as I'd done for years. It wasn't until I was half way home that it dawned on me what I'd done. I ran back to the post office but it was closed. I could see a light inside, though, and I hammered on the door non-stop until it opened. Unfortunately, it was only the cleaner, and she was cross at first, but to explain to anyone took a weight off my mind. And I must say, she was very understanding."

"Understanding?" Naomi paused in the bored act of picking something out of a back tooth. "And who, may I ask, gave Shirley Broughton leave to be understanding? *Understanding?*" She turned a look on Verity which made Michael Morey's tump seem inviting. "Who said presumptuous cows of cleaners should go around understanding people? I could be wrong, I may not have *understood*, but I don't think anybody ever said it, do you?"

That was the thing about the mad – you never knew what could set them off. Verity tried to be unobtrusive as she fumbled behind her for the door handle.

"I'm sure she didn't mean to be presumptuous. I remember her saying you especially would be kind. She said you'd realise it was the fault of those swipe-card things and that if we'd still had the old pension books that needed to be signed, it could never have happened."

The suddenness of Naomi's good mood was as unnerving as her bad one, merely reinforcing the likelihood of insanity. She grabbed Verity's hand and bounced it off her thigh in a friendly smacking.

"Of course I'd have realised. But you didn't give me the chance, did you, you naughty, saucy girl? Kept on quietly cashing it didn't you, you cheeky, sexy, pretty minx?

Ooh, just like Goldilocks, you are, with those lovely long curls. Come here, have a nice kiss."

Vile to be kissed by her. Verity offered her cheek as Naomi made for her mouth and ended up being kissed on the chin. She jabbered like someone demented.

"You must let me tell you all about it. Yes, I owe you that. But let's go home and discuss it over coffee. I'm dying for a cup."

"Sod coffee. And come away from the door, you'll fall out in a minute. Lean against me and snuggle in. Now, spill the beans, I'm all ears."

Verity snuggled and tried to hold her breath. "After I'd been to the post office I walked home to Maryford. Mummy's funeral was on the following day and I wanted to prepare a buffet in case people came back to the house. So I popped into the Co-Op to do some shopping. But when I went to pay, I found I had no money. In front of a packed shop I opened my purse and it was empty. I knew at once what had happened – Ophelia was stealing from me again."

"Ophelia – that's your daughter, is it? And she nicks your money?"

"I'm afraid that's the least of her misdemeanours, though probably the most inconvenient. All I can say is, it seemed like providence that I still had the pension. Almost as if Mummy were helping me. It meant I could pay for her little buffet. I fully intended to make it up from my ballet class money next day. Then I remembered – there was no class. I'd cancelled it because of Mummy's death. I'd have no money until my next class the following week."

It seemed she had got Naomi's attention with this. The stroking was definitely distracted.

"Why didn't you pay for the shopping by credit card?"

"Credit card? I don't earn enough for a credit card. But I can imagine what would happen if I did, and Ophelia found it. She finds my class money and takes it every week, no matter where I hide it. This week she even found it when I hid it in my umbrella. If I complain about it, she hits me." Why should putting it into words make her want to cry, she never cried when it happened? "I suppose the solution would be for my pupils to pay by cheque. But they haven't much money and like to pay cash for lessons when they can afford them." She closed her eyes. She was exhausted. "Well, there you have it, Naomi – that's why I kept on cashing the pension. I knew I'd never manage to repay that first week's money, so I thought I may as well be hung for a sheep as a lamb. It meant I could at least pay my bills at the post office as soon as I got it, and Ophelia would never know."

She jumped as Naomi licked her ear, then tried to turn it into surprise at her thoughts.

"I've just remembered – tonight Mummy said I must do what is right. And I will. I'm going to get in touch with the social security tomorrow and tell them what I've done. I'm going to pay back every penny." She took hold of Naomi's hand as it fiddled with her hair. "Please, let's get out of this terrible place and go home. Come and have a spot of supper with me. And don't worry. You won't be put in a difficult position. I'm going to own up first thing tomorrow morning."

With a doggy-eyed look of devotion Naomi brought the lock of hair to her lips. Then she nudged Verity aside with her elbow and started the car.

"Yes, let's get going, I'm desperate for a piss. Oops,

beg pardon, wee-wee, I should have said."

Like a hyperactive child at the wheel, she tore along haunted Burnt House Lane, laughing as she blared the horn at blind corners and giving Verity gleeful looks. They arrived at Maryford in a time worthy of the Guinness Book of Records.

Verity lived on a small council estate built in the 1930s. Most of the houses except hers were now privately owned. Here, her parents had lived all their married life and here, forty-two years ago Verity had been born. So many years, yet very little about the house had changed.

The two lilac trees her father had planted as saplings merged their branches over the gate. Beds of dahlias and late hollyhocks, which appeared every season, lined the path to the front door. In the face of such respectability it was impossible to believe deafening rap music was coming from these open windows.

"Oh, dear, Ophelia's home," she said as she rummaged for her key. "Still, I'm sure she'll turn her music off. Come in, won't you?"

The living room looked more like a country cottage of a hundred years ago than a council house. There were several parchment-shaded lamps with hunting scenes on them. Watercolours of English landscapes hung on the walls and the sofa had chintz loose covers and embroidered cushions. A piano stood in a corner and in the middle of a pembroke table was a large blue and white bowl of pot-pourri. But its perfume was over-powered by the stink of pizza and garlic bread, chewed chunks of which decorated the arms and seats of chairs.

A dark-haired girl of about twelve, lay on her back on the hearthrug next to an overturned can of coke. She jerked her hands in time to the music. A frowsty, gangly man perhaps in his early twenties sprawled along the sofa and shook his bare feet, the smell of them mingling with the smell of garlic.

Verity gave a nervous laugh. "Goodness, let's have that racket turned down a bit. There, that's better. Now at least we can hear ourselves speak. Naomi, I'd like you to meet my daughter, Ophelia." She indicated the girl, who stared at the ceiling. "And this is Darren Frost, Ophelia's friend…just a friend," she added, catching Naomi's knowing look, "a family friend, really. Put your legs down, would you Darren, then we can all have a seat? Now, everyone, what would you like – coffee, tea, fruit juice?"

Naomi asked for tea with three good sugars if it was a mug, but Ophelia and Darren refused her polite offer as if repulsing a beggar who has repeatedly asked for money. Verity pretended not to notice their unpleasant attitude and hurried to the kitchen.

On the table sodden tea bags leaked stewed tea, looking like little animals lying in brown blood. Ophelia and Darren must have had ten cups each, in a different mug every time. But to Verity the kitchen was as much a sanctuary as a church to the pursued. She scrubbed at the ear Naomi had licked and, while the kettle boiled, listened to all three of them shrieking and laughing and getting on like a house on fire. Now she was safe, she regretted not having been more assertive. But after tonight she need never set eyes on Naomi again. They must hold spiritualist meetings on other nights. She'd find out. She was desperate to shut herself in her room and talk to her mother. Before, she'd only *hoped* she heard her, now she *knew*. Not to be afraid of death, to know there *was* no death, made life a piece of cake. Speaking of which, she wouldn't give that awful woman supper. A few biscuits would do. She threw some custard creams onto a plate, picked up the tray and carried it into the living room. Naomi broke off mid-guffaw and stared at her.

"I knew I meant to ask you something. Did I hear it said tonight that you used to be on the stage?"

It was as if she knew the subject could drive Ophelia to a frenzy. Verity noticed Ophelia already had the sulky chimpanzee look she always got just before throwing a tantrum. Trying to avoid the inevitable she did her best at playing it down. "That's all over," she said.

Naomi rolled her eyes. "Well, I know that, don't I? But what were you? An extra or whatever you call them?" She looked as if she thought even that improbable.

The dismissive gesture made Verity furious. Old bitch, who'd never done anything with her life except stand behind a counter. She'd had enough of her. "I was a dancer." She remembered to stand like one, looking down as if she was of a different, higher species. "And an actress. I was once lucky enough to do Shakespeare."

"Well I never! A far cry from teaching ballet to council house kids, isn't it?"

"Unfortunately we all have to come down to earth at some point." She'd had her moment and could sense Ophelia getting restive. "Now, shall we talk about something else?"

"Never on the TV though, were you?"

Verity sighed to show Ophelia she took no pleasure in the conversation and was continuing only out of politeness. "On the contrary. I was on it many times."

"Go on! Will I have seen you in anything? Ever been

in Eastenders?"

"No. Brookside – I did a few episodes of that."

"Get away with you! Anything else?"

"Oh, a Sunday serial, various plays, a…"

She'd gone too far. Would she never learn? Darren gave a high-pitched giggle as Ophelia jumped up and brought her fist down on the top of Verity's head. Darren shook his foot as if trying to shake it off.

"Fucking shut it, will you?" The girl thrust her face into Verity's, which was red with embarrassment and the effort of not crying. "You've fucking ruined my life with your acting. Going off and leaving me for weeks on end with Gran. I notice you didn't say you gave it up for me. Well, I'm telling you for the last time, I don't want to hear about fucking acting, *ever*. OK?"

She flopped back on the sofa and slipped an arm through Darren's. He stared at Verity with his mouth open and jiggled his knee.

Naomi shook too, but from silent, side splitting laughter.

"Well," she announced when she was in control of herself, "I'd best be off. But I'll just get something settled before I go, Verity. Tomorrow's the day you cash your mother's pension, isn't it? Yes," she said as Ophelia looked at her darkly from the corner of her eyes, "been robbing the taxpayer, your mother has. That's me, the taxpayer. It's my money. So you can give it back to me from now on when you cash it, Verity. And no confessions to the social security, thank you very much. Come to my counter and pass your wallet over and I'll pretend to put the money in it. If you don't, I'll report that kid of yours and that paedo there to the powers that be. And I think we all know what that means."

Darren looked hurt at this description of himself and Ophelia, perhaps thinking it time she punched Naomi's head, jumped up again. But Naomi jutted out her long neck and glared.

"Try it and I'll blind you."

Ophelia sat down.

"Not going to school, are you? And having under-age shagging with that stinking skeleton. Do you know what'll happen if I send the authorities round here? They'll put Shakin' Stevens there in prison and you into care. You'll be a druggie and have to go on the game to get a fix. You're thick enough to find that cool, eh? Yes, thick as pig shit. That's why it'll happen to you. AIDS – that's what you'll die of. Or maybe a psycho'll torture you to death." She smiled, feet shuffling in excitement at the thought of what could be in store for the girl. Then she pulled herself together with a shiver of pleasure.

"Right, I think that's about all. Time for my beddie-byes. Nightie-night. Oh, and make sure you're in before my lunch break, Verity, because tomorrow's my half day. Bye, all."

The door slammed behind her. At the sound of water splashing on earth, Ophelia dashed to the window and pulled back the curtain.

"Christ, Darren, come and have a look at this. The filthy old hag's only pissing in the garden."

Three

Naomi Long had many peculiarities but one that disconcerted those who lived near her was her habit of moving around her house at night without switching on the lights.

A neighbour might be at their cottage window perhaps, relaxing at the end of a long day, when they'd see her with her characteristic loping walk coming home. They'd hear her door close and of course wait for lights to be switched on. But the lights never were. Though weird, they'd have forgotten about it and be thinking of something else when the hair on the back of their neck would rise – at a window a grey shape would drift across the blackness and they'd realise she was walking about inside like a spectre.

She lived at Holly Cottage in the village of Athercombe. Thirty years ago her parents had retired here from Wolverhampton and, never a night away from them since birth, Naomi had come with them.

The cottage, once the meeting place for smugglers, was three hundred years old. Legend had it that in the reign of George III a woman was tortured to death in its kitchen for betraying the bulk of their number to the excise man.

A yew hedge as thick as the walls of a church enclosed its garden and wisteria grew over its windows like drooping eyelids. But the holly that had given the cottage its name no longer stood in the middle of the lawn. Naomi and her parents had never been ones for trees, untidy objects, keeping out light. Not long after their arrival they chopped it down and balanced a pretend wishing well on its stump. Next, the small orchard at the back was dispatched for a 'paved area'. The wisteria and the yew hedge escaped only because both parents, perhaps worn out by their improvements, died suddenly within a month of each other. From that moment nature ran riot. And Naomi, always lazy, lived alone in the cottage, quite content.

Inside was a smell of clogged fat. The stone kitchen floor shone with trodden-in food and grease. The furniture in the sitting room was reproduction and enormous, like Spanish galleons at full sail with cobwebs for rigging. The bedrooms on the other hand, had the second-hand look of a student let. Rickety quilted headboards left smudges where they tapped on the wall in the night and old nylon bedspreads, full of static, clung like thistles.

It was Sunday afternoon and Naomi had been having a nap. She got out of bed just as the wall-mounted clock in the hall chimed three. She'd slept for an hour, fully clothed. Humming tunelessly she went downstairs to make a cup of tea. As the clock chimed the half hour she packed an old Polaroid camera and binoculars into a haversack, put on a green padded coat, tied a green scarf round her head, flung the haversack over her shoulder and strode from the house.

A walk across a field followed by a steep climb through woods, brought her to the start of St Catherine's Down. Leaden clouds sailed inland, though the sea from this height hardly seemed to move at all. Eight hundred feet beneath was Athercombe Bay – the Bay of Death.

Her destination was the Pepperpot, a lighthouse built in 1328. Like a burnt-out space-rocket it loomed over the drowned it had failed to save and who were now lying in Athercombe churchyard far below. Inside was a single chamber about four feet in width – enough room for a copulating couple.

Climbing toward it, Naomi spotted a lone car, tiny from this height, travelling along the coastal road. It stopped at the Viewpoint, a small car park only large enough for two or three cars, overlooking the sea. Through binoculars she watched as a man and a woman got out.

They crossed the road to a stile at the foot of the downs. The woman, who wore high-heeled boots and a short skirt, climbed it awkwardly. The man steadied her and they laughed then strolled up the flint-strewn hill stopping every now and then to kiss.

Naomi hurried on to the lighthouse. It was built on a Neolithic graveyard and one of the old burial mounds had half collapsed like an unsuccessful Yorkshire pudding. In her green clothes she was able to curl up obscured in its hollow and place her camera at the ready. Soon she heard voices. Dougie Benson's wife and her lover appeared to the right of the lighthouse. They were a handsome pair, both dark and tall, the woman with flowing black hair. They went inside.

Across the threshold was a wooden ledge about six inches high. Perhaps it was to keep out animals? Over it the woman hung her tiny skirt. And now the reason why she had climbed the stile so awkwardly became apparent – she wore no briefs. Her pubic hair was thick and lush and as raven as the hair on her head. The man unbuttoned her lacy shirt. Light streamed on to her breasts through the piercings in the tower's roof.

Naomi's camera whirred like a nightjar but the couple were too engrossed to notice. She examined the image which formed like magic before her eyes. The woman's face was turned away and in partial shadow. But clear as day were the long booted legs, the man's fingers in the hair, a pinnacled nipple touched by the tip of his tongue. Without doubt Dougie Benson would recognise them.

The woman cried out and Naomi listened rapt. That's how she'd sound when Dougie began to hurt her. But only when he began. He'd tie her to a chair in his workshop and use a wrench on her tits and by then she'd be screaming. Next he'd plug in his soldering iron and…she was so transported, she had to be stern with herself and deal with the matter in hand. There would be time enough later to have herself a ball. In an ecstasy of anticipation she took more photos.

At last the couple emerged from the lighthouse. Naomi ducked down and giggled into the grass. Enfolded in each other's arms they stood and looked out to sea for a few minutes. Then with a tender kiss they walked away over the brow of the hill.

Naomi, too, set off for home at a joyful trot.

Four

A few people still called him young Alec Johnstone (though he was seventy-four) to distinguish him from his late father.

He'd lived all his life at Westdown Farm. In Georgian times an ancestor had enclosed the Tudor farmhouse in a red brick facade. It stood like an abandoned doll's house on the remotest spot of the island. The land had gone, of course, sold to his neighbour. But Alec kept a few hens and allowed them the run of the garden.

Apart from his dog Shirley, he lived alone. Since the death of his wife he'd employed a cleaner on Tuesdays and Thursdays. He missed his old cleaner, Mrs Broughton, but this new one was lively. Kelly, she was called – a Londoner originally. No more than twenty-five, he'd have said, not married but with a three-year-old daughter, Jade. Well, that was normal these days, having children out of wedlock. Kelly always brought Jade with her when she came to clean. Today being Thursday, Alec was on his way to Shelbury to meet them off the bus.

Thinking to kill two birds with one stone, he put a tray of eggs for delivery to the old people's lunch club on the back seat of the car. Then promising Shirley he'd be back soon, he set off along the chalky track that served as a road on Westover Down. Along the way he stopped to let some fat black cattle stroll across and took the opportunity to look about him.

He was one of those people, rare nowadays, who love the place where they live more than anywhere else. In all seasons and weathers the down exhilarated him. On his right, like the tombstone of a giant's grave, rose the prehistoric Long Stone; on his left, five Bronze Age round barrows. Light and shadow fell in stripes on ancient terraced earthworks as a hawk hovered above the gorse with fluttering, excited wings. In the distance, between the black smudge of a wood and the blue smudge of the sea lay his destination, Shelbury. It was little more than a scattering of cottages, some thatched, with pale rounded roofs that reminded Alec of mushrooms in a meadow.

As he parked next to the churchyard wall, the landlord of the Bishop Ken pub came out to water the window boxes. He caught sight of Alec and raised his watering can in greeting.

"All right Young Alec? Coming in for a half?"

"Morning Terry. No, better not, it's my cleaner's day today. Just going to leave these eggs with Jean while I wait for the bus."

Giving Alec the thumbs-up, Terry returned to the gloom of the bar.

Alec pushed open the door of the village shop and made a bell jingle over his head.

"Morning Jean."

"Oh, morning Alec my love, brought the eggs, I see.

Just put them here for now. I'll take them through the back in a minute."

She moved aside a box of knitting patterns on the counter and in doing so jostled a box of Eccles cakes that in its turn knocked onto the floor a basket containing gigantic toy insects in lurid colours. With a skittering of paws a Jack Russell terrier appeared as from nowhere and pounced on a pink and blue spider, eyes alight and growling low as it shook the life out of it. Jean was round the other side of the counter in a flash.

"Give, Mitzi! Give! I say." She chased her down the vegetable aisle then up the aisle that held newspapers and set the stand of greeting cards spinning. "I swear Alec, she's had her eye on those things all week." She made a dart towards a bucket of cut flowers. "Give up at once, Mitzi!"

Mitzi streaked back to where she'd come from with her ears flat and the blue spider legs flying out behind her like streamers. It was Jean who gave up and watched her with her hands on her hips.

"Oh well. She'd better have it now I suppose. Sly as a box of monkeys she is." She turned to Alec a broad face flushed red and a grey corkscrew curl escaping from a hair grip above her forehead. "Look at me, all hot and bothered. Fancy a cup of tea now you're here?"

"No, thanks Jean. Just wanted to make sure you had the eggs in time."

"Yes, egg curry I'm giving them tomorrow. Cheaper than fish and makes a change. Oh, the price of fish lately, Alec, you wouldn't believe, and us on an island, too. And they're not fond of fish, old people. Like a bit of meat, they do, but the club can't afford that every day, either.

As bad as fish, it is."

If there was one thing Alec couldn't bear to think about, it was people not getting enough to eat. When celebrities sang about feeding the world, he wanted to shake them by the hand for doing so much good, and felt selfish that he'd had to be asked. Starving people in the developing world; suffering, emaciated animals; the old people in his village – he would have liked, and did his best, to feed them all. He reached for his wallet. "Here, Jean, take this for them."

"Fifty pounds? Oh, no, Alec, I couldn't take that. Goodness me, you don't think I was dropping hints, I hope? No, I couldn't take it, not when you give us the eggs so regular."

"Go on. Give them a bit of a treat. It does us all good, a bit of a treat."

With a show of reluctance Jean wedged the note between the eggs on the tray. "I tell you what, I'll pop up tomorrow night with some curry for your dinner. I'll keep a bit back specially. Ever had egg curry? You'll enjoy it. It's my own recipe."

Alec was in the middle of effusive thanks when a shadow passing over the length of the window told him the bus had arrived. With a wave over his shoulder to Jean, he hurried from the shop as much as his arthritis would allow him. Kelly and Jade stood by the car, waiting.

As usual when not doing something else, Kelly had a mobile phone to her ear. She was bony (a skeleton, in Alec's opinion), with pale opalescent skin showing blue veins. Her little nose was always pinched and pink. She never looked quite warm. Still, she looked very clean. She wore a white T-shirt, jeans in what Alec supposed was the newest fashion, and white trainers. Her mousy hair was fastened in a ponytail.

Jade, on the other hand, appeared to be in fancy dress. A wig of brown sausage curls made her head as wide as her shoulders and even at this distance her eyeshadow showed up bright blue. Her green mini-dress, tight at the bodice and flaring at the skirt, was printed with purple Celtic symbols. At the sight of Alec she pinned her arms to her sides and broke into a hopping and skipping on-the-spot dance, which looked to Alec as if she wanted to go to the loo.

"My word, who's a bobby-dazzler?" He held open the car door so that she could scramble into the back.

"It's Irish dancing tonight, innit, darling?" Kelly always spoke to Jade in a high-pitched voice. "First time, innit, Princess?"

"Wanna go now!" screamed Jade. She caught sight of Alec looking at her in the mirror, broke into peals of laughter, and drummed her feet on the back of his seat.

"Where does she go for dancing lessons?"

"Maryford." Except when she spoke to Jade, Kelly always sounded bored.

"Maryford? Do you know, I think that's where my daughter used to go for her ballet class. In the church hall?"

"Mm." She stared through the window and bit her nails.

"Yes, that's where my girl went. Pink leather ballet shoes she had and a black tutu. Used to give impromptu concerts in the sitting room. *The Little Wasp* was her party piece. And my goodness didn't her mother and I have to drop whatever we were doing? A born performer, she was."

"I took her out of ballet class." Kelly indicated Jade with a ragged thumb. "I hate the old cow what runs them."

"Old cow! Old cow!" sang Jade and kicked Alec in the kidneys. He started the car.

The hawk was hovering over the house as they returned. Alec paused to watch it while Kelly let herself in. Jade tore off her wig and swung it like a lasso as she gyrated up the path. One by one kitchen windows were flung open. Kelly was what his wife would have called a fresh air fiend.

"You park yourself," she told him when he came in, "and I'll get us a bite to eat." She bustled about like a whirlwind and the house seemed full of noise. "Coffee all right for you? And a ham sandwich? Jade, darlin, you want milk or squash?"

"Squashie! Squashie! Shake that arse!" chanted Jade and waggled her backside in a purple thong to an imaginary audience. It made Kelly giggle.

"I've just remembered," said Alec, "I've got to send an email. I'll have my lunch in the study if you don't mind, Kelly."

"Here it is, then. Give us a shout if you want anyfink."

She handed him his coffee and sandwich on a tray. He carried it into the study. Shirley, who went in terror of Jade's secret slaps, followed close behind.

A lark rose in song from the treeless down. Alec leaned back in his chair and looked out of the window. Someone appeared on top of one of the burial mounds.

He closed his eyes and thought about his daughter, praying that tonight, at last, he might dream of her. He jumped as the door flew open and hit the wall. Jade was grinning up at him, showing tiny teeth.

"A cuppah tea for yah!" she yelled.

With surprise he saw it was five o'clock. He had slept for over three hours, as deeply and dreamlessly as if he had ceased to exist.

"I done everyfink bar defrost the fridge and clean the windows," said Kelly as she handed him his tea. "I can do them on Tuesday if you like. May as well wash the nets as well and give 'em a freshen-up. Hey, you ain't eaten your sandwich. Want me to make you some toast before we go?"

"Me want toast!" Jade shouted.

"Go on with you! You've just had half a packet of biscuits. And we'll be having McDonald's tonight, after class." She rolled her eyes at Alec. "Ooh, costs me a fortune in that place, she does."

"You seem to give her everything she wants."

"Well, you do, don't you? Bet you was the same with your kids."

"I tried to…I tried to give her…"

"Oh yes, you was telling me you had a girl as well, wasn't you? What's she doing now?"

"She's dead." He felt so desolate, he might have heard of her death only minutes before.

"Dead?" Kelly sounded as if she didn't believe him. "She must have died young."

"She was thirty-six. Her mother died a year later of a broken heart."

"Yeah, I dunno what I'd do if anyfink happened to

my princess." She bent down and arranged the wig on Jade's head. "Oh, that reminds me, you don't know of a good babysitter, do you?"

"For Jade?" He looked at her squatting in front of Shirley checking from the corner of her eyes to see if he was watching. He was sure the child was planning to hurt the dog once his back was turned.

"Yeah. I gotta go to London the week after next. On Monday. Just for the day. I'll be back at night but I don't fancy trailing her on and off the tube."

"Oh, dear, I can't offer myself, because I'm expecting guests that week. In fact, I'm glad you've reminded me because I'd forgotten all about it. I won't need you for the next two weeks, so you can have a little holiday – paid, of course." With a whimper Shirley jumped up and slunk behind his chair. "But I'll do my best to find a reliable babysitter. Leave it with me, will you? If I come up with anyone, I'll let you know."

It was time for them to be taken to the bus stop. He handed Kelly the half dozen eggs he always kept for her and, to her bemusement, picked her a bunch of bronze chrysanthemums from the front garden. He was wrapping them in newspaper when he heard a familiar voice call him.

"Yoo-hoo! Evening, Alec!"

He shaded his eyes against the sun.

"Oh, Naomi, good evening. Don't often see you in this neck of the woods. Taking your constitutional?"

"Yes, it's my half day. Thought I'd be adventurous and stroll up here for a change. Bit of a long haul, mind." She rested against the fence till it creaked.

"This lady's a great walker," he said to Kelly. "Does

the monument to the Pepperpot every day in all weathers, don't you, Naomi?"

"That's my usual route. But like I say, I thought I'd vary it this afternoon. Nice to see you've got company." She scrutinised Kelly and Jade as if to commit them to memory. "Doing a bit of gardening, are you?"

"No, I'm just about to drop these two young ladies off at Shelbury. Kelly cleans for me and generally keeps me from sinking into squalor. I couldn't manage without her."

"Do you know, I could do with a bit of help myself in that department. A couple of hours a week would do. How about it, Kelly? You can fit me in, can't you? I'd pay over the going rate."

Kelly appeared to think about it. And the more she thought, the less she seemed to like it. She went purple in the face.

"Fuck off, bitch! Just fuck off, all right?"

Alec was shocked. With her head and jaw stuck out Kelly looked like an aggressive man about to attack. He took hold of her arm.

"How dare you? How dare you speak like that to this lady? And in front of your child. I'm ashamed of you."

Kelly pushed him away. She flung herself into the car and glowered at Naomi through the window. Jade climbed in beside her and glowered too. It made Naomi hoot with laughter.

"Well, what brought that on? All I did was offer her a job. Is she always like that?"

"I've never known it before." He looked towards the car as if a strange animal had jumped into it. "But I'm deeply sorry about it, Naomi. I'm going to insist she apologise. No, I can't let this pass."

Naomi pulled him back by his cardigan. "Oh, forget it and lighten up, you fussy old stick. Show a bit of tolerance, that's my motto. Anyway, they tell me cleaners are like gold dust and I wouldn't want you to find yourself without one because of me. But it's weird, isn't it? Look, she's still staring at me. Bonkers."

With a shrug she searched in her pockets for cigarettes, brought one out and lit it with satisfaction. "Well, better press on. Think I'll walk down to Hitherstone and treat myself to an early dinner at the pub. Heard very good reports about their meals."

"Yes, I can recommend them." He was distant with her, hurt at being called a fussy old stick. "Can I give you a lift? It's on the way."

"What, and get even further up Kelly's nose? No, no, I prefer the walk. If I go now, I'll get there while it's still light. Bye, Alec. Bye, Kelly." She waved and had another laughing fit as the scowl on Kelly's face deepened. With a wink to Alec she set off.

He got into the car. The arthritis in his neck made it difficult to turn his head so he looked at Kelly through the rear-view mirror.

"Would you mind telling me what all that was about?"

"Yes, I friggin' would mind, as it happens." Like all of her class she was ready and waiting for a fight, unable to let the smallest thing pass. "You took that bitch's part against me."

"Don't shout. And moderate your language. I did nothing of the kind."

"You fucking did. You said how dare I? Well, how dare you? You know nuffink about it. How dare she?"

"If I know nothing about it, tell me."

"You can fucking piss off!"

Her face and neck were so swollen, he thought she'd burst a blood vessel. On top of it all, Jade sat in the corner and screamed as if being slaughtered. With his head ringing he got out and walked along the track. It looked as if Naomi, alerted by the racket, was coming back. He called to her that everything was all right and watched with relief as she continued on her way.

"I'm sorry," Kelly sobbed when he went back to the car. "I didn't mean to shout at you, I really like you. I thought you was my friend."

"I am your friend," he lied. "Let's forget about it now, shall we?"

He realised now how he dreaded the days she came – how his house, far from being cleaned by her, seemed contaminated. No more. He'd give her notice. Not now. He'd phone her tomorrow when they were both calmer. At the thought of it, a great weight lifted from his life. But what about money? How would she manage? She'd manage. She had plenty of work. Still, to be fair maybe he should pay her a lump sum, a sort of redundancy money. He'd think about it tonight. He only hoped thinking about it wouldn't make him relent. It would be just like him.

"But you still like me, don't you?"

"Of course."

In the mirror he watched her gnaw her nails. Jade leaned back exhausted, her eyes fastened on her mother's face. But Kelly didn't notice. She stared after Naomi who, as they drove away, disappeared behind the Long Stone into the distant wood.

Five

Two years ago, while standing on the balcony of her Deptford council flat, Kelly had decided she fancied a change of scene. She'd thought of all the places outside London she'd been to and could remember only one, from when she'd been about five – a day trip with her mother and her latest lover to the Isle of Wight.

So, while her boyfriend snored, she'd crept round their tiny rooms and stuffed as many belongings as she could into the pink suitcase on wheels she'd nicked the week before from Woolwich market. Next she'd pocketed the wad of money she'd helped earn by flogging recreational drugs round the pubs of Greenwich. After fastening one-year-old Jade in a sling across her chest and without even a glance at the bloke asleep in bed she'd set off for the station and the first train to Sandown. There she'd been ever since.

Each Thursday she caught the bus to the island's main town of Newport to collect her Jobseeker's Allowance. Like the royal family, she looked on the nation keeping her as her right, her work as a cleaner being an optional extra. But given the pettiness of some people, she thought it made sense to cash her allowance in Newport where no one knew her. And until now there'd been no questions asked and never a hitch.

But since her clash with Naomi a week ago, she'd cursed not only her, but the fact that she, poor Kelly, was a bankrupt. A victim of the system, that's what she was. Why couldn't she have a bank account like everyone else? Not for saving, she didn't believe in saving, but to have her allowance paid in directly. They did that for you nowadays and it prevented old cows at the post office from sticking their nose in your business. Instead, thanks to that lousy system, she'd got caught out – literally on the job. She felt downright cheated.

Whenever she went to collect her allowance it was nearly always Naomi who served her. But would she serve her today? Maybe she'd refuse to hand over the money. Maybe she'd already reported her. Well, she couldn't prove nothing. For all Naomi knew, she might work for free. Yes, that's what she'd say if asked – that she cleaned old people's houses out of the kindness of her heart, so give me my money, you wrinkly old bitch! She screwed up her mouth ready for a fight, lifted the bewigged Jade onto her hip for moral support and swaggered into the post office.

Naomi was there, her part of the counter vacant. Kelly couldn't avoid her. But Naomi welcomed her as if they was best friends.

"It's Kelly, isn't it? Nice to see you again, petal. And this is little…what's she called? Jade, that's right. Gorgeous. Now, what can I do for you?"

Kelly handed over her card. Naomi took it without looking at it, all the time giving a stupid smile as she swiped it and counted out the money. Then she rested her chin that had a black bristle growing out of it on her hands.

"Where are you off to now? Somewhere to have lunch, eh? I bet that little one's peckish. Looks like she's got a healthy appetite with them dumpling cheeks."

"Can't fill her," said Kelly, thawing a bit. "She'll want to go to McDonald's, as usual."

Jade started screaming about Big Macs which made Naomi show big grey teeth that crossed over at the front.

"Ever been to the Quaker's House?"

Kelly frowned and wrinkled her nose. She didn't know what Naomi was on about.

"It's a restaurant in the market place. Lovely old building, it is – been there hundreds of years. That's where I go for my lunch. I tell you what, let me treat you as a friend of Mr Johnstone's. It's time for my break. Let's have lunch together. I'll pay."

Kelly thought she might as well give her that pleasure, though it didn't mean Naomi could link arms with her like they was lezzies. She gave her a nasty look for that. Only young lezzies was cool.

The Quaker's House on the corner of the cobbled market square reminded her of a picture in one of Jade's storybooks. It had those little diamond windows and was full of old furniture and old people. And the old–fashioned music coming from somewhere made her want to scream. When Naomi insisted on them sitting at a table next to the window she wished the sloping floor would swallow her up. She was sure all the young people outside were laughing at her. And worst of all, there was nothing she could eat. Nowhere on the menu was there a mention of a burger, a bacon McMuffin, or a nugget kebab. Even the word 'fries' wasn't there. She was not happy.

"I don't like nuffink."

"Bit too fancy, eh?"

"Yeah." She felt really, really, like pissed off.

"I know, how about pizza and chips? They're bound to have pizza."

Kelly gave a shrug, though inside she felt a bit better. She ordered Coke for her and Jade to drink while they waited.

"So, you help out Mr Johnstone with his cleaning?"

Oh-oh, here it came. Kelly was ready to say she didn't get paid but Naomi cut her off.

"It's a bugger to manage on just social security these days, isn't it? Especially when you've a child to bring up. There must be quite a few mothers like yourself forced to work to supplement their income. I bet the father doesn't contribute, eh?"

"Nah." It surprised Kelly, but Naomi sounded like really, really sympathetic. It made her feel a bit sorry for herself. "Nah," she said and shook her head as if a lot of thought had gone into the decision. "I don't want nuffink from him."

"Yes, I can see you're the independent type. Live alone, do you, you and the little one?"

"Course not." *What an insult. Only munters and pervs live without a man.* "I got my boyfriend. Works at the zoo, he does. Fantastic with animals."

"Oh? Is he a keeper?"

"A what?" Those pop-eyes staring at her were

getting on her nerves. She wanted to poke them.

"I mean, does he actually take care of the animals?"

"Dunno. He just sort of helps out."

"Sounds like a rewarding job. Going to marry him, are you?"

"Marry Darren?" She'd never thought of it before. But she wouldn't mind showing a garter on photos and being the centre of things for a day. She thought about it now.

Naomi took a paper serviette from a glass in the middle of the table and blew her nose on it. "I met a Darren last week. Talk about coincidence. Don't suppose it's the same one as yours, mind."

There was a bit of a pause while a fat old cow of a waitress brought their order. Naomi started straightaway to shovel in what she called Lancashire hotpot. She sprayed gravy as she spoke.

"Anyway, you were on about Darren…about marrying him…"

"Might do." Kelly speared a chip on her fork and wiped either side of her knife on the prongs several times. "Depends, don't it?"

"Depends on Jade, I suppose? Whether she'd like it or not?"

"Jade?" She wedged the chip in her mouth. 'Don't mean nuffink to her, do it?"

"Quite right. She's not going to marry him, is she? I must say, you're lucky having her for a companion."

"I know." Kelly smiled at Princess sucking tomato sauce off the cuff of her cardigan. "When I see other women with their careers, working in McDonald's and stuff, I think, I done better than you, though. I had her.

I done my bit."

"Yes, that's your contribution to the nation. An only child, is she?"

"Yeah, at least…" Careful, now. "Yeah, she is."

"Not planning anymore?"

"Not till she's going to school. Might have another then."

"Yes, one's enough at the moment, especially when you're working as well. Need to work a lot to make ends meet?"

"Work every day, don't I? I'll have to go in a bit. Got a pub in Wilfridstone to do this afternoon. Should have been at Mr Johnstone's but he's got guests this week."

"Well, if you ever need a babysitter, I'd be happy to help out. Free of charge, mind. Wouldn't dream of taking your hard-earned money. To be with the little one would be reward enough."

Kelly rested her elbows on the table and held her knife and fork on a level with her ears as if they were tuning forks. She gave Naomi a sideways glance and tried to work out if she might be a sex-offender.

"Like kids, do you?"

"Fucking adore them."

"Got none of your own?"

"Course not. I'm not married."

"You working Monday?"

"Why? Do you need someone then?"

"Yeah. I gotta go up to London. Business meeting."

"Business, eh? That sounds impressive. Am I allowed to ask what sort of business?"

"It's like charity work. I don't get no money. It's against the law. They're not allowed to pay you."

"Mysterious."

Kelly felt important. "Yeah, I won't say no more. It's in confidence."

"Don't say another word. I respect a person of principles."

"But if you happen to be doing nuffink on Monday?"

"I'll see if I can get the day off. I don't think it should be a problem. Write your phone number on this serviette. Oh, good, it's a mobile, easier to keep in touch. Better give me your address as well."

Kelly wrote it in her backward sloping writing that had capital letters in the wrong places. Naomi put the serviette in her bag and glanced at her watch.

"Bollocks! Must get back to work. It's normally my half day but I'm covering for someone this afternoon, otherwise I could have run you to your job in Wilfridstone. Anyway, stay and finish your drinks. I'll get the bill. I'll phone you tomorrow at the latest. I'll move heaven and earth to be free for this little sweetheart, won't I, treasure?"

She leaned over the table and pinched Jade's cheeks. Everyone in the restaurant clicked their tongues when Jade told her to fuck off. But old Naomi thought it was hilarious. She was still laughing when she left.

Kelly watched her go. She drank her Coke and swirled the glass lovingly as she held it in her fingers by the rim. Then she had an idea.

"Come on, sweetheart, let's go and get a Mars bar, shall us?"

Jade had cleared her plate of pizza and chips but she scurried from her chair with an excitement that touched

Kelly's heart. Her child would have something decent to eat even it meant she'd be late for work. She marched past the sweet shop towards McDonald's. Nothing but a McFlurry would do.

As they crossed the road hand in hand she did a double take at the person coming out of the paper shop. But no, it couldn't be, not in this place, and after all these years.

Six

Why is it places with the word 'seaview' in their name never get so much as a glimpse of the sea? Seaview Way, Sandown was no exception. Its only view was of the houses opposite. They had names such as Buena Vista done in wrought iron and spiky plants like daggers in gardens of pink and green squares. Some offered bed and breakfast, others were converted into holiday apartments or long lets. Kelly's flat was one of the latter, the top half of a pebble-dashed semi with a concrete drive.

It was half past six on Friday evening. In a room that reeked of happy-baccy and sweat, Kelly and Jade lay on a sofa covered with a soiled Indian bedspread. Jade sucked an ice-pop and Kelly drank a mug of tea as they watched Hollyoaks life size on a huge plasma screen.

"Darren!" Kelly shouted as the doorbell rang. "Someone at the door!"

Darren poked his head out of the bedroom. "What?"

"Doorbell." Her eyes didn't flicker from the screen. "Whoever it is, I'm not in."

Darren went to answer.

For a few seconds Kelly remained where she was. But curiosity getting the better of her, she put her tea on the floor beside the sofa and went to peep through the window. She didn't recognise the old green car parked in the drive, so she crept onto the landing and peered downstairs to see if she recognised the owner. A glimpse of Naomi in the doorway made her swear under her breath. She crouched down behind the banisters to listen.

"Well, well, if it isn't Darren Frost. I was hoping it would be. Small world, eh? Remember me, I suppose?"

Remember her? Why the fuck should Darren remember her? He didn't even know her, did he? His words, as usual, gave little away.

"What you want?"

"Just a courtesy call, sunshine – something beyond your understanding, I daresay. You're looking at Jade's new babysitter, you are. I've come to confirm dates. Didn't Kelly mention me?"

"Nah."

"Well, I *am* surprised. Still, I don't expect you told her about your date with Ophelia Shaw the other night, eh? Not a close couple, I imagine."

"Hey, don't you go say nothing about that."

Kelly noticed his knee start to jerk, the way it always did when he got worked up. Ophelia Shaw, eh? Right, he was dead. It gave her a migraine not to be able to fly downstairs now and tear his hair out. But she wanted to hear what else Naomi said.

"Have you out on your ear, would she, Kelly? I dunno, the risks some people take for nothing. Can't believe that Ophelia's much of a shag – too young to know any tricks. You should have a go with someone my age, for a change. Open your eyes, it would. Kelly in, is she? Let's go up, then."

Kelly dashed back into the lounge, flung herself on the sofa and picked up her mug of tea. She'd hardly got her breath when Naomi pushed past Darren into the room.

"All right if I come in? Not interrupting anything, I hope? I know I said I'd phone but then I thought it'd be better if I called – survey the lie of the land, in a manner of speaking." She glanced round the room. "Cosy. Wouldn't say no to a cup of tea, if there's any going."

Kelly didn't believe in being polite, she believed in doing what she felt like doing. And she felt in no mood for Naomi.

"We ain't got no fucking tea." She stared at her as if she was yet another nasty stain on the carpet.

Naomi opened her eyes to their full extent.

"Well, that's a surly attitude, I must say. What's that you've got there, if it isn't tea? Still, it's an attitude that makes my job easier. Yes, always easier to put the thumbscrews on arseholes is my motto."

She smiled in that snarky way she had but it didn't fool Kelly. Something was up and she had a feeling it was nothing to do with babysitting. She bit her nails.

"You'll know what it's about, of course – that Jobseeker's Allowance you're collecting. Always makes me laugh, that – load of mealy-mouthed crap. As if it wasn't an excuse for *not* seeking a job. Still, you've found one, so you won't be needing money for *seeking* anymore, will you? Seek and you shall find, like

Shakespeare says."

Kelly lowered her head and looked at Naomi from under her eyelids. "What you mean?"

Apart from *Jobseeker's Allowance*, she couldn't follow the rest. It used to get on her tits at school when the teachers jumbled up a load of words she couldn't understand, as if they were better than her. It got on them now and if Naomi wasn't careful she'd get a smacking like what Mrs Holmes got. But it didn't take words for her to know in her gut that Naomi would make trouble for her with the dole office. Well, you did, didn't you, if you got the chance? To try to avoid it, Kelly had already decided to move house. But she couldn't make out what Naomi was doing here, being so up-front about it and asking for a belting. A phone call to a special number where they didn't ask for your name was how Kelly had shopped people in the past. She decided Naomi must be really thick.

"You gonna report me?" she said. "That what you saying?"

"If you give me any nonsense, of course I will. But for now, I'll have the money to be going on with. You keep on cashing it but instead of putting it in your purse, you give it to me and I'll put it mine. That'll keep me sweet."

Kelly blinked. She had to think for a moment why her money should end up in Naomi's purse. Then she made sense of it. It was…kidnapping, was that it? No, the other one…blackmail.

She stood up. But Naomi must have been ready for it. A swat in the face from her bag knocked Kelly flat. While her mug of tea trickled down her neck, a storm of blows rained on her head.

"Get her off me, Darren!" she cried in a muffled voice as she hid behind her arms. "Fucking get her off me!"

She could see him in the kitchen doorway, his knee twitching fifty to the dozen. Jade had scrambled for safety to the corner of the room. The beating went on until Naomi was out of breath. Kelly saw her chest heaving.

"You've really pissed me off, do you realise that?" To show how pissed off she was, Naomi hit her again. Kelly whimpered against the sofa and rolled into a ball.

"I think you'll agree I tried to be civilised about this even though you hadn't the grace to offer me a cup of tea. It's my birthday today, and a bit of courtesy would have worked wonders. But no, cheek and violence was your answer. All right then, I'll try again. And this time fucking listen, OK?"

Kelly nodded while Darren and Jade stared with their mouths open.

"Thursday's your day at the post office, right? OK, you keep coming in as normal. You give me your card and I'll swipe it. Only I won't give you the money, get it? I'll pretend to, and you'll pretend you've got it. But I'll have it. OK? Got that, have you? I'll be running along, then."

With relief Kelly watched from under her arm as she walked to the door. She covered her head again as she walked back to the sofa.

"And don't go and let me down, will you? If I have to report you, you'll get in all sorts of trouble. Might even have Jade taken off you. Ask Darren. He knows all about it, don't you, Darren? He's shagging that Ophelia Shaw – under age she is. You want to watch that kid of yours if you ask me, or he'll be up her arse before you can say knife. Oh, and that reminds me – I won't be babysitting on Monday. Thought I'd let you know in time so you could get someone else. All consideration I am, not like some I could mention. Right, see you Thursday."

Before Kelly dared lift her head, she was off.

Seven

With what seemed like an endless source of money, Naomi regarded the world in a new light. Before, she had been parsimonious. To spend as little as possible was in her eyes an achievement. She owned no computer, no mobile phone and begrudged buying clothes more than anything. But now, everywhere she looked she spotted something she coveted. For example, she might notice the sea was like a blue opal, and would decide with her new found wealth to buy herself a ring that colour. So far it must be admitted she had bought nothing. The chief enjoyment was in anticipation. But it was extraordinary how the money mounted up. And having once given her mind to it, she realised there was no end of people she could blackmail. Her one regret was that she hadn't embarked on it years ago.

This Sunday afternoon St Catherine's Down was warm like a blanket, the hoof prints of animals baked hard as fossils by the sun. Naomi panted in the heat. She came out of the shady wood into a grassy clearing on the edge of the down. The monument to the battle of

Sebastapol loomed before her, as out of place in the loneliness as Nelson's column. She passed it every day but it never lost its menace. A monstrosity in a place so inaccessible, it seemed no human hand could have had a part in its construction. She liked to think about the men who'd built it, and to wonder from which direction they'd transported the stone. It was an effective reminder that the monument had no life of its own. As if to outface it, she leaned against its massive base and lit a cigarette. In the sparse shrubs surrounding it, magpies bounced from branch to branch in their clumsy, threatening way. Behind them the sea glinted in the light. She finished her cigarette and set off once more.

In the Viewpoint car park far below, a solitary, battered car made her think of the new one she would treat herself to – a dinky one in a pastel shade, which she'd give a name to – a woman's car. She strode along the spine of the down and cast a sly glance at the spot where a gibbet had once stood. The sheep grazing at the edge of the track trundled away from her then turned back to stare with an indignant expression.

The sun beat down. She stopped and took off her jacket, tying it round her waist by the sleeves.

The Pepperpot rose up from behind the hill like a warning finger. For the first time she wondered whether she could be bothered to walk so far. Yet in a superstitious moment it occurred to her it would be ungrateful, perhaps even unlucky, not to visit it. No need for a camera today, of course – it had done its work and earned her a tidy sum.

She had taken no more than a few steps when something moved behind her. Sheep, fleeing like a retreating army down the green terrace of an ancient earthwork. Ignoring the stupid creatures she carried on. A spark of light glanced off the weathervane of a distant church tower. A chough flew with a hoarse cry, turning its body in mid-air and flying on its back. On a far hillside rabbits dashed in and out of their warrens, and a wind surfer rode the tide of Athercombe Bay.

Why? she wondered, coming to a stop. Why had the sheep run? She looked behind. Nothing: nothing that is, that wanted to be seen.

Phobias come suddenly. Naomi's took her by surprise. For years she had exulted in this landscape that in one turn of the head had become loathsome to her. The down rolled before and behind, mile after mile. It was no longer open and reassuring. It was a place where there was nowhere to hide. She could go neither forward nor back. She could not decide in which direction danger lay. But she was certain danger was present.

With her eyes on the ground she forced herself to shuffle towards home. She hoped if she went slowly the presence would not notice her go.

She had reached a circle of gorse bushes – an odd, cultivated formation in this wild place – when it happened. A blow in the small of her back brought her to her knees. Her first thought was that she had been butted by one of the rams. She tried to scramble up but another blow sent pain through her entire body making her jaw chatter. She heard someone breathing heavily, grunting and giggling. It wasn't a ram. She was being kicked. Being kicked simultaneously in the belly and the throat.

"Don't go to Down!" yelled a voice inside her. So that was what it had meant. It was so obvious it was almost funny. But she didn't feel like laughing as a kick in the head smashed her teeth through her gums. She didn't feel like anything and she never would feel anything, ever again.

Eight

On Monday morning Kelly and Jade caught the train that stops at the end of Ryde pier for the passenger ferry to Portsmouth. In a fawn trouser suit and with her hair brushed out of its ponytail Kelly was attractive enough to make the men in the ferry bar look at her twice. It was the women who looked twice at Jade. With her black velvet coat, black velvet hat, white lace tights and black patent shoes she looked like a Victorian doll. Aware of the effect, she refused to let Kelly take her hat off even though it was as hot as midsummer. With a paper napkin tucked into her neck, she demolished a sausage roll, a bag of prawn cocktail crisps, a fizzy drink, a tube of Smarties, and a lolly like a gobstopper on a stick. Before the half hour journey was at an end she announced, "Ah gottah pain in ma belly!" and was rushed to the loo.

On the train to London Kelly sulked. She'd lost her mobile on the ferry. As if expecting to get stranded in the Sahara, she'd had a bottle of water in one hand and her phone in the other, thumb at the ready to caress it into life. Then Jade had got the runs. Kelly had slipped the phone into her pocket and in the ensuing scuffle it had fallen out. Now she glared through the window and bit her nails.

At twelve o'clock the train drew into Waterloo. A light drizzle fell. At Waterloo East they caught the Deptford train. It travelled along a viaduct higher than the chimney pots and looked down on streets strewn with rubbish. The wares of a flea market were spread out on the pavement along with the litter, and indistinguishable from garbage in the gutter. A high-rise block, where Kelly had been born, came into view. She pointed at it through the window.

"Wave to Nanny, sweetheart."

"Where? Where is she?" Jade was so intent on seeing her they almost missed the stop.

From the station a short walk through a stinking underpass brought them to the building's stinking lift. For once in working order, it took them to the stinking walkway of the third floor.

"There's Nan's door, darling. Run and knock."

A middle-aged woman opened the apartment door. At the sight of Jade she flung out her arms and squealed. Nan's belly and tongue were pierced and around her neck was a chain from which hung the name 'Liz' in chunky golden letters.

"Why didn't you ring me, Kell?" (She'd already spoken to her three times that morning.) "I been trying to get you since before eleven."

"I lost my fucking phone, Mum."

"Silly bitch. Isn't she a silly bitch, Jadey, my princess? Come and let Nan see how beautiful you are."

A dog howled on the balcony. She screamed at it to

shut up then turned back to Jade.

"She…is…gorgeous." She separated the words for greater emphasis. "Oh, leave her with me when you go out, Kell. Go on. You'd like to stay with Nan, wouldn't you, diamond?"

"Nah, Mum." Kelly flung herself into an armchair. "I been thinking – it's a good thing I had to bring her with me. She's a good advert for me. When they see her they'll be impressed."

Nan had to admit the sense of this. She held out her hand to Jade and led her into the kitchen.

Kelly looked round at her old home. She had left at fifteen when Mum had moved her new boyfriend in. Deciding it wasn't 'proper' for Kelly to stay under the same roof Liz had thrown her out, forcing social services to rehouse the teenager. It had seen quite a few changes since then. It was in minimalist or empty mode at the moment, with laminate floor like cinder toffee, plasma screen television and a black leather suite.

"Ooh, you've had them spotlights put in the ceiling, Mum."

"Yeah, had 'em done a couple of week back."

"They look great."

"Yeah."

Again the dog on the balcony howled.

"Shut up," yelled Kelly.

Jade scurried out of the kitchen and screeched through the window, "Shurrup! Shurrup! Shurrup! "

"You tell him, darling," Nan called. "I'll fucking fling him over the balcony the next time he starts."

Jade thought about this, seemed to decide it would be an amusing spectacle, and broke into peals of laughter.

"I dunno what you wanted a dog for," said Kelly. "Why don't you give it to that old woman what feeds them frigging pigeons? She's cracked about animals, she is."

"Ooh, I can't." Nan came in, drying her hands. "She got murdered the other night. I knew I had something to tell you."

"Who done it?" Kelly ceased to lounge all of a sudden and looked quite alert.

"It was four of them. Do you remember Stacey Conway? Well, it was her, and her little brother – they can't touch him for it, poor little mite, he's only nine – and Stacey's mother's boyfriend – West Indian, he is – and another girl. And there's been police and social workers crawling all over the place, coz they tortured her first – tried to scalp her, and a few other things, before they strangled her."

Kelly listened with her mouth open.

"Now," Nan folded her arms, "they done wrong but in a way she asked for it. Stacey had a air gun to shoot the pigeons with and the old woman threatened to tell the police. Well that must have got up Stacey's nose. And there's nuffink for kids to do round here, Kell. The government don't do nuffink for them. Mind, Stacey could do all right in the end. You been watching that programme *Naughty Girls*? It's a…what do you call it…a documentary? Yeah, it's a documentary about women what's gone to prison. True, it is. Well, you seen her what murdered that pensioner? Roxiana, she's called. I love that name, that's a name you wanna think about if you have another. Well, she's getting very popular with the public. And what Stacey done's no worse, is it? And she's better looking than that Roxiana."

The microwave pinged and Nan hurried off to serve up corned beef pizza with four-cheese topping. Jade rolled up her sleeves ready for eating.

"I had a call this morning to confirm your appointment," said Nan when they were settled with their plates on their knees. "I said you'd be there at half-four. Which reminds me, I got a new phone. Gonna start using it when everyfink's settled. I thought I'd like, cover me tracks. Don't want no comeback if things doesn't work out again. Don't let me forget to give you the new number before you go. You gonna tell them about the other…you know?"

"I'm not, as it happens." Kelly looked pained. "But there's no need for me to feel guilty about it, is there?"

"Course not."

"I mean, I done nuffink Mum." She began to get watery-eyed. "And it hurts…it really, really like hurts to talk about what I went through."

"Don't do it, flower. Always remember, whatever makes you feel good must be right."

"Yeah, that's what I tell myself."

They chewed in silence for a bit. Then Kelly said, "You still with Brian, Mum?"

"Yeah." Nan laughed behind her hand. "I might be wanting rid of him soon, though. I got a date tomorrow night. Don't tell no one, will you?"

All interest, Kelly, shook her head.

"You know where Fads is? Well, there's a new bloke works there. Black, he is. Been there about a month. Anyway, I was in there last week looking for tiles for the bathroom. Ooh, they've got some lovely ones, Kell. You know that pattern – fleur de loos, do they call it? They've got some in purple. The background's sort of smoky grey. I'm gonna get some for round the bath. Purple wallpaper they've got as well, sort of marble, like. Mind, they've got it in grey. I might ask for a sample first and give 'em both a try."

"But what about this bloke, Mum?"

"Oh, yes. He was helping me look and then he asks me out – just like that. We're having a meal at that new African restaurant. The thing is," she lowered her voice and moved nearer, "he's sixteen."

"Oh, Mum."

"I know," Nan squealed and covered her face. "He don't look it, mind. I think he's an asylum seeker. But that's why I'm telling you to say nuffink. Hey, look at the time. You'd better get going if you don't want to be late. I'll get Jade ready. Come to Nan, darling. Let's put your coat on."

A car below backfired and the dog howled.

"Fucking shut it, will you?" yelled Nan.

"Throw it over! Throw it over!" danced Jade with an unpleasant light in her eye.

"I will, darling, as soon as you've gone. Why you dancing? You want the toilet? Sure? All right, now have you got everyfink? Give me a ring as soon as you get back, Kell. Phone me from one of them call boxes at the station. Oh fuck, you'll need the new number. Here, I'll write it down on this bit of paper. I wish wasn't going. Don't know why you want to be on the frigging Isle of Wight."

"Actually, I was thinking of coming back, Mum."

"Great, darling. Think about it seriously now and ring me. Bye, Jade, my gorgeous. Blow Nanny a kiss."

It was half past three. Kelly had to run through the underpass with Jade in her arms to catch the train. This time they got off at Charing Cross and walked in the drizzle down the steps to Embankment. Here they caught a District Line train to Ravenscourt Park. By the time they arrived the rain was falling in torrents. For a few minutes Kelly watched it from the station entrance, hoping it would lessen. But time getting on, she held her handbag over her head, grasped Jade's hand and made a dash for the nearby park.

Not a soul, not even a jogger, was to be seen. The rain cast a greyish light over everything, like a reflection in pewter. On the left, just inside the park gate, was a garden centre. The entrance to it was through a narrow gap in a shrubbery of laurels. They grew for about fifty yards alongside the footpath. Behind them ran the station viaduct, forming one of the park's boundary walls. It was a secret place, this grove of viaduct and shrubbery. Perhaps that was why the voice whispered.

"Kelly. Kelly, come here."

She stopped and looked.

"I'm in here."

She stared at the hooded figure. The hand that beckoned wore a yellow washing-up glove.

"Come on. I've been waiting for you for ages." It backed deeper into the foliage. "Come under the branches. It's dry in here."

"What you doing in there?" She stepped on to the earth track that ran between the viaduct and the laurels. The ground was thick with dead leaves. "What you want?"

"So many trees," cried the figure, lifting up its face in the hood. "Unending torment. It was in full living leaf, yet for my love it became the Deadly Nevergreen."

Kelly was exasperated. "What you on about? You on somefink, or what? I can't stand around listening to this. I gotta go. I'm in a hurry."

So was the figure. It made a punching movement towards her stomach. Still holding Jade's hand looked down at the blood in disbelief. It was not until she was stabbed in the chest that she fell. The last thing she saw on this earth was the knife slice Jade's throat so completely her head was more or less cut off.

Nine

The British Spiritualist Association, known to its members as the BSA, was in London's Belgrave Square in what had once been one of the finest houses in the capital. Until recently its theology was Christian with eccentric overtones but thanks to what is known as 'the youthful element', the association now treated all philosophies with equal respect. Christianity carried no more weight than Numerology or the study of biorhythms. Old-fashioned psychic gifts were still practised, however. And Emily MacArthur, the visiting medium, gave what she was liked to call *satisfaction* with her demonstration of psychometry.

It was Monday afternoon and over a hundred members were gathered in what had once been the drawing room and was now the clairaudience chamber. The stage or platform, perhaps to confound charlatans, had no curtains, only a chair in the middle where Emily sat. She wore a pink and fawn crimplene dress and a jacket in Welsh tapestry topped off with a purple velvet hat.

Bert wore his best black suit and moved among the congregation with a basket as if taking the collection in church. One by one, each member placed an object in it –

a watch, a ring, sometimes a purse. Bert then passed the basket to Emily.

With closed eyes she scrabbled in it, the movement similar to one of those little cranes at a funfair that tries to grasp a soft toy. When she caught the object she held it to her bosom and, with her head tilted to one side, rotated it in her hands the way a squirrel rotates a nut.

The influence of its owner transmitted to her spirit messages, which, while her eyelids fluttered, she pronounced upon in the odd terminology spiritualists favour yet never use in their normal conversation.

"You'll be tipped up in a five. It could be five days or five weeks but no more than five months. Tipped up, they're saying. Go in peace."

It takes energy to be the conduit for a hundred spirits, all hoping to comfort or warn a hundred relations with a few well-chosen words. At the end of it Emily was ready for a cup of tea. With Bert ahead of her, she tottered down the back staircase to the basement passing the ghost of many a chambermaid and footman going up.

The café (with bars on the window) overlooked the gardens and the elegant back windows of the houses opposite. The proximity made her feel not quite real. To find herself among the elite – perhaps a cabinet minister or a duchess – to look through their drawing room windows and maybe even wave to one of them if she caught their eye was like finding herself in a country she'd thought existed only in myth. She ate her egg and cress sandwiches with as much enjoyment as if she were at the Savoy. When Bert went up to the counter to ask for their flask to be filled for the journey and the woman behind it gave him a bag of home made scones to eat on the way, Emily's sense of belonging was complete.

"A superb afternoon," said the president as she walked them to their car. "Truly inspiring. We'd be delighted if you could give us another demonstration before Christmas. We've a space in the second week of December to fill."

"I'd like that." Emily patted the hand that linked her arm. "But I won't promise. I'm not as young as I was. And to be honest with you, Bert finds the drive heavy, don't you, Bert? But we'll see. I've enjoyed today, anyway. A real treat, it was."

"So lucky living on the Isle of Wight." The president gave an ecstatic roll of her eyes. "The most haunted place in the British Isles, such fertile ground. One of our trainees in spiritual healing is from there, as it happens. But I hope you'll be stopping off at the New Forest to pay homage to Sir Arthur?" (Unlike 'the youthful element', she didn't pronounce 'homage' with a French accent.)

"Sir Arthur?" Emily stifled a yawn that made her chin shake.

"Yes, we showed you his portrait, remember? Sir Arthur Conan Doyle, the famous author and our most illustrious president."

"Oh, yes, Sir Arthur." Emily always thought of him as Sherlock Holmes. "No, I doubt we'll stop, pet. I'm fond of his books, mind. But it's *home James and don't spare the horses* for us. But we'll tip Sir Arthur a wave as we pass. Don't you worry, he's all right. God bless you now, pet, and thanks for a lovely day."

With relief she got into the car and removed her hat. Bert put it on the back seat with her walking stick. He waited until the president had gone back into the house before taking an envelope out of his breast pocket. He handed it to his sister and started the car.

"A cheque for two-hundred pounds, Em. And fifty for expenses in cash. Makes a change to get paid, eh?"

"It does, Bert." Emily put the envelope in her bag. "Makes you feel appreciated. Mind, our regulars appreciate us even if they can't afford to show it in the same way."

"No doubt of it, Em."

"But it's come just in time, this money. We can pay the chapel electric bill now. I've been frightened to put the fire on and it gets cold up there these autumn nights."

"Yes, we'll be all right now, Em. Oh, but London's a terrible place, isn't it, when you leave the posh bit? They look like a lot of medieval peasants with those hoods on their heads. And look at him – the gusset of his trousers is round his knees. So many foreign faces, like another country, it is. I couldn't live here. But they must like us to want to live among us."

"Oh, yes, I expect so. But we're blessed where we are, Bert."

The green fields began and they were in *their* England once more, with flocks of white birds against a grey sky and herds of red cows that sauntered to an unseen milking shed. Night fell on the New Forest and the trees stood like ghosts of themselves. A wooden signpost pointed to the village where Sir Arthur lay. But Emily was asleep.

She opened her eyes as the masts of Lymington marina came into view. Bert offered her a boiled sweet.

"We're here, Em. The ferry's waiting for us. Can you make out this one's name?"

She put on her glasses. "Wight Star. Was that the one we came on?"

"No, I think that was Wight Sky, or something. Here we are, got your sea legs? Mind how you go up those stairs, now."

They sat at the fore next to the window and ate their scones with a cup of tea. The lights of Yarmouth winked in the distance and waited.

"Well, I've enjoyed today, Bert. Like a holiday, it's been. And I'm glad we came this way instead of Portsmouth. A good idea of yours, that was. Much pleasanter."

"Yes, we'll do it always now, shall we? I like to see those New Forest ponies. Oh, dear, we're nearly there, Em. I'll just make a quick dash for the toilet."

The ferry glided towards the quay next to Henry VIII's fortress. At a snail's pace, they made their way to the car, ready to disembark.

"Got your seat belt fastened, Em?"

"Yes. I'm all settled, Bert."

"Here we go, then. Well, drat it all, can you believe it? I've lost my best hat. I bet I left it in the café at the BSA. Yes, I remember, I put it on the chair beside us when we sat down for tea. What a nuisance."

"We'll phone them tomorrow and ask them to put it in the post. They were nice people, they won't mind." She brought a hand to her chest. "I'll be glad to get home. I don't know what it is, but I've come over queer all of a sudden. Oh, my goodness, Bert, someone's walked over my grave."

Ten

Inspector Thomas Chaudhuri was thirty-two but still lived with his father in the terraced house in Maida Vale where he'd been born. Most people seemed to find Thomas an unusual name for a Hindu. A very few thought he must have been named after India's Christian martyr. But since he was the first of the family to be born in England, his father had deemed it right that his name should in part reflect his nationality. And his mother, dead these fifteen years, had thought her husband the wisest man in the world for thinking it. So the inspector's name was Thomas, though most people called him Tom.

It was half past five and still raining when he arrived at the scene of the crime in Ravenscourt Park. The bodies had not long since been discovered by the owner of the garden centre. At ten to five that evening, expecting no more customers, he'd shut up shop, propping his bike against the wall while he locked the gates. When he turned to mount he saw the head amongst the leaves and thought at first it was part of a broken doll. But in his heart he must have known what it was or he would have left without a second look. When the truth of what he was looking at had sunk in, he ran away screaming.

A preliminary search of the crime scene showed the murder weapon, most probably a large kitchen knife, to be absent. And there was nothing to identify the victims. In the fashionable black handbag, expensive compared with the victim's cheaper-quality clothes, was a selection of blue and pink makeup and a set of keys on a Bart Simpson key ring. A zebra-striped fake-fur purse contained thirty-two pounds, seventy-six pence along with a day-return ticket to Sandown. But no diary, address book or mobile phone. On a bit of torn paper was written in a childish hand *Mum's new mobile*, and then a number, the sevens crossed in the continental fashion. Chaudhuri rang it. A voice welcomed him to the Vodaphone answering service and invited him to leave a message. The phone was switched off.

"I bet she's watching *Emmerdale*," said Detective Sergeant James, apparently touched by the thought. "And after that it's *Eastenders*. I bet she's switched it off so she can't be disturbed while they're on."

"OK," said Chaudhuri. "Get her name and address from the company, would you, James? As soon as we have that, we'll pay poor Mum a visit."

An hour later, the coroner's officer having taken the bodies for post mortem, Chaudhuri, James and PC Janet Ellis set off to call on Elizabeth Parker of Benbow House, Wharf Street, Deptford.

On the walkway of the third floor the end theme tune of *Coronation Street* could be heard coming from almost every flat. At a block opposite rap music blasted from a wide-open window and sounded like a lunatic yattering to himself.

Liz answered their knock. She peered round the edge of the door, not in a timid way but an unwelcoming one. She was eating something. At the sight of Chaudhuri's warrant card she held up a hand signalling him to wait a bit, fixed her eyes on the doorpost and chewed with a will. At last she swallowed and looked at him.

"What you want?"

"Mrs Elizabeth Parker?"

"Ms."

"I beg your pardon. Do you think we could have a few words?"

"What about? No one here's done nuffink. Brian," she called over her shoulder, "there's a couple of frigging coppers here wants to have a word. You done somefink you shouldn't, Brian?"

"Nah," replied a voice obstructed with food.

"There you are, no one's done nuffink. And if it's about the old bird woman what got herself murdered, I've already told you all I know. So piss off, if you don't mind."

"Ms Parker," Chaudhuri leant against the door before she slammed it shut, "it's about your daughter."

The change in her was immediate. And it was obvious she expected the worst. Chaudhuri had noticed it was always the thickest, least imaginative types who did – the ones who also believed they'd win the lottery. He put it down to reading too many 'true' magazines. She seemed to hunch as she backed away, her eyes pleading.

"My Kell?" she whimpered. "What's happened to my Kell?"

"Let's go in and sit down, shall we?"

"Oh, God," she wailed, his tone confirming her fears. "My Kell's dead. Oh, God, Brian, it's Kell. She's dead."

Brian was sat in front of the television with a plate of tortilla and noodles on his knee. He looked pained at the interruption. He moved his eyes towards Chaudhuri then back to his plate, debating whether to finish his meal. With a sigh, he put the plate on the floor.

"All right, what's happened? Let's hear it."

Chaudhuri waited until PC Ellis had guided Liz to the sofa before speaking.

"Ms Parker, the body of a young woman was found this afternoon in Ravenscourt Park."

"Oh, God, not murdered. Oh, God. Oh, God. Oh, God."

With reluctance Brian got up to comfort her.

"Because she carried no identification the only way we could trace her to you was through your telephone number, which she'd written down and kept with her."

"Yes, I wrote it for her. Oh, God. I gave it to her just before she left. It's a new number. Oh, my God."

"Now, Ms Parker, for this reason we can't be sure before a formal identification that she is your daughter. It appears this young woman had travelled this morning from the Isle of Wight and intended to return there tonight. We found a return ticket to Sandown in her bag."

Liz flung herself back in the sofa and hid her face. She seemed hardly to breathe. Even Brian looked at her with concern. Outside the window a dog moaned.

"It's my Kell," she said at last. "She lived at Sandown. She didn't like it, though. She was gonna come back here."

"Kell? That's short for Kelly, is it?"

Liz nodded and hid her face once more, rocking herself to and fro. When she was still, Chaudhuri asked,

"How long had she lived at Sandown?"

"A couple of year, maybe."

"Do you know if she had a boyfriend?"

"Course. Darren Frost, he's called. She thinks the world of him."

"Did they live together?"

"Course they do. I told you, he's her boyfriend, isn't he?" She flashed him a glance of irritation, and resumed her weeping.

"Did Kelly often come to London?"

"She ain't been here for more than a year – not the Christmas just gone but the one before that."

"Is that the last time you saw her?"

Liz looked at him with contempt through her tears. "I told you – I saw her today, didn't I? She come here for her lunch before going to her meeting."

"I see. What time was this meeting?"

"Half-four."

"And what time did she leave here?"

"Half-three. I remember coz she had to run for the train."

"You didn't go with her?"

"What, to the meeting? Course I didn't."

"Stayed here, did you?"

"Course."

"Do you work?"

"Yeah. I'm controller for Star Cabs over at Thamesmead." He knew she would refer to it as her 'career'. "I got the day off today, though."

"This meeting of Kelly's… what was it about?"

She was on the point of speaking but stopped herself and sighed instead. "I dunno," she said at last.

"Do you know who it was with?"

"What, you mean like names and stuff?"

"Yes, what was the name of the person she was meeting?"

"I dunno."

"But you knew where it was to take place?"

"Nah, she didn't tell me nuffink like that."

"But just now, when I mentioned where the body had been found, you seemed immediately to associate it with Kelly."

"Coz you'd already told me it was her."

She glared at him. He said nothing and she wept again.

There was something wrong. Normally, the bereaved used their grief as a reason to avoid questions they couldn't or wouldn't answer. And Liz was the type who obstructed the police on principle. Why didn't she tell him to piss off, as she'd done earlier? Because she hadn't been afraid then. Now she was. It was as if she expected to be questioned and was amazed he hadn't asked what she dreaded to answer. The desire to keep him on the wrong track made her co-operative.

"We haven't found her mobile," he said. "I assume she owned one?"

Liz nodded. "She lost it on the journey. Probably all

that jiggling on the fucking ferry."

"We'll need the number of her phone. Do you have it?"

She quoted it from memory and James copied it down.

"Ms Parker, we have reason to think Kelly was not the victim of a random attack. We think she knew her killer."

"It can't be the people she was going to meet, then. I know for a fact she'd never set eyes on them before."

"People? She was meeting more than one person?"

Liz bit her lip as if she'd made a slip of the tongue.

"Come, Ms Parker, how many people was Kelly meeting? She must have told you."

"She told me nuffink."

"Was it something to do with the hospital? There's one on the outskirts of the park. Did she have an appointment there that you know of?"

She leapt up and made PC Ellis start. "Where's my Jade?" The plate of food next to her foot skimmed across the laminate floor. "Where is she?"

"Jade was Kelly's daughter?"

"Where is she?" Her hands, in fear, came up to her mouth. She looked at him in terror. He hesitated.

"They never murdered my Jade, an' all?" she said with pathetic incredulity. "You ain't telling me I ain't got no Jade no more?"

They stared at each other. Then she threw back her head and howled.

"They gone and killed my Jade. They gone and killed Nan's princess. She could have been a glamour model. And they gone and killed her."

The dog on the balcony howled in sympathy.

"Arsehole," she screeched. "I'll toss it over. Jade wanted me to do it, and I will. I'll do it if it's the last fucking thing I ever fucking do."

She made a dash for the balcony door. They could barely restrain her. At last they got her onto the sofa again, where she lay wide eyed, her cries like someone humming tunelessly. While they waited for the doctor, Chaudhuri questioned Brian in the kitchen.

Brian had tow-coloured hair but the ruddiness of his skin suggested it had once been ginger. His dark hazel eyes also had a touch of red, like a bloodstone. He said he worked in a picture-framing factory at Woolwich docks, where he claimed to have been until five that evening. Regarding Kelly, he gave as much information as he could, which was scant.

For reasons of her own she had been known as Kelly Houghton since moving to the Isle of Wight. She was forever changing her name, he said. That and her address was all he seemed to know about her and he gave the impression he had no desire to know more. But a recent photo left Chaudhuri in no doubt about her identity. The purpose of her visit to London remained a mystery, however.

There was a knock at the door. The doctor had arrived. Within a few minutes he and PC Ellis could be seen guiding Liz upstairs to bed. She walked as if asleep. Chaudhuri thought she enjoyed making it difficult for them. He turned to Brian, who was watching their progress with a scowl.

"So you'll identify the body after the post mortem? I doubt if your partner will be in a fit state. At any rate, you should at least accompany her."

"You send us a car, then, mate. I ain't got no time to take no half day off work, waiting for frigging trains to London. I ain't gonna pay no train fares, neither."

"I see. By the way, shall I take the dog off your hands? It seems to get on your partner's nerves. I'll find it a good home."

Brian handed over a chain leash from the back of the kitchen door. Chaudhuri took it and went out onto the balcony.

The dog was a mongrel, auburn coloured, with fluffy ears like a fox and eyes outlined in black as if it were wearing eyeliner. At the sound of the door opening it sat up neatly with an alert enquiring expression. Then it remembered to be afraid and cowered. Its resignation brought a lump to his throat. How much more tenderly it would have been treated had it been a bull terrier. Liz would have revelled in gaining the respect of something vicious. She was the type who married murderers in prison.

He stepped carefully among mounds of excreta and gently slipped the leash over the dog's head. It went with him compliantly and lifted its paws high like a deer.

"She's hiding something, isn't she?" said James as they left. They took the stairs in preference to the reeking lift. "And it must be dodgy if it means more to her than helping us find her grand-daughter's killer."

Chaudhuri nodded. "We'll check and cross-check Kelly, both in the names of Parker and Houghton. Make that the priority when we get back, James. I want her mobile phone records, including reverse, as well. And get someone to phone her mother tomorrow and find out if Kelly had a job. It slipped my mind in there."

He looked around with distaste.

"Either of you ever been to the Isle of Wight?"

PC Ellis said she had and it was paradise.

"Great. The very place for James and me to spend a few romantic days together. You'll be looking after Dad," he told the dog. "That's your job for the next few days."

Its nose, which had been dry and flaky-looking, was already beginning to shine as if someone had been at it with shoe polish. He longed to cuddle it but not while James was around. When they got back to the station he'd buy it a pie from the canteen.

"Did Greene get the security videos?"

"Yes. From the tube station as well as the park."

"OK. Let's go and have a look at them."

Eleven

Like someone suffering a recurrent nightmare, the video recordings from the CCTV cameras played and replayed Kelly and Jade's advance towards death. Always with the same inescapable end. An end which Chaudhuri and James could not for the life of them explain. What they saw was so incredible, that were it not for the insistent eye of the camera they would be forced to conclude their own eyes deceived them. There was nothing for it but to look at each recording again.

Again they watched the 4.15 train arrive at Ravenscourt Park. The doors opened and Jade appeared in the distance, a doll-like child jumping onto the platform with both feet, Kelly soon following. No one else disembarked. Apart from these two, the platform was empty. Hand in hand they walked out of the camera's range.

The next recording covered the street outside the station and the entrance to the park. A cul-de-sac. Now and then cars turned into it from the main road, hoping to find a parking space but unsuccessful, they drove away again. Throughout the afternoon a few people arrived on foot and all of them went into the station. No one went into the park.

Chaudhuri and James watched as it started to rain. According to the camera, the time was 2.17pm. A small red Fiat arrived and squeezed into a gap by the kerb. A tall, middle-aged couple got out. Arm in arm, they strolled into the park, the rain falling in torrents.

At 2.32pm a young mother with two children in posh school uniform hurried along the street and through the park. They were using it as a short cut to one of the large Edwardian houses that bound it. They had been recorded by another camera, leaving by the far gate at the hospital end of the park. They were the only people to use that gate all afternoon.

At 2.49pm the middle-aged couple, laden with trays of plants from the garden centre, returned to their Fiat. They took their time, untroubled by the rain, and placed the plants in the boot. Five minutes later they drove away.

3.26pm. A woman in a black ankle-length coat with a hood approached wearing heavy shoes and walking with shuffling, hurrying steps. She, too, went into the park.

For almost three quarters of an hour no other person appeared. The camera, to whom the animate and inanimate are all one, continued to record the relentless rain and the soaked, deserted street. Chaudhuri fast-forwarded to the point when, at 4.18pm, Kelly and Jade came once more into view. They'd left the station. Their back was to the camera. Kelly still had hold of Jade's hand and her handbag was over her head to keep off the rain. They dashed into the park. But no one followed. Chaudhuri and James waited and watched until long after they knew Kelly and Jade to be already lying dead inside the park. But not a soul either approached the park or left it.

They turned to another recording. This viewpoint was now from inside the park, looking towards the gate. Here was the mother with the children, running out of view to the gate at the far end. There were the couple with the plants heading back to their car. And here came the woman with the hood. She hesitated. She stopped. She looked towards the garden centre. From this angle its entrance was hidden by the shrubbery and here the bodies had been found. The woman with the hood seemed to come to a decision and went in.

Fast-forward forty-five minutes. Kelly and Jade came into view, Kelly still with her bag over her head. Like the woman in the hood, they stopped near the garden centre and looked. They too appeared to go in. But Chaudhuri and James knew they had turned off before they reached it and instead went into the space between the bushes and the viaduct wall. The murderer was already there.

Now, out of sight, Kelly was being stabbed in the stomach and chest. Now Jade's throat was parting. On tenterhooks, and determined this time to miss nothing, Chaudhuri and James watched for the murderer to emerge. For five minutes they sat there and stared at the shrubbery, ten minutes, twenty, thirty. In the dusky light the owner of the garden centre appeared, running. This was where they came in.

But when and how did the murderer get out?

Twelve

It was after midnight when Chaudhuri got home to Kilburn Park Road. A light in the living room told him his father was still up. He always was. But tonight was special – he was waiting excitedly for the dog. Not that he intended to keep it, he'd pointed out when Chaudhuri had phoned him earlier. He couldn't face another dog after Silkie but this one could stay until a permanent home was found.

It stood now on the doorstep and stared at the door with its head on one side. Chaudhuri, clutching its lead and a sack of dog biscuits, fumbled with his key.

"Dad, I'm back."

Something stirred on the sofa. A smooth black head and two round black eyes looked at him over a cushion. The dog's tail wagged.

"Is that Tamal? What are you doing here? Bit past your bedtime, isn't it?"

"He's staying the night." Mr Chaudhuri came in from the kitchen. "His father's taken his mother to the airport and won't be back till maybe the early hours, so he's staying with us." He looked at the dog. "This is the poor little thing, is it?" The dog's tail wagged even more. "Come on, then, girl, come here."

It trotted to his feet and with a gymnastic flourish rolled onto its back. Not wanting to seem a pushover, Mr Chaudhuri tried to stop his smile. "What's her name, then?"

"Good God, I forgot to ask. Still, I don't suppose it matters. I don't think she'll have heard it very often where she came from."

"I don't like dogs," said Tamal, still peeping over the cushion. "My dad says they spread germs."

"Spread germs?" Mr Chaudhuri looked scornful as he tickled its tummy. "Of course they don't spread germs. People in this country have always had dogs. They never caught germs from them, did they?"

"My dad knows," Tamal insisted and sat up. "When we went to Bournemouth he wouldn't let me go on the beach coz the English let their dogs run round. He said it shouldn't be allowed."

"Don't know how he gets on in Calcutta then, when the humans defecate in the street." He gave Chaudhuri a wink. "Right, let's get this little creature something to eat, Tom. Is that dog food you've got there? I'm glad you thought, because I couldn't leave Tamal to go out and get some. You coming to help feed the dog, Tamal? All right, stay there like a good boy till I can get you to bed. We won't be long."

They went into the kitchen. Chaudhuri flopped into one of the old easy chairs next to the boarded-up fireplace.

Even on the brightest day this room was dark, its only window facing the wall of the back yard. As ever, it was clean and tidy but utilitarian – not so much as a plant on the windowsill to bring a bit of cheerfulness. It had been different in his mother's time. Now the room reflected his father's honest but puritanical character.

A brown teapot in a black and orange knitted cosy stood ready on the table. Chaudhuri poured himself tea into a mug with a picture of Princess Diana on it. "Hasn't Tamal got school tomorrow?"

"No, he's being kept off, Tom." Mr Chaudhuri glanced at the kitchen door then closed it. "The thing is, he won't go to bed. Wanted the telly on. I wouldn't have it. All violent stuff at this time of night. And he went into a sulk when I said we didn't have Zee TV. I offered the *Blithe Spirit* video but he wouldn't even answer me."

Chaudhuri burst out laughing. "Noel Coward for a seven year old boy? I'm not surprised. You need your head examining, Father."

"You liked it at seven. One of your favourite films, it was."

"Exactly. And look at the result."

Laughing, Mr Chaudhuri filled a plastic sandwich box with water for the dog. Then he became serious again.

"She's pregnant, you know – Tamal's mum." His eyes were magnified behind his glasses so that he looked like an owl. "A girl they're expecting, apparently. Tamal says she doesn't want it. You'd have thought it the most natural thing in the world, to listen to him. When I asked him if he wouldn't like a little sister he looked at me as if I'd gone mad."

"It's the age." Chaudhuri took a mouthful of tea that puffed out his cheeks like a hamster's. "All boys hate girls at that age. I know I did. Bloody hated them."

"Oh, Tom, you know it's not just that. I tell you, there's something funny going on." He passed Chaudhuri the Scottish castle biscuit tin. "Mind you, I don't know how far gone his mum is, but why is she going to Calcutta all of a sudden and keeping Tamal off school? He didn't go today and he won't be going tomorrow. I offered to take him but they said not to bother. It's my belief she's gone for an abortion."

"Like that, is it?" Chaudhuri swallowed a Jaffa cake nearly whole.

"Exactly. Well, she won't be able to get it done here, will she, if she's beyond the time? Definitely not, if the only reason for not wanting it is that it's a girl. She's going for a month, apparently. Quite a long time when you're pregnant. And she's not strong – had a couple of miscarriages before, if I remember."

He sat in the chair on the other side of the fireplace and gestured for the dog to come on his lap.

"Of course, she's got plenty of family in Calcutta. The in-laws will look after her well. But I bet it never occurs to them to wonder why she's getting rid of a girl when she lives in a country where they're not an economic burden. I bet you any money they'll just think she's lucky to be able to get rid of it in more comfort than they could afford."

"Oh, come on, Dad." Chaudhuri started on the grapes. "You don't know for certain."

"No, of course not. But if it's not happening in this case, it's happening in another, isn't it? I wish we could somehow put a stop to it."

"It's India's problem, not ours. Though by all

accounts there are quite a few Asian doctors in this country not above flexing their cultural muscle in the abortion department." He got up and stretched. "Think I'll have a quick shower. Shall I try to get Tamal up to bed?"

"Yes, have a go. I'll make up a bed for Baby in the meantime."

"Baby? Who's Baby?"

"The dog." Mr Chaudhuri looked sheepish. "Well, it'll do her till someone gives her a proper name."

Chaudhuri went out sniggering.

Seeing no one was bothering with him, Tamal had fallen asleep. Chaudhuri carried him up to the spare room and five minutes later came down from his shower, smelling of Badedas.

His father was in the living room, the dog on one knee and the complete works of Shakespeare on the other. He was watching Macbeth.

"Always put the best films on at this time in the morning. Shall I switch it off?"

"No, I'll watch for a few minutes, Dad – help me unwind."

He looked at a beautiful Lady Macbeth, Francesca Annis, he thought it was, who berated her husband for hesitating over murder.

I have given suck, and know
How tender 'tis to love the babe that milks me:
I would, while it was smiling in my face,
Have pluck'd my nipple from its boneless gums,
And dash'd the brains out, had I so sworn as you
Have done to this.

It brought Jade's severed head to mind. He looked away and spotted a box of chocolates on the mantelpiece. He got up to help himself to a few. Next to the box was a photo of someone he'd never seen before.

"Who's this, Dad?"

Mr Chaudhuri looked up over his glasses. "Oh, I forgot. That's yet another match for you. Tamal's father put it there."

It was a studio portrait of a young woman, stiff and solemn in all her finery.

"It's his cousin from Calcutta – wants an English husband with a decent wage packet. I told him English policemen aren't allowed bribes but he thought you might still come up to scratch."

"Dad."

"Yes, I told him he was wasting his time but he was insistent."

"Well, if I was going to be cajoled into an arranged marriage, I'd want something a bit more tempting than this."

"No need to talk like that about the poor girl, Tom. You can afford to be generous."

Chaudhuri examined the woman in the photo. Her dowry dangled from her ears and her nose, the soberness beneath this frippery assuring all comers she would be a good wife.

"I can't do it, you know, Dad. Get married for the sake of it, I mean." He sat on the arm of his father's chair and leaned against him.

"Wouldn't want you to, Tom."

"But you don't feel offended? I mean, you and Mum

had an arranged marriage."

"Yes, and as chance would have it, it was a fortunate one. But it's too important to leave to that sort of chance. When I think of some of the men she might have been bound to, some of the men I know, I thank God she ended up with me – not that I'm being big-headed, mind." He looked up, worried he might have seemed so. Chaudhuri laughed and kissed his nose.

Mr Chaudhuri stroked the dog thoughtfully. "We all want romance, Tom, more than anything else when we're young. The dreams I had…well, I'm sure they were no different from any cockney lad's. A man feels just as disappointed as a woman in an arranged marriage. And naturally he takes it out on her. 'Oh, but she learns to love him', Tamal's dad said to me tonight. Yes, I told him, that's why so many Indian men become tyrants – they're contemptuous in their hearts of such a woman. They know there's no truth in it. 'At least no one in an arranged marriage gets divorced,' he said. Because they're not allowed to, the silly idiot, that's how much faith they have in them. Even in this country they can't because they daren't. Look at all these honour killings – shameful what they've brought into a civilised country. And he thinks I'd want something like that for you? Oh, he made my blood boil."

It sounded to Chaudhuri as if his father had repeated these arguments often in his defence. He kissed him again, guilty he might be the cause of friends giving him a hard time.

"I know what it would do to you if I had a failed marriage, though, Dad. And being a copper…well, it's almost a foregone conclusion. In my case, I can understand it if you think nothing but an arranged marriage can work."

Mr Chaudhuri took his hand. "The only test for a true marriage is if you're allowed to end it. The ordinary English have been marrying for love for most of their history and doing it very successfully. All right, I agree divorce is now too easy. But that's what they've got wrong, not marriage."

"What about those who don't believe in marriage?"

"Those who have a different partner every other year, you mean?" He looked as disgusted as if Chaudhuri had just farted. "I'm not bothered about them. They think lust's love. That's why they can't stay with someone five minutes. Love means as little to them as to those who believe in arranged marriages."

"A lifetime's too long to be with the same person, they'd say to you."

"And I'd say what sort of love takes that attitude?" He turned his face up in indignation and the ceiling light flashed on his glasses. "Would you say that about your children – I've loved you for ten years and I've had enough of you now? Or your parents?" He glared at Chaudhuri as if the argument were his. "If it's love, it lasts forever. So what's wrong with making a proper commitment and getting married?"

"It's only a bit of paper."

"And I say that's only an old chestnut."

Chaudhuri had to bite the inside of his lip so as not to laugh. But his father was too carried away to notice.

"To marry for love is a wonderful aim, even if it fails. Think of all the literature it's given birth to. Think of all the poetry. I bet your 'bit of paper brigade' never write any. As for arranged marriages, it's no coincidence in my opinion that they happen in countries where there's no poetry worth the name. Power and money and damned arrogant meddling, that's what they're about. No reason for them otherwise."

"Can I have a drink of water?" Tamal peeped through the banisters of the living room staircase.

"Go back to bed. I'll bring it up."

The dog had fallen asleep, curled into the shape of a croissant. Mr Chaudhuri stood up with it and put it back on the chair like a cushion.

"Oh, by the way, Jacqueline phoned," he said, coming back from the kitchen with Tamal's glass of water. "We had a bit of a chat. She said not to bother ringing her back because she's having an early night. But she wants you to ring her tomorrow."

"OK Dad. Thanks."

Jacqueline was a solicitor. She lived next to the Thames at Canary Wharf in a building called The Cascades. It looked like a Machu Pichu pyramid made of glass. Chaudhuri tried to imagine marrying her and bringing her to live here. The wooden armed three-piece suite was so old it was becoming fashionable again, the beige folk-weave curtains and orange-shaded lamps likewise. Only the patterned carpet of green and yellow leaves was too ugly to be revived.

He'd known these things all his life. His mother had chosen them and for that reason his father would keep them and care for them until they dropped to bits. But what woman of today would want them? Or want his father, come to that? The woman in the photo? It could, in the end, be enough to make him marry her.

He listened with half an ear to Macduff bewailing the murder of his children.

All my pretty ones?
Did you say all? – Oh hell-kite! – All?
What, all my pretty chickens, and their dame,
At one fell swoop?

This imaginary suffering brought a lump to his throat more readily than the actual suffering of Liz. Was eloquence a measure of feeling? It was certainly a guarantee of sympathy.

He looked up at his father coming downstairs, clutching the banister like an old man.

"Think I'll turn in, Dad. I'll put the alarm on for five o'clock."

"Don't bother, son. I'll wake you. I'll take Baby's basket up to my room, just to keep an eye on her. You go on up. I'll settle everything down here."

Chaudhuri was half way up the stairs when his father called to him.

"Lady! That's the name."

"Sorry, Dad?"

"For the dog – Lady. Good thing I put this film on. It's given me the idea. What do you think?"

"Perfect, Dad. Couldn't be better."

He remembered just in time to brush his teeth again after the chocolates. He had hardly lain down when he was asleep.

Thirteen

The waning moon was lying on its back, hanging like an ill omen over the shabby house of spirits in Ryde. The mermaid door-knocker leered and rapped with her tail. A light came on in the hall. The door opened.

"Mr MacArthur, I'm sorry to bother you like this but could I have a quick word with your sister?"

"Of course." He was eating something. "Come in. You're fortunate to have caught us. We got back from London not half an hour ago."

"Really? Then you must be tired. I won't keep you long."

"Oh, don't worry about that. I was just making a spot of supper. Do you fancy a bite? Haven't got toothache, I hope, with that scarf round your mouth?"

"No, just a bit of cold. I shan't bother with supper, thanks. But could I use your loo?"

"It's that little door there, under the stairs. Come along to the kitchen when you're ready. Emily's there."

Lock the lavatory door. Take off the woolly hat and gloves.

Take off the jacket and the shoes. Put on the hooded coat that stinks like meat, the Wellingtons and the yellow rubber gloves still slippery with blood.

In the kitchen a kettle whistled as if to warn them. The room was dingy but cosy. A cast-iron range covered one wall but the fire was unlit. An electric bar fire glowed on the hearth. A birdcage hung in the corner by the window and a green budgie hopped from perch to perch.

Emily sat in an armchair, her hands folded in her lap. She looked up, ready to smile. But her smile became puzzlement.

"Bert."

Bert turned from the worktop where he was cutting up tomatoes.

"All right, now? Ready for a cup? What's up then, fancy dress?" He started to laugh then his face fell and he groaned at the sight of the knife.

He will fight to the death for his sister. Kill him first, now, in the chest, and hope to hit the heart. Bone. Try again for flesh.

Bert struggled.

Oh, God, in the shoulder, close to his hump.

Bert tried to get away but the knife came down in his eye and his cry was terrible.

Throat, throat, throat.

"Oh, Bert, Bert." She couldn't stand. Moaning she crawled to him. The knife entered her back. She fell beside him and tried to lift his head from the floor and rest it on her arms. The knife entered again as she kissed Bert's blood.

She is dead. He is dead. We are dead.

Switch off the fire and the light. Take the newspaper from the chair and spread it on the floor of the hall. Take off the hooded coat, the gloves and the Wellingtons. Bundle them in the bag with the knife. Stand on the newspaper and put on hat, gloves, jacket, shoes. Open the door and step outside. Pick up the newspaper. Put it in the bag. Leave.

Fourteen

The next morning Ravenscourt Park was grey and sombre but radiant compared to the owner of the garden centre. He was one of those Londoners – usually found selling newspapers outside tube stations – who are permanently sour. If he ever smiled it would be as grim as his scowl. He was overweight in a flabby way. His shoulders and arms were thin but his belly hung over the top of his trousers as if he'd stuffed something into the waist of his T-shirt. The jowls of his cheeks sagged and were covered with long grey side-burns, which made up for the lack of hair on his head. His name was Tony Smart.

"I'll be wanting compensation for loss of earnings, besides counselling," he said to Chaudhuri who along with James had just arrived after an early briefing with the team at Hammersmith Police Station. "How much longer are you lot gonna keep the place shut down?"

It was not yet eight o'clock but for the last hour Smart had hung around the cordoned-off entrance to the park, glaring at the SOCOs and bewailing his plight to any passers-by who found time to be curious at a crime scene. For the past ten minutes he'd sat with a cup of tea in the mobile incident room at the end of the cul-de-sac.

"All being well, you should be able to open tomorrow morning, Mr Smart," said Chaudhuri. "If you've time to spare, we'd like to ask you a few more questions about the customers you had yesterday afternoon."

Smart had plenty of time as well as the inclination. He put his cup on the table and sat back ready to be obstreperous. "You've already asked me about customers and I've already told you."

"True, but events have moved on a bit and I think this time we can be more specific. I noticed your shop doesn't have CCTV."

"That's right. Don't need it, don't want it."

"Really? You're very lucky. Not much troubled by shop-lifters?"

"Not round here. Wealthy area, isn't it? No blacks."

Chaudhuri refused to be side tracked by that one. "Surely you've quite a bit of passing trade, being so close to the station?"

"Not much. The entrance is obscured by them bushes, see? Don't know about it. Don't notice it. And plants is not like sweets and chocolate. Don't appeal to most people. I cater for the locals and a few regulars at the hospital. They're keen gardeners round here. Got a base of regular customers and that keeps me going."

"All right. You had a couple in yesterday, about three o'clock. They bought quite a bit from you. Do you remember them?"

"That would be Dr and Mrs Templeton. Tall,

distinguished looking couple? Wife wears a very expensive sapphire and diamond ring? Antique, none of your Argos stuff."

"I'm afraid we didn't notice her ring, Mr Smart. They arrived shortly before three and stayed over twenty minutes. They were in a red Fiat."

"That's them. Got a Jag as well, mind. The Fiat's just a run-around. She wanted winter pansies for her London garden as well as the house in Herefordshire. Yellow ones and white ones she chose. And a few narcissi bulbs."

"You've got a good memory."

"Have to have if I want to offer a decent service."

"Do you remember the customers you had after that?"

"I do. That's an easy one. Coz I didn't have none." To express a negative, even a double one, seemed to afford Smart untold pleasure. He sat in his chair as smug as if he'd just won Mastermind.

"None? Are you sure?"

"Course I'm sure." He bridled at being doubted. "And I'm telling you I didn't have none. I knew I wouldn't once it started to rain. That's why I shut up shop a bit early. If I hadn't been expecting a delivery at four I'd have gone as soon as the rain started and might have been spared quite an ordeal."

"Delivery?" Chaudhuri wracked his brains for the memory of a delivery man on the CCTV but to no avail. "Did he turn up?"

"At long last. Waited till nearly quarter past, I did, and then had to help him unload coz he couldn't find no space for the van and was parked out there on a double yellow line."

"Out where?"

"It's too late to do him for it now, mate," Smart beamed lugubriously. He pointed with his thumb over his shoulder. "He parked out there in King Street, right next to the gate for quickness."

"The gate to King Street? It was open? I thought you said yesterday it was always locked."

"Well it was open in the afternoon," Smart snapped. "How else do you expect me to get my deliveries? Don't expect him to take the trouble to come to the customer entrance, do you? Not him. Pigs might fly."

"I wish you'd told us this when we spoke to you last night." Chaudhuri gave Smart a disappointed look which only succeeded in making him scowl the more.

"Now you hold your horses, mate, hold your horses. I'd just had a nasty shock, see? I'm still not over it. When I think about murderers on the loose, running round cutting heads off, me blood curdles. It could have been *my* head, I hope you realise. You should be asking what you can do for me instead of sitting there interrogating me and casting aspersions."

"No-one means to cast aspersions, Mr Smart."

"You just hinted I withheld evidence."

"I didn't intend that, believe me. I'm sorry if you're upset. Your account is invaluable to us and I'm very grateful to you for taking the trouble."

With a grunt Smart conveyed he would overlook the offence this once but not to go and try it again.

Chaudhuri said, "Would you do me the favour of coming with us and showing us exactly how the gate was propped open?"

"Will I be able to get my computer back?"

"All in good time. I know you want to help as much as you can and your list of customers and their familiarity with the garden centre and its environs could be important. Just pop these protective covers over your shoes, would you?"

The garden centre was bordered on two sides by high walls, one on the cul-de-sac or station side, and the adjacent one on King Street. They were spiked and over twelve feet in height. The third side was formed by the gable-end of the house next door and the fourth by the station viaduct. Entry from the park was through a door in one of its bricked-up arches. Perhaps the garden centre had originally been some sort of store yard for the station. Now it looked like the extra-large back yard of a terraced house whose owner was mad about plants. The little glass lean-to where Smart sat behind his till might have been the potting shed. The delivery gate, which was at the far end in the King Street wall, was hidden behind a variety of trees in enormous pots and was in effect invisible to anyone unaware of it. With surprising strength Smart dragged the pots aside and opened the gate wide. The tumult of the street was as if an opening had been made in a wasps' nest.

"I see," said Chaudhuri, inwardly cursing. "No one could miss that. Yes, you can close it again. How long was it open for in all?"

"Just for the delivery. Like I said, I don't want every Tom, Dick and Harry wandering in off the streets. I've got my regulars and that's enough for me."

"And how long did the delivery take?"

"Can't have been much more than fifteen minutes. I

propped the gate open a bit before four. Then when he finally put in an appearance I helped him unload, as I generally do. Didn't take long."

"And you say he arrived at quarter past four?"

"Thereabouts. I weren't clock watching."

"So in that time anyone could have come in here by the park entrance and noticing the open gate, gone out that way?"

"I'd have seen them, mate," Smart protested as if slandered.

"Did you see a lone woman in a long dark coat with a hood? She came in here after Dr and Mrs Templeton had left."

"I tell you there weren't no one!" he cried, almost beside himself.

"All right, Mr Smart. Thank you for your help. I must ask you to leave now but I'll try to hurry my colleagues along and get business back to normal for you."

"These plants need a drink."

"What, after yesterday's downpour? I'm sure they'll survive. We'll reimburse you for any losses, of course. But we'll be as quick as possible. And I really would urge you to think about getting security cameras. As you say yourself, you're very isolated here. If ever you should have trouble at least you'd have evidence of the perpetrators."

"So that you could catch them, you mean?" Smart was scathing. "You're having a laugh, aren't you, mate? No, I'll carry on as I am, thank you very much. No point in going to unnecessary expense. And that *would* be unnecessary."

They saw him off beyond the cordon and watched him wheel his bike towards the main road. James had a look on his face of extreme distaste.

"Know what I'm thinking? I'm thinking the camera *did* pick up the murderer leaving the crime scene. But forty minutes after he'd committed the murder. I'm thinking it picked up Smart when he came haring out after finding the bodies – *allegedly*."

Sergeant Bailey James (who Chaudhuri always called by his surname, claiming it should have been his given name) was newly promoted from constable. In reality the best-natured bloke in the world, Chaudhuri was accustomed to him casting suspicion on those he saw as obstructive or uncooperative witnesses. It was compensation for not being allowed to shake information out of them. Though never intended to be taken seriously even by James himself, it could sometimes throw up interesting ideas always welcome at this stage of an enquiry. "No blood's been found in the garden centre," he pointed out.

James gave a derisive snort. "So far. But now we know about that open gate we'll have to do a forensic search in there as well, won't we?"

"There was no blood on Smart last night – not even a whiff of it."

"He'd have washed it off, wouldn't he? Plenty of water in there. And anyway, that crafty bugger would have worn protective clothing."

"Where is it, then? And where's the weapon?"

"Stuffed in the delivery bloke's van? Or in the bag on the back of his bike?"

"No, Greene had a quick check of his bike last night

while we were questioning him. And any weapon found on or near the premises needn't have been put there by Smart – not now that we know our lady in the hood escaped through the garden centre."

James ignored this. "And here's a funny thing – how did Smart know what time the crime was committed?"

"What do you mean? I don't follow."

"He claimed just now that if it hadn't been for the delivery, which he admits he was expecting at four, he would have left early and been spared an ordeal. That means he must know the murders took place after four and not earlier."

Chaudhuri thought for a moment. "It's understandable for him to assume the murders took place after three, otherwise the Templetons would almost certainly have found the bodies. I think he's just making an innocent assumption."

The word 'innocent' made James snort again.

"But if he did it," Chaudhuri went on, "he must, as you say, have covered himself up. Which implies pre-meditation. And my gut reaction…oh, hell, I promised myself not to say that anymore, sounds like I'm complaining of diarrhoea – my instinct tells me you don't plan to murder two people practically on your own doorstep. And there's no evidence he knew Kelly and Jade, not according to his computer, anyway. And in Greene's view Smart seems to have used it to store every bit of information under the sun – one of those oddballs who see his computer as his friend and confidant. And most important," he raised his voice to drown out James, "if he had a delivery when he said he did – and the CCTV from King Street can settle that easily – then he simply didn't have the opportunity."

"He'd've had a couple of minutes. More maybe. The killings couldn't have taken long, after all. Seconds, at most."

"Are you serious? Smart plans a murder on the same day and at roughly the same time as he's expecting a delivery?"

"OK," James was reckless by now, "the murder wasn't planned. Purely spur of the moment psycho stuff."

"Really? He sees the delivery van off, thinks, *I've got a couple of minutes to fill, I'll just dash into the bushes and see if there's anyone to stab to death before I go home*?"

The look of exasperation on James face was so hysterical Chaudhuri was proud of himself for managing not to laugh. "No, James, I'm far more interested in our disappearing lady. Especially since we now know how she disappeared."

A tent had been erected to cover the crime scene. They went into it to speak about the new development of the open gate to the crime scene investigation officers. One of them was bagging up a mushed, gory-looking leaf found under the bushes at the far end of the shrubbery. It was betel nut.

"Asians chew it, don't they?" said James.

"Only lower-class ones." For Chaudhuri, snobbery was a virtue.

James had another brain wave. "Hey, you don't think that's what our hooded lady is? Asian, I mean. I thought that coat looked a bit weird. Maybe it's her everyday wear when she goes out, rain or shine. Maybe she walked up and down the shrubbery here while she waited for Kelly and Jade and had a good chew on that betel nut stuff to calm her nerves and then spat it out when she heard them coming."

Chaudhuri shook his head. "She didn't walk up and down. Apart from the spot where the bodies fell, the ground's untrodden and probably has been for years. The betel nut was more likely spat into the bushes by someone walking along the main road at the hospital end of the park. And look at these footprints in the blood." He squatted down to peer at them. "They've a deep wide tread, rather like the tread of a Wellington boot, according to Forensic. That strikes me as being part of the protective clothing rather than the sort of thing someone would wear every day – especially an Asian woman. I've never seen one in Wellingtons, have you?"

James had to admit he hadn't. "She reminded me of some of the women Sam and me saw on our holidays in Turkey." Sam was James' obese but alluring wife. He grasped any opportunity to talk about her. "Did I tell you about this Turkish bloke who came up to me and asked me how much money I wanted for her? I said just give me a pint, mate, and she's yours." He roared with laughter all the way to the car.

"So," said Chaudhuri, "what sort of picture's forming in that fecund mind of yours, James?"

James frowned in concentration, like a little boy in school. "Her in the hood – Asian or otherwise – waits for Kelly and Jade in the bushes, kills them, has a quick look through the door of the garden centre to make sure no one's seen her, sees the gate to the street's open and decides to use it for her getaway. But unless she took the coat off after the killings, someone'll remember her. She'd be bloodied. Even in London they'd notice. And as there are no obvious footprints in the garden centre she most likely took the wellies off, too."

"Well done, James. But something else has just occurred to me. If the murderer used the gate as a way out of the park, he or she could also have used it as a way in."

"What?" James looked at him in dismay. "Someone else besides the woman in the hood, you mean? What was she doing for half an hour before the gate was opened, then? Look, she arrived at three twenty-six pm. From the CCTV it looks as if she went into the garden centre but she can't have done because Smart would have seen her. She must have been waiting for Kelly and Jade."

"We can't take it for granted, James. What if Smart's wrong about the time he opened the gate? What if he opened it at, say, ten to four, since he was expecting the delivery at four o'clock? What if before that he went for a pee? It's like a forest in there. Our hooded lady could have gone in unnoticed and remained so while he was occupied shifting all those pots away from the gate. When he opened it, she could have left that way long before Kelly and Jade even got off the train."

James rallied. "OK. Let's look at the CCTV from King Street, like you said. If it picked her up, it'll tell us exactly what time she left. It'll also tell us if anyone else used the open gate as a way into the park."

"Right. Phone Greene now and tell him to get onto it immediately. And make sure someone visits that hospital – The Imperial Masonic, is it? Get them to enquire whether Kelly Houghton or Parker had an appointment there yesterday. Unlikely, I admit, since it's private, but you never know. Once we discover why she was in London everything else will fall into place."

He reached into his pocket for a fruit sweet and offered one to James.

"What we can say, despite the unexpected opportunity of the open gate, is that the killing was well planned, wasn't it? It was no passing, random attack. Our murderer expected Kelly and Jade and waited for them. And they knew her. They had no fear of her. Was she the one they were going to meet? Or was it someone, possibly from the Isle of Wight, who knew about the meeting and considered it a good opportunity to kill them well away from their own patch? When Kelly and Jade stopped and looked towards the bushes it was because someone was calling them, wasn't it? And they didn't hesitate. They went like lambs to the slaughter. And speaking of slaughter, James, it's nearly ten o'clock – time for the post mortem."

Fifteen

Chaudhuri thanked his lucky stars for Clare Mayhew's timely phone call. It was the perfect excuse for not attending the post mortem. Clare was Liz Parker's family liaison officer and, as she put it, Liz had 'talked'. Stoked up with brandy it would have been more accurate to say Liz had rambled, and all about Paki bastards and princesses with broken necks.

"From what I can work out, sir, one of Kelly's boyfriends killed one of her kids. According to Liz the boyfriend was Pakistani. It was some time ago but he was convicted, so there'll be a record. There seems to have been a little boy as well, who Liz claims was killed by her boyfriend's dog – that's Liz's boyfriend, I mean. No name, unfortunately, but if it's true, he'll have done time."

With a sense of relief neither man would admit to, Chaudhuri and James turned their back on the mortuary and headed for the incident room. A quick consultation of CRIS, the Met's Crime Report Information System database, rewarded them with rich if sickening food for thought.

Five years ago Zia Haq, identified as Kelly's boyfriend, had been found guilty and imprisoned for the manslaughter by shaking, of Latisha, Kelly's ten-month-old daughter. Three weeks into his sentence, he was murdered by a cell-mate in what was believed to be a race crime. Two years later, Lucas Obromski, Liz's boyfriend was imprisoned after his pit bull terrier savaged to death Kelly's four-year-old son Todd. Obromski was still serving his sentence.

Zia Haq's family lived above their halal butcher's shop on Harrow Road. It was midday when Chaudhuri and James found a parking space in one of the poky side streets comically named Fifth Avenue. Piles of battered cardboard boxes and sacks of rubbish littered the entrance to the shop. Chaudhuri, who didn't eat meat, averted his eyes in horror from the organs for consumption, arranged on white plastic trays in the window. He would have preferred the post mortem, not being expected to find it a mouth-watering sight.

The place stank like a charnel house and looked none too clean. Perhaps it was simply the unpainted dreariness that made it look dirty. He nearly burst a blood vessel trying not to breathe in the smell while James did the talking.

They'd phoned in advance and were expected. But the two brothers behind the counter pretended to know nothing of this. They carried on serving customers whilst looking at Chaudhuri and James as if they were something nastier than the goods on display in the window. Eventually one of them led them through a door at the back, which opened onto a built-in staircase. This was the entrance to the house above.

A staccato, hectoring voice could be heard. The speaker was an elderly man, berating a woman who was perhaps his wife. She sat in the corner of a sofa, her face hidden in the end of her shawl. The man stood in front of her, his hands clasped behind his back and his belly pushed forward. He was hardly five feet in height and wore a long buff-coloured waistcoat and white crocheted kufi. His grey beard grew only on his jaw-line, the rest of his face clean-shaven. As Chaudhuri and James entered he turned his irate little eyes to look at them.

"I'm telling her all this is her fault," he said to Chaudhuri in Bengali. "Zia was a good boy. All my boys are good boys, so why not him? Because of her." He jabbed a finger towards her and made her cower. "She thought he should be brought up like western people. Western people! I hate them. Pigs! All thieves and prostitutes. They made my boy a bad boy. They are responsible. And her. I will always blame her."

He stopped to get his breath. Chaudhuri took the opportunity to speak to him in the man's native tongue.

"You know why we're here, Mr Haq. We're investigating the murder of Kelly Parker, otherwise known as…"

"Why didn't she die before?" he screeched in fury. "My boy might never have met her if she'd…"

"Mr Haq could we discuss this calmly? Let's sit down, shall we?"

A heavy three-piece suite still in its polythene cover stood in a straight line along one wall. In one of the chairs a girl sat with a baby, its eyes outlined in black. Was she its mother? She was so tiny she looked prepubescent. With equanimity, almost smugness, she had watched the haranguing of the older woman. Behind her was a garish picture of Mecca, painted on black velvet edged with tinsel. A gaudy rug topped a fitted carpet, its pattern dulled with what was probably blood from the shop. Under the window – the curtains knotted in the middle – stood a teak dining table and four unmatched chairs. Chaudhuri and James sat here, Mr Haq on the sofa as far from his wife as possible.

The man who had shown them up stood in the doorway like a diminutive bouncer expecting trouble.

Mr Haq eyed Chaudhuri with interest. "You speak my language. Are you Bengali?"

"I am."

"Moslem?"

"No. And before we go any further, I think it would help my sergeant here if we spoke English. You speak it, I presume?"

"I speak. See? I bother learn their language. Why they not learn mine? This multicultural society, yes? Then why they not speak Bengali? Should be law. Everybody make speak Bengali."

"Would you mind telling me where you were yesterday, sir, from two in the afternoon till six in the evening?"

"I here in shop. All day. I go nowhere. You ask customers."

"And you, Mrs Haq?"

"She no go out, never," he answered for her. "She stay in home." He made it sound like house arrest.

"How many other people help you in the shop?"

"My sons help. Good boys."

"And they were here all day?" He looked at the man by the door. "You work full time in the shop, do you?"

The man nodded.

"Would you tell me your name, please?"

"Aziz. I didn't go out nowhere. Couldn't have done, even if I'd wanted to. There was a bomb scare yesterday morning. Someone threatened to blow himself up in Somerfield. Surprised you don't know. Your lot had the street closed off at both ends nearly all day, looking for Al-Qaeda. Me and Ali did what we always do – opened the shop at nine and was here until we closed at ten-thirty at night. Anyone'll tell you." He grinned at Chaudhuri, revealing the red-tinged teeth of a betel-nut addict.

Chaudhuri turned to Mr Haq once more. "How many sons do you have?"

"Four. Fifth son Zia dead. Two sons now in this country, two in Bangladesh. Businessmen in Bangladesh. Ver..r..ry rich!" He put extraordinary emphasis on the word 'very', widening his angry eyes. "Bangladesh good place. Here no good. No money made now. And fifth son dead. He killed by filthy racist white person in cell. But Zia no kill baby. He good Asian person. Asian love childrens. English make child abuse. All make it. Kelly, she kill baby. It not hers, so she kill it."

"What do you mean, it wasn't hers?" put in James. "Whose was it?"

"I no know. She steal baby. Zia tell me."

"Zia said nothing of this at the trial, Mr Haq. I'd say it's the first anyone's ever heard of it. It's not so easy to steal a baby in this country and get away with it."

"Yes," nodded Mr Haq, as if far from having

contradicted him he and James were in full agreement. "She get away with it because she English. Then racist white police blame my son. She fault!" he thundered at his wife, this time stabbing her with his finger. "She want be like English. She bastard."

Chaudhuri looked at the woman. Had this been going on for five years? It might simply be a one-off thing, the result of painful memories roused by their visit. But somehow he thought not. The way she accepted it suggested this was part of her daily experience.

He turned once more to Aziz. "Do you live here? In this house, I mean?"

"Yeah. We all do. Me and me wife got a room on the next floor." He glanced at the girl in the chair. "Me brother and his family's on the floor above. When did she die, then, Kelly?"

"We found her body yesterday. Did you know her?"

"Never set eyes on her. We didn't get involved in Zia's life after he left home. We wasn't allowed to."

"You were older than him?"

"A year."

That would make him twenty-six. He had the stolidity of someone thirty years older. Chaudhuri stood up.

"I'm sorry if we've revived painful memories but we'd no option, I'm afraid. We may speak to you again, Mr Haq, but for now we'll leave you in peace." He reached down and took the hand of the woman. "Goodbye, Mrs Haq. I'm sorry about your son."

So browbeaten was she, she glanced apologetically at her husband for this undeserved kindness. Chaudhuri had no doubt she'd pay for it when they'd gone.

Outside, the racket of traffic and humans was deafening. There was a Gregg's nearby so James bought a couple of meat pies for himself and a couple of cheese and onion slices for Chaudhuri.

"Would that bloke wait five years to kill Kelly?" asked James as they sat together eating in the car. "I shouldn't think he'd wait five minutes. What an arsehole. Too short to be our lady in the raincoat, though. They all are, unless they were on stilts. Best check there really was a bomb scare, mind."

"Makes no difference." Chaudhuri said through a mouthful of pastry. "None of them had an opportunity. That doesn't mean they couldn't in some way be involved, but as you say, they're all too short to be our hooded lady."

James looked thoughtful as he started on his second pie. "There couldn't be any truth in what Haq said about Zia being set-up, could there?"

"About as much truth as in the assertion that the child wasn't Kelly's. It's a lot of paranoid bollocks. Zia shook the baby so much he broke its neck." He looked round for a tissue and not finding one wiped his fingers on the paper bag from the bakers. "No, I'm not shedding any tears for Zia – if you live by the sword it's only right you should die by it. What I want to know is who the baby's father was. Also who fathered her other kid – Todd? Could be something there. Get Greene to ask Liz about it. And get him to check Brian's alibi while he's at it."

Chaudhuri took a couple of oranges out of the glove compartment and passed one to his sergeant. "What puzzles me is why Liz didn't tell us about Zia last night. Weird, that, don't you think?"

"Maybe she'd forgotten. Five years ago, after all."

"Maybe. You'd think a thing like that would never be far from your mind, wouldn't you? But there was something else our Liz's mind last night, I reckon. I reckon she knows who Kelly was meeting and she knows it wasn't the Haqs. I think she deliberately sent us on a wild-goose chase. Anyway, let her stew for a bit. She'll tell us what she knows in time. Let's see if identifying the bodies loosens her tongue. No, our murderer's from the Isle of Wight, James. I'm convinced of it."

For a moment he was distracted by a young beautiful Asian woman with hair to her waist, who crossed the road in front of the car. Could she be *the one*? He'd reached the age where he was always looking for *the one*. Well, if she was it, he'd missed it. He turned back to James, "Finished stuffing, have you? Right, let's see what Greene's come up with from the CCTV on King Street."

They played and replayed the video footage countless times but always with the same result. At 4:13 the delivery van for Smart's garden centre arrived on King Street. While the gate in the wall was open, no one but Smart and the delivery man used it to enter the garden centre. They did this three times, carrying plants from the van. But on the fourth, a few seconds behind them, a third man left by it. He wore what looked like a tweed coat, a flat cap and a scarf wrapped round his neck and half covering his mouth. He carried a dark holdall and walked, almost strolled along the street. As Chaudhuri and James watched, he crossed the road and disappeared down a side turning. It was 4.33.

"The hooded coat's obviously in the bag," said James. "But at least we know we're looking for a man."

"I'm not so certain."

"Come on! That's definitely a man."

"Really? This person is very aware of the effect of the camera. So maybe that's what we're meant to think."

"Get it enhanced, then?"

Chaudhuri nodded, "And see where that takes us."

Sixteen

It was Tuesday evening and the church clock was striking seven. The door of the parish hall burst open freeing Verity's ballet pupils to squeal their way home. Inside, their teacher was sitting at the piano using its lid as a desk as she addressed an envelope to herself. Once done, she put her ballet class money into it, sealed and stamped it ready to post in the post box outside. It would arrive through her door early on Thursday morning, meaning she'd be able to set out with it to pay the rent and council tax well before Ophelia woke. Last week she'd paid the phone bill the same way.

The alternative was to keep the cash in the house overnight and if she tried that she might as well just hand it to Ophelia the second she walked in. She hated to think how much money she'd lost that way until at last it had come to her in a flash – to use the post box as her bank. Like all good solutions it seemed obvious once she'd thought of it. There was nothing Ophelia could do to get money out of her if she didn't have it. That didn't mean Ophelia would do nothing, of course.

There was still a lump on Verity's hip from the kick

she'd got the first time she'd come in empty handed and a bald patch on the side of her head where her enraged daughter had pulled out her hair.

Ophelia had gone so berserk on the second night Verity would have smashed the post box to get the money back if she'd been able. But not being able was the whole point. Now that there was no pension to fall back on, she had to defeat Ophelia and herself in the only way she could think of – by having no choice. And it had worked.

Whether she'd worn Ophelia down or whether the lack of booze and drugs had done the work she didn't know, but this second week the violence had stopped. And with Darren absent, no doubt seeking his free supply of pizza and stimulants elsewhere, there had come a rare period of calm in which to think. Living in daily fear had rendered her incapable of any thought except how to propitiate. But now that the fear had lessened, resentment took its place.

Why had she allowed Naomi to blackmail her? If Ophelia ended up in care, so what? She'd probably prefer it. And Verity would find it a relief. Smarting from countless humiliations, she detested her daughter. Better to let her go. In years to come they might meet as friends. But she could never love her again. She'd made her feel powerless, a coward and for that Verity could never forgive her. So last Friday she'd done what she'd meant to do before that fateful journey home with Naomi and owned up to the social security about the pension.

All too late. If only she'd done the right thing from

the beginning, got out of the old weirdo's car that night and walked home rather than be intimidated then Ophelia would never have met Naomi and wouldn't have murdered her. The stupid, spiteful, degenerate little bitch denied it of course. She'd laughed the same way she had when Verity heard her discussing with Darren how much fun it would be to torture Naomi to death. But Verity knew. And she knew what she was going to do about it.

As she emerged from deep in thought her eyes focussed on a spider with a body like a currant speeding to the edge of its web stretched across one of the sills where it seized a fly as if in an embrace. Shuddering, she fled from the hall, dropped her envelope in the post box and began the steep climb towards the castle.

Twice a week, after each ballet class, she returned the hall key to Mr Smythe-Pryce, the churchwarden. Calling at his house and being invited in for a glass of sherry was the highlight of her week. But she could as soon make small talk tonight as betray Ophelia to the police. The thought of dealing with the police so terrified her she could barely speak, as if someone had glued her tongue to the roof of her mouth. She would slip the key through the letterbox and sneak away unseen.

Mr Smythe-Pryce lived with his sister along a country lane at the foot of the downs. His house was so hidden by trees that when they were in full leaf strangers didn't know it was there. It had once been a humble manor house. It was long and low and painted white and faced the lane obliquely. In front of it was a little stream with a couple of modest Saxon mounds clinging to its brink like limpets and you reached it by crossing a tiny bridge.

At the sight of the open door, panic seized her and she turned to run. But he was watching for her from the drawing room window and with a wave trotted out, glasses on forehead, finger marking the page in a book. He wore a fawn knitted waistcoat over a shirt and green woollen tie. He was elderly – a sweet, scholarly bachelor too gentle ever to have been attractive to women. Verity suspected he was in love with her. He was so self-effacing, however, she knew he'd never dream of declaring it.

"Come in, Verity, my dear. Don't stand there. Come in and have a drink."

She loved his house. The drawing room ran the length of it and had latticed windows at either end. If she reached up she could almost touch the moulded ceiling. The walls were panelled in parchment-coloured wood and above the fireplace someone long ago had carved what looked like the face of Mr Punch in high relief. The chairs were big and fat with foxglove-patterned covers, the floorboards two feet wide and black and shiny.

"Now, what's it to be? Sherry? Glass of wine? Gin and something?"

"Nothing, thank you." She handed him the key and stroked her hair to check the missing bit was covered. "I really can't stop."

He blinked and his glasses fell from his forehead onto his nose. "Oh, come, now. You need a rest after that walk and you may as well have something to drink at the same time. What's it to be?"

Yes, she needed a rest. She hadn't noticed the shakiness of her legs until now. But if she didn't sit down soon, she'd fall down.

"Would a cup of tea be too much trouble?" It would give her a few minutes to compose herself while he made it.

"No trouble at all. Just what I was fancying myself. Make yourself comfortable. Shan't be a tick."

Still clutching his book he bustled off as if to prevent her changing her mind. She heard him in the kitchen telling his sister Dorothy that she had arrived. A second later Dorothy put her snow-white head round the door. She always wore pearl stud earrings the colour of her hair and pastel-coloured clothes. Today her jumper was powder blue.

"How's our actress?" As if to make up for her brother's diffidence, Dorothy was assertive and generally not popular. "Taken the weight off your feet? Jolly good. Tea's on its way."

Actress – nowadays she forgot that was what she'd been until people reminded her. She felt so different, it was like thinking of someone else – like an old person who marvels they were ever young and loved by their children. She leaned back in her chair and looked around.

The shelves either side of the chimney held heavy, learned-looking books. Mr Smythe-Pryce was a Classics scholar. Like him, she could have gone to Oxford. She would have lived in a house like this and read those books. There would have been no Ophelia. She'd have had her aborted. But there would have been a man.

She longed for one. She could hardly believe there'd once been so many – so many, she hadn't a clue which one of them was Ophelia's father. And at the time she couldn't have cared less. Like the best femme fatale she'd treated them badly, though they'd never seemed to mind. Ironically Ophelia had turned out to be a worse punishment than anything those forgiving men could have imagined.

There it was again – Sunday night – Ophelia's face torn, her clothes smeared with blood. She'd said she'd been in a fight with Darren's girlfriend, had laughed hysterically when Verity had asked if the blood came from Naomi. But Verity had gone to check and… Oh, God, let her not think about it. Head shaking – that was the only way to get rid of the image – shake her head like those…head-bangers, was it? Shake her head. Shake it till it felt almost shaken off. The door opened and she stopped a little too slowly. Dorothy was giving her a peculiar look. Verity pretended to be shaking out her hair.

"Isn't this a glorious evening?" Dorothy set the tea tray on a low table. "I bet it was sweltering in the church hall. No matter how many windows you open, it never seems to make a difference, does it? Mrs Bevis almost fainted the day of the summer fair. I had to take over her stall while she sat outside for a bit. And you, you poor thing, pounding away at that piano for hours on end. It must be like running the marathon. You ought to get a pianist, though I expect they charge the earth. Anyway, a cup of tea'll cool you down. No sugar and milk, that's right, isn't it? Robin, pass this cup to Verity, would you?"

The cups were wide and shallow, made of what Verity thought was called *Satsuma* in shades of topaz and amethyst with a beaded gold rim. They seemed to give a special fragrance to the tea. She wanted to listen forever about gardens and the church and the castle where until he'd retired Mr Smythe-Pryce had been curator. The house was enchanted and would hide her so that no one would ever find her again. She looked up to see brother and sister staring at her.

"I'm so sorry, were you speaking to me? I was miles away, I'm afraid."

"That's all right. We were just asking how the class went tonight."

"To tell you the truth, it's completely drained me."

"Yes, you look a bit tired. Hungry, I expect. You young women are always on starvation diets. I think she should stay to dinner, Robin."

She longed to accept because she was famished. Since yesterday morning she'd eaten nothing but a bowl of bran flakes. But she was in no state for small talk and couldn't be sure she wouldn't say something dangerous if she let down her guard. "No, it's terribly kind of you, but I must get back to Ophelia."

"Ah, worried about the murderer?" This was Mr Smythe-Pryce.

"Murderer?" She took a quick drink of tea and scalded her tongue. "I didn't know…has there been a murder?"

"Yes," said Dorothy, "a dreadful affair." She stood up. "I'm going to pack you a few home grown nectarines, Verity. They're from Robin's greenhouse – best crop we've ever had. Shan't be a tick."

Mr Smythe-Pryce watched her go. "She can't bear to hear about things like that. Last night, it was. Up on St Catherine's down. A woman called Naomi Long. It's all in here." He reached down the side of his chair, took out the local paper and leafed through it. "Yes, here we are. 'Miss Naomi Long, age 65, of Holly Cottage, Athercombe. Her body was found not far from St Catherine's Oratory, popularly known as the Pepperpot.'" He looked at Vera over his glasses.

"How did she die?"

He shook his head. "It doesn't say. Perhaps the police haven't released that information yet. But what a terrible thing. The church'll say prayers for the poor woman. I can't remember when anyone was last murdered on the island, apart from that poor Danish student, of course. But her murderer was from the mainland, wasn't he? A tourist. Perhaps this one is too."

"They think it was a...what's the expression...a random attack, do they? She was simply in the wrong place at the wrong time, so to speak?"

"Goodness knows. The way poor lunatics are allowed to wander about these days, it's more than likely."

"And she was...murdered last night...on Monday evening?" She tried not to hope. But Ophelia had stayed in all day Monday.

Mr Smythe-Pryce referred to the paper again. "Found, it says. Found on Monday evening. Might have been dead for days. It's lonely up there at this time of the year."

Verity put down her cup. It made a little tinkling noise in its saucer. "I'd better be going now and let you have your dinner."

"Why not stay? Dorothy would be delighted." He looked, but didn't say, he would be delighted too.

"Thank you, but I really must get back. If there's a murderer about, I don't want to bump into him after dark. Though it wasn't dark when Naomi… at least, I suppose, not necessarily…"

Was he looking at her with suspicion? It terrified her that she could barely control her thoughts. If she were like this with Mr Smythe-Pryce, how would she manage with the police? And they would come. It was only a matter of time. She gritted her teeth to pull herself together.

"I mean, if she was walking the downs when she was murdered it must have been light. The paper says she was discovered in the evening, doesn't it? I wonder what time? It must still have been light or you wouldn't find a body, would you?"

"I doubt it. You're perfectly right. It must have been light. And no sane person would walk the downs after dark. Though by all accounts Naomi was a most peculiar woman."

"Really? In what way?"

He hesitated as if he'd revealed more than he intended then dropped his voice to a whisper. "Don't want to say anything in front of Dot – she loathes what she thinks of as prurient talk – but I heard something tonight a bit unsettling. In fact, I don't mind saying it's knocked me for six."

"Yes, you don't seem your usual self. What was it?"

He glanced towards the door to make sure it was shut. "You know David Bell, the church organist? Well,

I was in the church earlier this evening when he came in to practise. The concert's tomorrow night by the way, if you're thinking of going, I've got a spare ticket in case you're interested. Anyway, we got to talking about the murder and he told me something he'd heard apropos of it. A few years ago a poor woman hanged herself in some woods not far from here. There was a sad story behind it I gather, though he didn't get round to telling me what, because Mrs Crystal came in with some flowers. But the main thing was, on the day this woman hanged herself, the person who found her saw Naomi Long there too. And here's the awful thing – she was watching her as she died. Yes, watching her and…well, there's no need to go into detail." To cover his blush he took out his hanky and pretended to blow his nose. "To think she might have saved the woman and didn't. It doesn't *bear* thinking about, does it?"

Her feelings must have shown in her face, though he misinterpreted them. "Oh, my dear, have I upset you? I shouldn't have mentioned it. Dot's right, one shouldn't dwell on these things."

She shook her head. "You haven't upset me at all. I'm glad you've told me." Now it was her turn to glance at the door. "But do you think that's why Naomi was killed? Some relation of the woman who hanged herself taking their revenge?"

"I don't know. It seems rather late in the day, doesn't it? It happened years ago. Ought I to get in touch with the police?"

She thought for a few seconds. How many people apart from Ophelia might have wanted Naomi dead? Here was one, out of the blue. And with justification.

Horrible, merciless, twisted, bitch. There could be scores of others for the police to concentrate on. She looked into Mr Smythe-Pryce's troubled, earnest face.

"I suppose you could just have a word with the police. I take it the woman in the wood did actually kill herself? There's no suspicion it might have been murder?"

"No, they were sure it was suicide according to David Bell. She must have left a note, I suppose."

"Still, I think the police should be told. It was very odd behaviour on Naomi's part. It's the sort of behaviour that could make some people…"

"Ah, Dorothy." Mr Smythe-Pryce jumped as his sister entered. "We were just talking about the concert. Where did I put Verity's ticket? I'm going to run her home in the car. She mustn't be allowed to walk those lanes with this murderer on the loose."

"Heavens!" Dorothy handed Verity a carrier bag of nectarines and a tin containing a home made sandwich cake. "Quite right, Robin. Don't let her do it."

Seventeen

The Solent was the colour of peppermint ice. Chaudhuri and James stood on the deck of the car ferry, letting the wind buffet the dust of London from their pores. Seagulls flew alongside, black legs limp against bodies of such dazzling white, it almost hurt to look at them. Like a hump-backed monster The Needles drifted out from the headland in the west.

They landed at Yarmouth. At the village of Caulfleet they stopped at traffic lights – the arched bridge across the stream was too narrow for cars to pass both ways. While waiting Chaudhuri admired a manor house on their left and an ancient church on the opposite side, its massive squat tower veiled by yew trees. A notice near the lych-gate announced Sunday to be harvest festival. He pictured the vividness of fruit and flowers against carved stone and wood. If there was time, and he was still on the island, he would go to the service. He'd once had a girlfriend he'd followed everywhere, even to church and he'd been surprised to discover he enjoyed it, especially the hymns and the kindly prayers. But he wouldn't let on to James, who thought to be a Christian was to discriminate against other religions. Chaudhuri had noticed the daft bugger didn't think the same about Hinduism. Or if he did, he thought it better not to say so. Well trained.

The traffic lights turned green and the car swooped over the bridge towards Newport. The first call was police headquarters where Superintendent Jefferson expected them.

He was a tall, good-looking man with thick auburn hair in a glamorous, leonine style. Only a high-ranking officer could get away with looking like that. Chaudhuri couldn't help wondering how the Superintendent would fare with the drunks in Shepherd's Bush on a Friday night. He was a Bristolian, educated at Clifton Boys' School, and seemed delighted to hear Chaudhuri had been to university there.

"Ah, it's a wonderful city. The suspension bridge. Clifton gorge. Did you know Clifton is described as the most beautiful suburb in the world? Fully deserved, too. But to my mind there's nowhere like this island. A bit of a change from London, eh?"

A knock on the door interrupted Chaudhuri's reply. A huge, blond, Viking of a man entered. Jefferson introduced him as Chief Inspector Trent. Behind him a uniformed officer carried a tray of tea.

"So," said Jefferson as he handed round cups, "this murder of yours – you think you're not dealing with a random attack? You think your victims knew their killer?"

Chaudhuri bit a custard cream (his favourite) in half and swallowed it with a gulp of tea.

"What I will say from looking at the CCTV is that

the murder was well planned. Whether or not Kelly and Jade were the intended victims is debatable. I think, though, the location and the time of day militates against its being a random attack. The place is bristling with security cameras which in view of the care taken to mask her identity the murderer seemed to expect. Though James here disagrees, I think we're looking for a woman. And a highly intelligent one at that. Anyway, we've given her or him the name of Raven for the sake of argument. I've brought a copy of the CCTV. We've had it enhanced, though it doesn't seem to have helped much. Would you like to see it? I'd value your opinion."

The video was switched on. Black-clad Raven entered the park.

"There now, what's your first impression – man or woman?"

"At first glance I'd say female. It's the coat that does it, of course. You wouldn't expect a man to wear it."

"Yes, yes, that's true. Now watch closely – here's where Raven stops and appears to hesitate. It looks to me as if she's deciding whether the shrubbery might be a good place to hide. The point is, if she were familiar with the park – if she was a Londoner – she'd have already decided. She wouldn't hesitate for a second. I think she planned the location simply by consulting a map – probably an A-Z."

He was struck, as he was each time he looked at her, by the sinister shuffling walk, so different from later, when she left the crime scene. Obviously it was another part of a well-thought-out disguise. He fast-forwarded.

"Now, here come Kelly and Jade. They stop too, just where Raven stopped earlier. Why? Is she calling to them? Kelly's saying something – to her or to Jade? Is Raven feigning illness, perhaps? Is that why Kelly goes to her? It may be prejudice on my part but from the little I know of Kelly, I doubt it. I don't think she'd put herself out for a stranger who appeared to be in distress. I think she knows Raven. Is it the person she's come to London to meet? We've yet to discover that, although from what her mother said, she was meeting more than one. But to my eyes Kelly and Jade are the intended victims and Raven well known to them. Now, if you've a couple more minutes, I'd like you to take a quick look at this. This is the CCTV of Raven leaving. This time, as you can see, she's wearing an overcoat and a cap. Not very clear, I'm afraid, but the general impression this time is of a man."

"Yes, that's a man without doubt."

"You think so?"

"Without doubt."

"Right. You see my problem? Master of disguise, this one. I've some enhanced stills here, though they're hardly more helpful. No hope of you being able to identify her, I suppose?"

Both Jefferson and Trent shook their heads.

Jefferson took a drink of tea. "What makes you think Raven is from the island?"

"Kelly had been away from London for more than two years and gone back only twice in that time, which implies she'd no longer much involvement with the place. However, she was planning to return, which I can't picture her doing if she knew she had an enemy there. Was the enemy in fact here? Was the island becoming an uncomfortable or even a dangerous place for her?"

"Well, as far as we know she wasn't up to anything. I stress, as far as we *know*. She'd got no record, either as Houghton or Parker, but resources being what they are, we'll all agree that means little or nothing." Nodding their heads ruefully, they all did. "By the way, what about CCTV from the ferry terminals? If Raven hails from here they'll have picked her up. Unless she's got her own boat, of course."

"I've got one of my men at Portsmouth as we speak, going through them. Now, sir, there's a boyfriend of the name of Darren Frost I'd like to question. Same Sandown address as Kelly. I'll call on him straight away if he hasn't done a runner. And if you've no objections, of course."

Jefferson gave his consent with an expansive wave of the hand.

'I'm wondering," he said, "if the fact that Kelly was meeting more than one person might point to a connection with a case Trent here is in charge of. On Sunday we had a murder of our own." He looked rather proud of it. "A rare thing on the island but not unknown. And this one was a bit unpleasant, as it happens. A Miss Naomi Long – elderly woman – kicked to death by two people on a particularly lonely part of the downs. We didn't find her body until Monday evening. I wanted Inspector Trent to hear what you have to say because three people from the island murdered within a day of each other – albeit two of them in London – well, it's so singular, a connection seems obvious."

Chaudhuri turned to Trent. "Have you made an

arrest?"

"We haven't, unfortunately."

It was the first time Trent had spoken. His voice was so deep Chaudhuri was startled. He attempted to turn his look of surprise into a friendly smile.

"As in your case, Inspector Chaudhuri," Trent smiled back, "we don't know whether they were male or female, only that they were wearing trainers – size six and size seven."

"Smaller than average feet for a man. Do you think they were women? Or one of them was?"

Trent shrugged. "It's possible. Even probable. But whoever they are, they must have been a gruesome sight walking back to their car. Yes," he raised his eyes to the ceiling in contempt, "that's what they did. They trailed blood all the way back to the car park. Does that mean the murder was spontaneous? A bit of psychotic fun? If it was planned they must be as thick as two short planks. I know it's the end of the holiday season but there's nearly always somebody out walking those downs on a Sunday. But thick or not, we think it was pre-meditated. The victim's cottage was broken into late last night."

"Last night? And she was murdered the day before?"

"Yes. Weird, isn't it? If it's the murderers, why wait a day? And though they made one hell of a mess, it doesn't look as if anything's been stolen. Not the usual stuff, anyway. Jewellery, even money, it's all there."

"They were looking for something specific."

"But what? She was a law-abiding spinster. What could she have that was of more interest to a burglar than money?"

Chaudhuri had no ready answer to that one. But he

felt his senses tingle. Kelly's murderer was here on the island. And the people she'd been expecting to meet – were they the two who had murdered this Naomi Long? Had only one of them, for whatever reason, followed Kelly to London? But why London at all, if they lived on the island? Well, that was the crux of the case. Once he knew why Kelly had gone there everything else would fall into line. But in this sleepy place where according to Jefferson murder was almost unheard of, was it possible the deaths of Kelly and Miss Long were unconnected? Highly unlikely. He and Trent were after the same culprits. They could work together. But the one Chaudhuri wanted was the woman.

Jefferson broke into his reverie. "It might be useful for you to drop in at the incident room and see what Trent's team has come up with. Want him to go with you to Sandown first and help with the boyfriend? He could drive on ahead of you and show the way. It's not far." He got up and pointed at a map on the wall. "Here's Sandown – about a fifteen minute journey and very pleasant, as it happens. How long would that distance take you in London – an hour and a half? Longer? Thought so. Talk about the pace of life in the capital. A snail's pace. Takes half an hour to buy a bloody stamp."

He looked quite smug to have got that off his chest.

Eighteen

There was no doubt Kelly's flat was deserted. From experience that had become second sight the three men could tell when someone was in but not answering the door. If the boyfriend Darren Frost still lived here, he wasn't home. Neither was there any response from the flat below. A look through the windows showed it to be unoccupied and empty of furniture. So James was left to watch from the car in case Darren returned while Trent drove Chaudhuri to the incident room in Athercombe.

"It'll be useful for you to meet my team. With a bit of luck, one of them might know something of your Kelly Houghton. I can show you our crime scene if you like, as well. It's a bit of a trek, mind." He stole a glance at Chaudhuri's immaculate suit and glossy shoes. His own were always scuffed, which his mother used to say was the sign of a dubious character. "On second thoughts, it'll soon be dark, so maybe we should leave it for another day. How long are you staying?"

"I'd like to say as long as it takes, though that might tempt me to drag my feet. Magical place, isn't it?" Like a little boy, Chaudhuri twisted round in his seat to prolong the sight of Old Walpen. "Look at the pheasant on that roof. Is it real? Oh, no, it's made of thatch. I've never seen that before. There's nowhere like England in my opinion, especially on a day like this. Nowhere."

Trent was pleasantly surprised. He'd always associated ethnic minorities with resentful anti-English whinging that masked downright racism. He'd often been tempted to vote for the BNP as a result. But like most reactionaries, he could very quickly sway in the opposite direction. "Got somewhere nice to stay while you're here?" He was prepared to put Chaudhuri up at his house if he hadn't.

"The Painted Plough in Newport. Any good?"

"Oh, yes, it's a nice old-fashioned inn. She does a great steak and kidney pie. Attractive woman, as well." He gave Chaudhuri a grin. "You married, by any chance?"

"Afraid not. Never met a woman stupid enough to have me."

"Parents going to find you a nice Indian girl, I expect?"

"What, an arranged marriage, you mean? No, no. That's not for me. I prefer to make my own mistakes, Trent. How about you?"

"Bachelor like yourself." He sighed. "Never any time to meet anyone in this job, let alone fall in love."

"Yes, that's about it."

"Call me Bob, by the way."

"All right, Bob. I'm Tom."

"Thomas – the patron saint of India."

"Really? I didn't know that. I only know he was the doubting one, like me."

"Not a bad attitude for a policeman."

They were silent for a while. Trent thought Chaudhuri had fallen asleep. But again he was gazing from sea to countryside as if entranced. He caught Trent looking at him.

"Funny there are no people, eh? I mean, you can see their handiwork all around neat as a new pin but the people are nowhere in sight."

"Yes, you're right. I'd never really thought of it before. You see the odd tractor. But if I saw a person in the fields it would seem peculiar."

"Live in Newport, do you?"

"No, I've a cottage over near Ashbury – that's the witchcraft village, or was in the past."

"Witchcraft village?" Chaudhuri shook his head, incredulous. "It's like a fairy-tale here. Though I suppose the poor women they condemned as witches didn't think so."

Trent shrugged. "Shouldn't have broken the law, then, should they? They knew the penalty. Putting the evil eye on people and making pacts with the Devil. It's not exactly fighting for human rights, is it? Hardly the stuff of martyrs."

Chaudhuri laughed, the whiteness of his teeth making his face even brighter. "Our modern-day witches will have you tied to the ducking stool if they hear you. By the way, there was something I meant to ask you – how do you know Miss Long's cottage was broken into on Monday rather than Sunday?"

"The man who found her on Monday – actually, it was his dog – the body had been kicked into some bushes. A bit similar to your case in London, now I think about it. Anyway, the man who found her called at her cottage on both Sunday and Monday evening. Ted Britten's his name. Lives in the same village, not many doors away. He was concerned about her. On Sunday she didn't go to church for either the morning or the evening service. He's churchwarden."

"A regular churchgoer, was she?"

"Never missed, apparently. On Sunday when she hadn't turned up for the evening service he called on her about eight o'clock. There was no answer, so at ten he tried again. She wasn't in – well, he wasn't to know she'd been lying dead about five hours by then – but the point is, there was no sign of any break-in. He wasn't worried, exactly – a bit puzzled because her car was there but no more than that. He thought maybe she'd been invited out somewhere for a change. If she would be having a drink she'd leave her car to be on the safe side. Anyway, on Monday he expected to see her leave for work as usual but at ten o'clock in the morning the car was still parked. He called on her again and got no answer. Had a good look through the downstairs windows but nothing seemed amiss. He did the same at five before he went for his walk on the downs. And that's where he found her body. I spoke to him again this morning and he swears that at five o'clock on Monday there was no break-in. But when I sent some of my team down to the cottage at eleven that night, the back door had been forced and the place ransacked."

The sun, which had dazzled them by being on a level with their eyes, sank like a beach ball into the sea. Darkness would come quickly now.

Chaudhuri said, "How long had she lived on the

island?"

"Nigh on thirty years, apparently, and always in the same house. Came from somewhere up north with her parents when they retired. They've both been dead for donkey's years, though. She's lived alone since."

"And how soon would you have expected news of her death to get round?"

"Hard to say. Ted Britten was in no state to go and gossip in the pub. In a right state, he was. Of course, these things do get round quickly but Athercombe's a remote village. We're nearly there, by the way. Why do you ask?"

"Well, it seems as if your burglar took the first opportunity to break in when he knew he'd have a couple of hours undisturbed – in other words, when he knew Miss Long was dead. But if he was also one of the murderers he'd have broken in on Sunday, wouldn't he? Did she have her keys on her, by the way? She did? There you are, then. Why would the murderers need to break in? So she wasn't necessarily murdered for what was hidden in the cottage. It might have been broken into by someone who'd only that night heard of her death and knew you'd be searching eventually. He had to get there before you."

Trent shook his head. "I simply can't picture a law-abiding spinster having so many enemies. It doesn't ring true. And her murder was so messy and inept it might have been a random attack. Imagine choosing to kick someone to death. Why not stab them, if you've planned it? Because it wasn't planned, that's why. I think it was a spur of the moment thing and after it they panicked. I don't think they were calm enough or even basically intelligent enough to think about taking her keys. Murder, that's all they could think about. And once they'd done it, they scuttled off home as fast as they could. I think breaking into the cottage was an afterthought. They'd got over the shock of killing her by then and thought they might make something out of it. As it happens she had nothing any villain would want. But they weren't to know that, were they? And having omitted to take the keys from the body, they'd no choice but to break in. They left it till night because they'd be seen in the day – lot of retired people on the watch in these villages, not like London. That to me seems the likeliest explanation."

"Yet they didn't touch her money? You said earlier you'd found money at the cottage."

"Just a bit of change in her bag." Trent shifted uncomfortably. "It's odd they left it, I agree, but her bag was on the floor wedged between a chair and the dining table. Maybe they were so busy pulling the place apart they didn't notice it. Or missed it in the dark. We've already established she had no credit cards with any of the banks on the island, just a savings account at the post office branch where she worked. But yes, it's odd about the money." He narrowed his eyes as if squinting against the sun. It was what he always did to show he was thinking. "Alternatively, here's another theory for you – they were, as you say, looking for something particular, that's why the money was left. And why the delay between the murder and the break-in? Because on Monday they were in London. Maybe even travelled there on Sunday night."

"You mean the murderers of Naomi and Kelly are

the same? And their priority before they broke into the cottage was to get Kelly out of the way?" Chaudhuri pouted a bit as he considered. "Could be. We know Kelly was expecting to meet more than one person. In the event her murderer was alone, however."

"Maybe one of them was injured in the attack on Naomi. We got samples of two different blood groups at the scene."

Chaudhuri leaned his head back. "I'd like to believe it, Bob. It would make everything so much easier if our culprits were the same. But the methods – they were completely different. Kelly's killer, cool, precise, full of foresight. Naomi's, as you say, slapdash. They didn't even take a weapon with them. And yet," he conceded, "that's no reason why the same person couldn't have committed them both. Kelly's murder could have been planned first, though she was killed later. Maybe they didn't have time to plan Naomi's killing. Anyway, they're definitely connected. I can feel it in my bones." He grinned. "Not much of a substitute for DNA but it's all I've got at the moment."

They had come to the outskirts of the village. Trent stopped the car.

"Look up there." He got out and pointed to a ridge that sloped upwards towards the sea. It was black against the dying light of the sky. "That's where we found Naomi, about half way to that tower that sticks up there on the right. We call it the Pepperpot. It's a disused lighthouse. Hundreds of years old, it is. She used to walk up there every day – twice a day, sometimes. We'll go there tomorrow, if you're interested. Anyway, lets pop into the incident room and then, if Kelly's boyfriend still isn't home, I'll take you to have a look at Naomi's cottage."

There was no village green. The heart of the village was the old church on top of the cliff. Many a drowned sailor, even a smuggler, was buried in the churchyard with an anchor for a headstone. The road inland curved round by the churchyard wall. On either side were houses and cottages, some down narrow lanes, hidden in the thickness of the trees.

The incident room was in the wooden village hall. A tea urn hissed in a corner. The table on which it stood was littered with plastic cups and spilled sugar and greasy paper bags. There was an aroma of bacon sandwiches but, Trent noticed with regret, no sign of any. He introduced Chaudhuri, explained why he was there, and requested he should receive as much help as he needed. Did anyone know anything concerning Kelly Houghton or Parker, for example? No one did. Anyone ever heard of her? No one had. Neither, in the past couple of hours, except for crank calls, had there been any developments in the Naomi Long case, now known as 'Lighthouse'. There was DNA but no match on the database. Trent decided to take Chaudhuri straight to the cottage.

In the dusky light it looked as if it were half asleep. But inside things were not so peaceful. Every room been had ransacked. Not vandalised – the perpetrator had either had no time or no inclination to smash things. But a hectic search for something had taken place in every drawer and cupboard and under every rug and mattress. From a fall of soot on the hearth it seemed the intruder had even checked the chimney.

Trent handed Chaudhuri a pair of protective gloves. "Whoever it was, they wore gloves and worked by torchlight, which might be why they overlooked her bag. None of the neighbours saw any light at all. We've found only two sets of fingerprints, Naomi's and Ted Britten's. Sad that, don't you think?"

"Bit of a loner?"

"Yes, one of a dying breed. Typical spinster, as I think I said before. She worked in the post office at Newport. Been there years. Oh, and she went to séances." He laughed. "You know, crystal balls and all that stuff. Ted Britten told me. Apparently he didn't approve. Disturbing the dead was how he saw it. But what harm if it gave her comfort? Disturbing nobody, to my mind. And she didn't have many friends, obviously."

"From choice or because she was unpopular?"

"Maybe not either. Maybe just because of living in a village. The staff at the post office didn't mix with her much but they're all a lot younger so you can't expect it. Apart from that they'd no complaints. Mind you, Ted Britten did tell me something a bit strange – apparently she hardly ever put her lights on, which is why you can be sure the neighbours would have noticed if our burglars had. Many a time Ted's seen her come in from work on dark nights and never a glimpse of a light. He put it down to eccentricity."

"Eccentricity? It's positively weird."

"That's what I thought. And another thing – she never listened in church, he said. Used to get on people's nerves, apparently."

"Never listened? How, exactly?"

"Fidgeted, according to Ted – in the sermons and

the bible readings. Fishing in her handbag, shifting around in the pew, sometimes even catching people's eye and grinning at them and stuff. Just as if she wanted to spoil it for them. Then when the hymns came on she sang louder than anybody though she was tone deaf, he said, and never kept in time with everyone else. Must have driven them mad, though it makes you want to laugh, thinking about it."

He saw Chaudhuri's mouth twitch.

"Oh, and her language was another thing. Swore like a trooper and Ted was sure it didn't always slip out by accident. Did it on purpose most times, especially when the vicar was about. Enough to drive any man of the cloth to murder, in my view. Better call on him next."

They doubled up with laughter and in the process Chaudhuri accidentally kicked a wooden casket which lay open on the floor. He picked it up. It was roughly the size of a shoe box and made of a grainless, soft wood, easy to carve and inlaid with brass.

"Well, would you believe it. When I was little one of my aunts had a casket like this. They sell them to the tourists in India. Hers had a secret drawer. You see this bit of wood round the base – it looks like beading, doesn't it? Well, if you slide it – bingo, there you are."

A concealed drawer shot out from the side. Uppermost was a neat parcel wrapped in tissue paper. Chaudhuri handed it to Trent, an action which lifted him even further in the latter's esteem. He opened it and brought out a handful of photographs.

"Christ, it's Darius Field." He scrutinised the pictures by the light of the window. "He's got estate agent businesses all over the island. Probably owns half of it."

Chaudhuri peered over his shoulder. "Do you recognise the woman?"

"Can't make out the face." Trent held the photos at all angles. "No, I don't recognise her. What a little cracker, though. I look forward to interviewing her, whoever she is."

"What's that building they're in? Looks like a castle tower."

"That's the Pepperpot. The old lighthouse we were talking about, up there near the crime scene."

The eagerness in Chaudhuri's eyes Trent knew to be reflected in his own. He turned his attention to the box again. An envelope contained £1,300 in cash. There was a small diary, blank except for some recent entries for September. The inscription *VS – £150* occurred on the Thursday of the first and second week. On the Monday of the second week was written *AB – £1000*.

Chaudhuri said, "Did she have an address book? Or a mobile phone? We might be able to match the initials to a full name."

"Our intruder evidently thought the same. There's no address book anywhere, though I'm sure she would have had one. No mobile, either. There's no computer socket so she obviously didn't bother with a PC, which is a big shame from our point of view. There was only the purse in her handbag, a couple of library books and a packet of fags."

Chaudhuri studied the photos again. "She was a blackmailer, wasn't she? Are these what the burglar was searching for?"

"Well, it's just occurred to me that we've turned up

no camera. If it was in the house and our burglar took it, it looks like an act of desperation – he couldn't find the photos, so takes the camera to be on the safe side."

Chaudhuri picked up the diary. "No mention of Kelly Houghton, not even her initials. The woman in the photos, is she *VS* or *AB*? How much would she be willing to pay to keep these photos secret, a hundred and fifty pounds a time or a thousand? Impossible to say until we know her."

"We know the man, though," Trent reminded him. "And he's the island's biggest landlord amongst other things. What are the chances of his being Kelly's?" He looked at his watch. "Eight o'clock. I'll get someone to give Field a ring and make sure he's home. I think it would be a good idea for you to come with me if you're not too tired. We could have a bite to eat first. We do fantastic fish and chips here, as you'd expect. Or we can get a curry if you prefer."

"It'd be a sin to come to an island and not have fish and chips. I'll have a large portion of both if it's going."

Fantastic bloke, Trent decided. He became expansive as they made their way back across the road to the incident room.

"Field lives at Corve Manor, not far from here. It's a spooky old place – fourteenth century or thereabouts. He often has guests, I believe, but we'll just have to risk interrupting a dinner party. My sergeant will drive us and take notes. By the way, do you want to tell James to knock off for the night? I'll get one of my team to take over and give him a break. It's early. The boyfriend still might show. But if he doesn't, there's nothing to stop you letting yourself into the flat tomorrow, is there?

Have you got keys? There you are, then. No need for a warrant."

Bats swooped against the night sky and from somewhere, some cottage garden, came the scent of tobacco flowers. There was silence except for a faint sound which might have been the breeze in the trees or the sea.

Nineteen

He didn't know whether it was the sea air or being full of mushy peas, haddock and chips but Chaudhuri could have done with a nap. He didn't want to offend his new friend Trent, however. So after a cup of coffee strong enough to keep him awake all night if need be, he felt more than ready to call on Darius Field. He sat beside Trent in the back of the car while Sergeant Cooper drove.

The night was full of stars. Above him rose the giant constellations he'd learned as a boy to recognise from books and which with a shiver of unease he now saw for the first time. The earth was a shadow against the sky. Sometimes the dark bulk of a cottage or farm was passed, clinging to the road as if craving company. These winding English lanes are very old and full of ghosts.

In the twisted black hedgerow that reminded him of witches' brooms a gap appeared. It was flanked either side by a stone gatepost topped with a crumbling griffin. The car drove between them into a tree-lined drive. A single light shone in the distance; sometimes obscured by the grove of trees, sometimes visible, as if it watched then hid. They entered an open court, half gravelled, half formal garden. High box hedge cut in the shape of a sphere at the corners flanked a path that led to the long, low house – Corve Manor.

Built in the time of Edward III, its windows in its massive walls were tiny, save for the one where the light shone. This was disproportionately wide for its height. Its leaded panes bulged out as if buckling beneath the weight of stone. Inside could be seen the flickering of a fire.

Chaudhuri was a bit disappointed when Field himself and, not a butler, answered the door. He noted that Trent was deferential as he showed his warrant card.

"Yes, I got your phone call," said Field. "Come in." His voice, though low, was resonant.

They stepped into a hall whose floor was of white stone, bevelled in places by centuries of feet. A wide uncarpeted staircase branched off left and right to a gallery above. Field was about forty, tall and with the darkness of a Celt. His casual but beautifully cut clothes showed a slim, powerful body as he led them into a well-lit room.

The stone fireplace, above which hung an old carved panel, reached almost to the beamed ceiling. The carving over the fireplace showed Adam and Eve being expelled from Eden, mouths turned down in sorrow and Eve pulling out her flowing hair. The panelling on the rest of the walls was painted with figures so faded they looked like wraiths neither fully materialised nor completely dissolved. The fire, though burning convincingly, was gas. There was something comforting about this link with the present. Chaudhuri and Trent sat on a long lemon-coloured sofa close to it, while Sergeant Cooper took a seat near a small table to take notes. All declined the offer of a drink.

Trent said, "I'm sorry to disturb you so late, Mr Field, but we're investigating the murder of Naomi Long."

No response. He tried again.

"You must have heard about it. It's been front-page news in the local paper. She was found on Monday on St Catherine's down."

"Yes, I read about it." He sat elegant but relaxed, his elbow on the arm of his chair, hand covering his mouth. "But why should you think I can help you?"

"Anyone who knew her can be a help to us at this stage."

Field moved the hand with a flourish. "Then you've literally come to the wrong house, Inspector. As far as I'm aware, I never set eyes on the woman in my life."

"Really?" Trent sounded unconcerned. "Well, that's unfortunate. I was hoping you could help us. Her cottage was broken into. Did I mention that? Not a common or garden burglary, mind. No, whoever did it was looking for something particular. You might be interested, Mr Field, to have a look at this."

He reached into his pocket and brought out one of the photos, now in a clear, sealed bag. Field took it. He gazed at it for so long he might have forgotten the existence of everything else.

"Which one of you paid the blackmail money? You or the lady in the photo?"

"I did." He spoke without hesitation. "The demand was sent to Abby but I gave her the money."

"Abby? Would you tell me her full name?"

"Why?" His eyes gleamed like jet as he looked up at Trent from beneath black brows.

"We'll need to talk to her, I'm afraid. This is, after all, a murder enquiry."

"Are you trying to tell me you suspect her?" As if to show contempt he tossed the photograph onto the table between them. "Why should Abby murder Naomi? Do ordinary people murder blackmailers when the far easier alternative of paying is available?"

"Ordinary or not, they often murder at the prospect of having to pay more."

"Then suspect me."

"Perhaps I already do, Mr Field. But I'd still like you to tell me the lady's full name."

Field got up and went to the many-paned, bulging window. In the darkness there was nothing to be seen but his reflection and the reflection of the room behind him. The muscles of his arms were outlined beneath the primrose-coloured sweater as he put his hands in his pockets. He said, "Her name's Abigail Benson."

"And where can we find her?"

"She runs a beauty salon – *Abigail's* in the market square at Newport. If you must talk to her, it would be better to do it there."

Trent gave Chaudhuri a glance. Apparently he too thought they sounded an unlikely couple. Though the woman in the photo was undoubtedly pretty, there was something incongruous about a glorified hairdresser. In Chaudhuri's opinion Field could have had any woman he wanted. Then why not a more sophisticated one – not to put too fine a point on it, someone more of his class?

Trent said, "How long have you known Abigail Benson, Mr Field?"

"Over a year. She used to come here to give my wife some sort of beauty treatments."

"But she doesn't now?"

"No."

"Why?"

Field turned from the window and leaned against the stone embrasure. "In the circumstances, it would be in rather bad taste, don't you think?"

"Your wife knows about her…her friendship with you, does she?"

"She hasn't said. But she probably suspects. Why are you so interested? Is infidelity a crime now in this Orwellian country?"

Trent was unperturbed. "I'm simply trying to get a bearing on the situation. Tell me about the blackmail, if you would. When did it begin?"

"The Sunday before last – the day that photograph was taken."

"Am I right in thinking the place is St Catherine's lighthouse?"

"Yes."

"Did you go there a lot?"

"We did. Fairly often in the past though not so much recently – except for that Sunday, of course."

"All right. Tell me everything you can remember about the blackmail, if you would."

A scream made Chaudhuri jump. It seemed to come

from outside the house and at a distance. But it was moving. With a speed outstripping anything human it came closer, passed beneath the window and without pause faded into the night.

"Our vixen." With a grin at Chaudhuri, Field turned to watch it, cupping his hands on the window and peering closely through the glass.

"The blackmail, Mr Field…"

"Oh, yes." He rubbed condensation from one of the leaded panes and continued to look into the dark. "I think Abby said it was eight o'clock that evening. She was home by herself when she heard someone at the door – not knocking, just fiddling with the letterbox as if they were looking through. It frightened her."

"Lives alone, does she?"

"No."

"Married?"

A definite hesitation this time, "Yes."

"And the name of her husband?"

"It's Doug." From the movement of his neck muscles it seemed he clenched his teeth. "Doug as in slug."

"Doug Benson? Very well, Mr Field. Carry on, would you?"

Field threw Trent a glance of resignation mixed with disgust. "An envelope had been pushed through the letterbox. There was no stamp on it, only Abby's name. She thought it looked like a greetings card and that's exactly what it was. It had a picture of a Labrador puppy on the front. But inside was a photo similar to the one you've got there. There was also a note from Naomi. She asked for a thousand pounds by Friday or she'd send the rest of the photos to Abby's husband."

"I see. Very worrying. So what did Abby do?"

"She phoned me." He came back to the fire and sat down. "I was at The George in Yarmouth. My wife and I were having dinner with some friends from Italy. I told them it was a business call and went outside to take it."

"Abby wanted you to give her the money, did she?"

"Yes. Poor darling, she said she wanted to borrow it. She was adamant she'd pay it back."

"And you agreed?"

He reacted as if Trent had committed a *faux pas*. "Not to being paid back. But I didn't think she should pay it at all. I told her to burn the photo, say nothing and leave Naomi to me."

"I thought you said you didn't know Miss Long?"

"I didn't. But I wouldn't have needed a private investigator to find her."

"And when you found her, what did you intend to do?"

"What I'm sure you'll agree is the most effective thing." He looked mischievous as he smiled. "Report her to you."

"But you didn't. Though it would have been the best thing for all, you didn't do it, Mr Field. Why?"

Again Field rested his elbow on the arm of his chair. He stroked his lower lip with his forefinger and appeared to sum Trent up. After a few seconds the stroking stopped.

"Have you ever lived in terror of someone? Have you ever dreaded another person so much you hardly dare think when you're with them in case they're able to read your mind? I suppose you haven't. I suppose only a woman or a child would feel such an emotion. But that's what my beautiful Abby has to put up with from the slug. It's because he's a slug and she's beautiful that he hates her. Simple as that. He's one of those men who, once he's got a beautiful woman wants to destroy her out of jealousy. You're probably wondering why in that case she runs the risk of seeing me. It's because she wouldn't have anything to live for if she didn't – well, that's what she says, anyway."

His smile was embarrassed, as if he feared he'd been conceited. That vulnerability made him suddenly very likeable. Chaudhuri wasn't surprised Abby had fallen for him. What amazed him was that she was still with her husband.

"The slug already suspects, of course. A couple of weeks ago he came in from one of his séances..." He leapt up suddenly and strode again to the window, drumming with his fist on the side of his thigh then lifting it as if he would smash it through the glass. Instead he pressed the fist to his mouth, keeping it there for a few moments until he was once more master of his words. "He beat her. He'd had a 'message' from his spirit guide, he said, telling him she was unfaithful. Christ, I wish his spirit guide would haunt him to death and drag him by his ponytail to Purgatory." The outburst had drained him. He came back and slumped in his chair. "Since then we've been extra careful. We went to the Pepperpot that Sunday only because the slug had gone to the mainland. Usually I follow him to these spiritualist meetings in Ryde to make sure he goes in then drive to Abby like a bat out of Hell. We sit and hold hands in the garden shed so she can slip into the house if he comes back unexpectedly. So much for being unfaithful. But it's enough for me. It'd be enough for anyone who knew her."

He pointed to the photograph.

"But those things are in a different league from the slug's spirit messages. This time he'd probably have killed her. And such is her terror of him, if I hadn't promised to pay the blackmail she'd have confessed to him the minute he walked through the door. I didn't try to talk her out of it for long, believe me. Instead we arranged to meet in Newport the following morning when I'd give her the money and she could take it straight to Naomi."

Trent shook his head. "Very misguided, if you'll allow me to say, Mr Field. If Abby is suffering marital abuse she should report it to us and let the courts deal with it."

Field laughed as much for emotional release, Chaudhuri thought, as from amusement.

"I don't think we'll need to trouble you, though it's kind of you to offer. I'm more than capable of avenging Abby the second she wants me to."

"If that means you intend taking the law into your own hands, I would advise strongly against it."

"All right. I'll bear it in mind at the opportune moment."

He laughed again. Trent looked at him like a stern schoolmaster.

"The money you paid Naomi Long – was it in cash?"

"Of course. That was one of the stipulations. Another was that Abby should go to the post office where the bitch worked and hand it over in exchange for the photos. But she didn't get them. Naomi hadn't expected her so soon, she said, and hadn't brought them with her. She kept the money, though. She told Abby to call for the photos on Friday. Abby did but this time Naomi said she'd forgotten to bring them."

He looked from Trent to Chaudhuri.

"I know what you're thinking. But it never occurred to us to kill her. Abby's incapable of it. And I was beginning to see if it finally got her to leave her husband it was a blessing in disguise. I was willing to pay through the nose until she started to feel more guilty about me than him. Then she'd leave him. I know her, you see."

"But do you know her, Mr Field?" Trent spoke as if in a heated discussion of great interest. He leaned towards Field with his forearms on his knees. "Surely now Miss Long's dead there's no urgency for Abby to leave her husband? She's still with him, you tell me. Isn't that because she's happy for things to continue in secret between you? The danger's past, isn't it? She can have her cake and eat it, as the saying goes."

Had this thought also occurred to Field? He sat still, perhaps fearing by the slightest movement to betray the anxiety Trent's words aroused. Trent turned the screw.

"I mean, not only did you pay the blackmail money for Abby but someone very conveniently murdered Miss Long and put an end to her threats for good. The only remaining danger from Abby's point of view was that the police might come across these photos in Naomi's cottage. And someone did their best to make sure we shouldn't. Where were you on Sunday, by the way?"

"Sunday?" His relief at the change of subject from

Abby to himself was palpable. "Why do you want to know? I thought you said the break-in happened on Monday?"

"I didn't mention a day, actually."

He was unfazed. "Didn't you? Then I must have assumed it occurred on the same day as the murder. That was on Monday, wasn't it?"

"That's the day we found Miss Long's body. So where you were on Sunday?"

"I was in London."

"All day?"

"All weekend. I got back on Monday night, about ten o'clock."

"Where did you stay in London?"

"At my house in Belsize Park."

"Business trip?"

"Hardly. My wife had promised to take her niece to an audition for stage school on Monday afternoon. Karina – that's my wife – used to be an actress. The niece is following in her footsteps. Being incapable of using public transport, they needed me to drive them."

"Your wife doesn't drive?"

"She does but she can't be bothered with the London traffic."

"Yes, a menace, isn't it?" Trent sat back and crossed his legs. Chaudhuri saw he was about to link his hands at the back of his neck then thought better of it. "How did your niece get on at her audition?"

"She was accepted." The mere tone of Field's voice revealed how presumptuous he found Trent's interest.

"Ah, congratulations. A good school, is it?"

"If you consider the greatest achievement in life is to

be applauded by a lot of strangers, it's adequate. Estelle will leave it hardly able to write her name but probably with a Ph.D. in Theatre Studies. She's only twelve, by the way."

"So it's a boarding school? What's it called?"

"The Wanda West Academy, if you can believe." He grinned despite himself. "It's in Hammersmith."

"And you accompanied your wife and niece?"

"As I said."

"How long did the audition last?"

"We arrived at two-thirty. The audition was at three and lasted over an hour. What with one thing and another it was after five when we left. We took Estelle home to Holland Park and headed straight for the motorway."

"And the earlier part of the weekend?"

"We went with friends to a concert at the Royal Festival Hall on Saturday night. On Sunday we had other friends to supper."

"I'll need their names and addresses, if you don't mind."

"You'll what?" Field looked as if contemplating whether to kick Trent through the door. "What the fuck are you playing at?"

"I'm sorry, Mr Field, but in a murder investigation we can leave no stone unturned."

Field scowled at the fire. "Speak to my London housekeeper, then – Mrs Ferguson." He rattled off a London phone number. Chaudhuri was aware of Sergeant Cooper behind him writing frantically to keep up.

"I'll require your niece's address, as well."

Field sprang to his feet as if this were the point at which Trent would be evicted. Instead he went to a desk at the far end of the room. It stood against a wall completely lined with books except where a space had been left for it. He took a couple of business cards from a drawer and threw them at Trent. Trent caught them and put them in his pocket.

"Have you been in contact with Abby since you got back from London?"

"Only by phone."

"Right. Well, we'll have to ask her a few questions, as I said, but we'll try to spare her every inconvenience by doing so at the salon. Inspector Chaudhuri, have you anything you'd like to ask?"

Chaudhuri said, "Do you know anyone of the name of Kelly Houghton? Sometimes she called herself Kelly Parker."

Field shook his head.

"She'd lived in Sandown for the past two years. Don't own any property there, do you? Seaview Way?"

"No, I own no property in Sandown."

"Got a list of your tenants, by any chance?"

Field went to the desk once more and handed Chaudhuri a stapled document.

"Thanks. Kelly Houghton was originally a Londoner. She was found murdered there on Monday – in Hammersmith, as it happens."

"As what 'happens'? Is this some coy way of telling me you suspect me of her murder too?"

"Did you know her, Mr Field?"

"No."

"Very well. If we need to talk to you again where can

we contact you?"

"My office is here."

"Really? I wish I had an office in a place like this."

With hardly any change in his expression Field managed to imply he thought it would never be likely.

They rose to leave. As they entered the hall an odd sight met them. On the shadowy stairs a woman was standing as still as a statue. Her face was beautiful but haggard, deep lines running from her nose to the corners of her mouth. Her eyebrows slanted like a wicked queen's in a fairy tale, her eyes similarly slanting and pencilled in black. Her pouting lips were carefully painted a shiny fuchsia and her red hair hung almost in elflocks to her waist. She wore a short, wrap-over tunic which might have been the top half of a pair of silk pyjamas. It revealed her long tanned legs nearly to her groin. For a moment Chaudhuri thought he heard her snarl. Then realised his mistake when a border collie slunk out from behind her, head lowered, one delicate forepaw lifted ready to spring. Its mistress showed no inclination to stop it.

"It's all right," said Field, though whether to the dog or the woman was unclear. At his approach the dog lay down. "This is my wife, Karina." He stood in front of her on a lower step. Chaudhuri and Trent wished her good evening receiving only a stare in return.

There was nothing for them to do but leave. At the door Chaudhuri turned back. Field was still standing in front of his wife. Chaudhuri wondered whether he was protector or gaoler. He closed the door.

On their way to the car Trent stretched and yawned so much his eyes watered. "Christ, it was hot in there. I could hardly keep myself awake. And you must be knackered, Tom. Shall we get you straight back to your hotel and have a drink? Or, sorry, maybe you don't?"

"Sometimes I wish I didn't. But it's just what I could do with."

Trent tore off his tie and threw it on the seat between them. "Hope you didn't find all that a waste of time."

"On the contrary, I found it very interesting. Interesting that both Field and Kelly should live on this island and that he should be in London on the same day not a ten minute walk away from where she was murdered."

"You're joking? That close?"

Chaudhuri nodded. "It could be coincidence, of course. But I wonder if he'd have admitted it if he'd known I was investigating Kelly's murder?"

Trent laughed. "It'd be ironic if his alibi for Naomi's murder made him a suspect in Kelly's. But if that alibi holds water, and I've a feeling it will, there's no way he could have killed Naomi himself."

"Himself? You're thinking he might have got someone else to do it?"

"Always a possibility with the wealthy. When you can afford anything it must be irresistible to believe everything has a price."

Chaudhuri took out his pencil torch and beamed it over the list of tenants Field had given him. "If his wife was to find out about his affair with Abby Benson – and I got the feeling she hasn't – she'd get half his fortune if she divorced him."

"Yes, a lot to lose, even for a woman you're madly

in love with, but an intolerable amount if that woman won't leave her husband. It must have come as a shock to Field when even blackmail wasn't enough to make her do it. He paid the first demand. But would he really have been willing to pay a second?"

Chaudhuri switched off his torch. "It's very odd, isn't it? You'd expect any woman to move hell and high water to be with him. Especially if she was married to an abusive slug."

Trent made a snorting sound. "And he's a right slug, our Dougie, let me tell you."

"You mean you know him?"

"Oh, yes. Didn't I say? Used to be one of our special constables. Right weirdo. Has a cottage over the way from Naomi's'."

"And like her, into spiritualism."

Trent's eyes sparkled in the light from an oncoming car. "Yes, wonder if that's significant?"

"Could be. Something else I'm wondering, Bob – why did Naomi blackmail Abby instead of Field?"

"You mean she could have asked for more money from him? Maybe she thought he wouldn't pay it. Or maybe she didn't realise who he was. It would only be a matter of time before she'd find out, of course. Fascinating bloke, isn't he?"

"Yes. Something enigmatic about him."

"Enigmatic." Trent repeated the word with relish. "That's a good description of him. Used to be a surgeon in London. Was becoming quite famous, I believe, when there was a family tragedy. His mother, I think it was. Died suddenly. Anyway, he came back here to be with his father for a bit and never went back. Carried on the family business. Not your typical property developer, Darius Field."

"No. Surgeon suits him better."

"Is Kelly's name on that list of tenants he gave you, by the way?"

"Unfortunately not. I'd like to talk to his wife, Karina, if that's OK. Get her version of the weekend in London."

"Karina?" Trent blew out his breath with a whooshing sound. "A bundle of trouble, that one, if I'm any judge. But yes. Good idea. We'll both have a word."

Chaudhuri's mobile phone beeped. He dug into his pocket for it and looked at the text message from James.

"Seems like all this speculation regarding Kelly and Field might not be relevant anymore." He pointed to the text. "Boyfriend Darren's done a runner. He definitely hasn't returned to the flat. Doesn't augur well for him, does it."

"The old story, eh? So you'll be round there early in the morning? Well, I'll be in Yarmouth most of tomorrow. Suspected forged currency racket. Christ, I hope we never get a bridge link to this island or every petty villain in the south'll be popping over to claim a patch. Anyway, don't hesitate to phone if there's anything you need."

It was after midnight and the end of an exhausting day but Trent seemed in no hurry to bring it to an end. He left the young sergeant to return to the police station and write up his notes while he himself joined Chaudhuri at the bar of the Painted Plough.

It was good to see James waiting for them and even better to set eyes on the glamorous if somewhat androgynous landlady, also in no hurry to shoo them off to bed. At least she looked as if she was more than ready to shoo Chaudhuri but without thoughts of letting him get much sleep.

Twenty

At six-thirty the following morning Chaudhuri and James arrived at Seaview Way. As a formality Chaudhuri rang the doorbell, though he was sure no one was there to answer. He was about to use Kelly's keys when James pointed to an upper window – a skull-like face was peeping through a corner of the grimy pane. Chaudhuri rang again, this time keeping his finger on the bell. After half a minute the door opened an inch or two and the skull squinted through the gap.

"Darren Frost?" He held out his warrant card. "I'm…"

The door made an attempt to slam itself shut. Chaudhuri kicked it against the wall and hauled a prone Darren off the stairs by his T-shirt.

"As I was saying before I was so rudely interrupted, I'm Inspector Chaudhuri and this is Sergeant James of Hammersmith and Fulham Crime Management. We'd like a few words with you. Top floor, is it?"

Squawking protestations, Darren was chivvied up the stairs. His bare feet were the colour of toadstools. He'd obviously slept in his T-shirt and tracksuit bottoms and looked as if he hadn't washed his greasy black hair for a month; maybe it wasn't really as dark as that, maybe it was the grease.

With a sideways lean he scurried round the living room door ahead of Chaudhuri and flung himself onto the sofa as though it was the last seat in a game of musical chairs. Pimples glowed like rubies in the sparse black down of his beard. With his right ankle on his left knee he shook his corpse-coloured foot convulsively.

Chaudhuri knew the type. They could never be still, always jerking as if they'd bumped into an electrified fence. He stalked round the room, Darren's eyes following his every move, and examined its contents with the air of a disgusted auctioneer. Making a sudden lunge at the sofa he yelled, "Where's Kelly?"

From the way Darren jumped he might have just touched five thousand volts.

"Dunno, mate." He gave Chaudhuri a startled rodent stare and drummed the fingers of both hands on the seat of the sofa. "I ain't been here, have I? Just got in, ain't I?"

"I'm not fucking clairvoyant. You tell me."

"Nah, I ain't been here, have I?" His Adam's apple moved like a walnut stuck in his throat, shell and all.

"Where've you been?"

Darren looked evasive. The foot and fingers raced. "I just been here and there."

"Like where? London?"

"Nah, I ain't been there."

"Kelly has, though."

"Yeah."

"Why did she go?"

"Went to see her mum, didn't she?"

"And who else?"

"Dunno." He looked as if he really didn't which probably meant he was telling the truth. He was too thick to lie well, though Chaudhuri knew he would spend most of his life doing it.

"Where is Kelly now?"

"Dunno. Out cleaning, I suppose."

"Cleaning? That's her job, is it?"

"Yeah."

"When did you last see her?"

After much inward struggle as to the best reply, Darren decided on, "Dunno."

"Did you see her on Monday afternoon?"

"Monday? Nah, I was working Monday."

"Where?"

"At the zoo."

"Is that in Sandown?"

"Course."

"Fond of animals, are you?"

"I couldn't give a monkey's, mate. It's just a job, see? They're a fucking pain, actually."

"And you were there all day Monday?"

"I said, didn't I?"

"At the risk of giving offence, we'll still check."

"You fucking do what you want, mate."

"Oh, I will. It wouldn't be the first time an air-headed little toe rag like you hasn't bothered to get himself an alibi for murder. Thick as pig shit murderers are. That's why the stupid fuckers do what they do."

"Murder?" That rodent look again, the little red mouth open to show little sharp teeth, "What murder? I don't know nothing about no murders. Don't you come here bothering me, mate. I ain't done no murders. I ain't staying to hear this."

He made a run for the door. James propelled him back into the room.

"Your girlfriend's dead and you don't want to know about it? Christ, what an arsehole." Chaudhuri shoved him on the sofa with his foot.

"My girlfriend?" Darren managed for a second to be still. "You mean Kelly?"

"She was your girlfriend, wasn't she?"

"Yeah." It might have been something from years ago that he'd just this second remembered. "She get killed in London, then?"

That other people lived and died meant nothing to him. It was nothing more than words. Chaudhuri stared with loathing.

"I been staying with another woman." Darren was eager all of a sudden to account for himself. "I been staying with her since Monday night. I been to work all day but after that I been to stay with her. Hayley Ashley her name is. I got her phone number."

With a grin he produced the latest model in mobile phones and brought up Hayley's number on the screen. He held it out to James. As if it were alive with infection, James glanced at the number then used his own phone.

At the mention of Darren Frost Hayley broke into a torrent of shrieked abuse accompanied by the shrieks of a child.

"Tell him I was with you, Hayley!" Darren zoomed in next to James head and yelled into his mobile. "Tell him, you frigging stupid slag!"

Unable to withstand such blandishments Hayley admitted he'd been with her from six o'clock on Monday evening until six this morning, when they'd argued and she'd thrown him out.

Chaudhuri couldn't hide his disappointment. "We'll also check you were at work when you claimed to be."

"Yeah, you do that, mate." Darren's knee shook with relief. "But I been there every day, you'll see. You check. It don't bother me." Dancing on the spot he reached for a packet of cigarettes on top of a CD stack and inhaled smoke with enjoyment.

"The child was murdered too."

Darren appeared not to understand. Then it dawned on him.

"Oh, Jade? They killed Jade?" With an insincerity that was comical he put on a sad face. "Ah, that's a shame, innit? I'm really, really like sorry to hear that."

He hung his head and glanced up to see if Chaudhuri was watching. He was.

"How many people did Kelly clean for?"

"Dunno. Loads."

"If there were loads, she must have had a list. Find it."

"There ain't no list," he insisted, becoming a pedant, "only a few names on a calendar. It's in the kitchen, through there."

He pointed across the landing. Chaudhuri gave him a push towards it, signalling as he did so that James should search the rest of the flat.

Like someone whose mental development had stopped at the age of eleven Kelly had chosen a Kylie

Minogue calendar. Below various dates, in writing that looked like printing joined up, she had written various names. Darius Field's wasn't among them. Chaudhuri put the calendar in his pocket and looked round the room.

No curtains at the window overlooking the waste-ground garden; everywhere a patina of grime. Cheap, unclean cutlery jumbled in dusty drawers, a pedal bin that stank of rotting rubbish. A sink full of used tea bags and worktops littered with empty take-away cartons, remnants of food clinging like snails.

In the bathroom: crumpled washing over a shower rail with a scummy grey curtain, dirty laundry in a black bin-liner, a toilet it was better not to think about. In the main bedroom: flat-pack furniture coming apart, drawers already emptied in James' search. In contrast Jade's room was a bower with pink fairy lights still switched on and draped over the pink and white princess bed.

"How long have you known Kelly?"

"About two month."

"And how long have you lived here?"

"About two month."

"So you'll know where she kept her things – address books and such like."

"Nah." From his tone they might have been illegal. "She didn't have nothing like that."

"Computer?"

"Nah."

"What's this then, you lying little turd?" James came out of the bedroom with a shiny black laptop under his arm.

"Hey, you put that back. That's mine, that is. You ain't got no right."

"Yeah, shame, isn't it? He should report us to a higher authority, shouldn't he, sir?"

"He won't do that, will you, Darren? You'll be a help to us for once in your life. Just tell us the computer password, mate."

"I dunno, do I? It ain't my computer, is it? It's Kelly's."

"You're an idiot, Darren. You've just said it's yours."

"Yeah, I mean I paid for it, like. Kelly like used my credit card for it, didn't she?"

"The same as she did for her mobile phone?"

"Yeah. She weren't allowed no bank account."

"A right sugar daddy, you are. The computer password?"

'Dunno. Ow, that fucking hurts! It's house, OK?"

"House as in home?"

"It's like what you call out at the end of bingo."

Appropriate. On-line bingo was the main use the computer had been put to and had superseded a half-hearted attempt at Facebook. There were various porn sites, some uploaded pictures in which Kelly and Darren exposed themselves, and many more of Jade, all of an unquestionable innocence.

"Who lived here with Kelly before you?"

"Dunno."

"Had other boyfriends living in, did she?"

"Must have done." Jealousy appeared to have no part in his noble nature.

"Friends? Girlfriends she saw from time to time?"

A shrug.

"Got the landlord's number?"

"What, for the flat, you mean? Dunno. Don't mean nothing to me."

Chaudhuri went into the kitchen to wash his hands.

"Right, for now we'll love you and leave you. But we haven't finished with you by a long way. So let us know if you change address. You'll have to if you want your computer back. Sorry, mate," he ignored Darren's objections and gave the computer a pat, "there could be vital information on here. Don't want to get done for obstructing our enquiries, do you? You'll get it back in a couple of days. And a word of warning –try doing a runner and I'll break your legs before you've taken one step."

Darren laughed, deciding to take this as Chaudhuri's bit of fun.

"No worries, mate. I ain't got no reason to run, have I? I ain't done nothing."

He followed them into the hall and called over the banister, "You come here as often as you like, mate. I ain't done nothing, I haven't."

They closed the door on him.

"Did you find anything of interest apart from the computer?"

James shook his head. He looked mulish. "I don't think we should have taken it without a warrant, sir. We should have brought one."

That *sir* irritated. He didn't need reminding he was in charge and answerable for any misconduct. "Don't be such an old woman, he won't make a fuss." He glanced at James' offended face. "Not one for the written word, was she? Not a single book in the entire flat. If she made

176

a note of the people she was meeting in London, the only place it'll be is on this calendar or that computer. As for Darren, he's got an alibi for Monday which I've a feeling his workplace will corroborate."

James paused to look back at the house. "It's weird, but it's as if he hadn't expected Kelly to come back. She should have got back on Monday night. Yet he spends it with another woman."

Chaudhuri didn't even pause before replying, "I don't think it's weird. I think it's exactly the sort of thing he'd do if he felt like it. Why would he care about her just because he was living with her? Or her him? They'd rut like a couple of animals without any feeling at all for each other. Can you imagine their life together? It must have been sheer hell. There's some justice in the world, then. Anyway, let's check the ape was at the zoo when he says he was. It's a wonder they let him out. That's what's wrong with this country of free education, James – it suffers fools so gladly you'd think it was their human right. I know one thing, though – he was scared half to death when we first arrived and highly relieved about something before we left. We didn't ask the right questions, did we? But we will. Oh yes. We will."

Twenty-One

A couple of miles north of Sandown stands the village of Wilfridstone, once a medieval port but now stranded in reclaimed farmland. With its winding old high street and sheep grazing on the downs above it looks the picture of pastoral peace. Yet everywhere are reminders of a history full of horrors. The iron ring to which bulls were tethered for baiting still nestles among the cobbles of the market place. By the churchyard steps is the lock-up where humans were bound to stocks and whipping post for the sport of every passer-by. And in the thatched cottage opposite, effigies in the waxwork museum recall medieval tortures so terrible you must laugh at them to stay sane.

It was difficult to associate these things with a building as cosy as the White Hart pub. Yet it stood when they were happening and stands today when we dwell in disbelief on those times.

At half past nine the landlady was having breakfast. It consisted of dry crisp bread and a small portion of cottage cheese served on a dinner plate, sprinkled with black pepper and eaten with a fork. This was how she fooled herself she was having a proper meal. She'd lost two pounds since last week, which left a spare thirty-six to go.

On a blackboard at the side of the bar was chalked a list of dishes from every country under the sun except this one and all claiming to be freshly made that morning. If the list never changed, her pretensions changed by the week. As she pecked at her cheese to make it last she looked round dissatisfied at the refurbished bar.

Like many country pubs, its exterior was exciting and its interior a disappointment. When she'd moved in two months ago, a traditional English country theme had seemed the obvious choice. But being a Londoner and never having left it except for foreign holidays, her ideas of how this should be achieved all came from DIY programmes on TV.

So she had torn down the old tapestry curtains and replaced them with boudoir pink so heavily swagged they shut out almost all the light from the bottle glass windows. The Constable prints in their thin, mass-produced frames refused to hang straight on the rough stone walls and the blue silk flower arrangement in the fireplace had a tendency to get caught on her tights if someone was sitting at that end of the bar and she had to squeeze past. Already she was sick of Olde England and it didn't attract the locals, either. Morocco would do it. Or Australia. Yes, she'd start on an Australian theme this weekend. She'd look on eBay for a stuffed kangaroo.

The door opened and two tall men in suits came in.

"Ms Goodall?"

She looked up at the very good-looking Asian one over her designer glasses. "That's me. Call me Trish. You're the police, I take it?"

"We are. I'm Inspector Chaudhuri and this is Sergeant James."

"I've been expecting you. Come in. Sit yourselves down. Have a coffee?"

She spoke in a world-weary manner, which though the norm in London seemed misplaced here, Chaudhuri thought. Her movements, too, were both sluggish and slapdash as if everything were tedious and hardly worth the effort. She sauntered to the bar hoisting up her jeans and pulling down her T-shirt as she went. She poured weak filter coffee into thick white cups and tossed a paper straw of sugar and a tiny carton of milk into each saucer. Then she placed, half shoved the cups in front of them and sat down with a sigh. Propping her elbows either side of her plate she went back to her cottage cheese.

Chaudhuri looked round. "This is a fascinating old place."

"Yeah. Needs a lot doing to it, though."

"Must be very rewarding."

She snorted. "That's what I thought at first. Doesn't take long for reality to set in, though."

"Business good?"

She looked up from her plate and with her fork dangling from her fingers pushed spectacles too small for her face more firmly onto her snub nose.

"It's the sticks, here, innit? Not like London. They don't want to try nothing new here. Backward. Still, it's the end of the season. I missed the holiday rush, unfortunately. Maybe next summer'll be different."

"You're not from round here, then?"

"What, me? I should say not. Wandsworth born and bred."

"You must find things very different?"

"You can say that again. Dead, it is, after the London hotels. That's the 'sector' I used to work in." She flexed her fingers in the air, for some reason to imply inverted commas. "You know Uxbridge Road? I was manageress of three hotels along there. All owned by the one man, Mr Yang. Back-packers we catered for, mostly. Never no vacancies."

Her eyes misted over in reminiscence. Then she slumped over her plate again. "Anyway, thought I'd find a run-down place in the country and give it the benefit of my experience. Since coming here I've done my best to introduce a bit of culture. You can see that from the menu, can't you?"

She pointed with her fork at the blackboard as if a poem or a quotation from Shakespeare were chalked up. But she meant the meals.

"You've got plenty of room, anyway. Opening that bit up, are you?" He indicated what had once been a separate room, its dividing wall demolished.

"Yes, that's going to be the restaurant. Scandinavian-style décor, a bit like a sauna, sort of, though what I'll do with those walls I've no idea." She glared at the old stone. "Still, it's always been my dream, a gastro pub. It's worth making an effort. I love good food," she added virtuously.

"You've taken on a lot of work. I can see why you'd need a cleaner to help."

"Yes, it's a shame about Kelly, isn't it? Fancy getting herself murdered. And the poor little girl as well. Terrible, it is."

"Did you know Kelly well?"

"Only met her the once – the day she come here to clean. A Thursday, it was. I remember because she said she normally worked somewhere else on a Thursday, so I'd have to arrange another day if I wanted her to come on a regular basis."

"And did you?"

"Oh, yes. We agreed she'd do all day Saturday, starting the following week. She'd help in the bar a bit, as well. She could bring her little girl. I'd no objections. Thought it might shut the others up for a bit."

"Others?"

She rolled her eyes. "The ghost kids. At least, it sounds like kids. One minute they're laughing, the next crying. Sometimes it goes on all night. It's doing my head in. And someone breathing in the dark and sitting on the bed. It's a bloody nightmare. Well, I wish it was, actually."

"Must be very unpleasant. You're not on your own, are you?"

"You offering to keep me company? I'd feel safe with you. Truncheon at the ready and all that."

She ogled him lasciviously then remembered herself. "No, luckily I've got my partner. He's at the cash and carry, just now. Still, alone or not, it's a bloody creepy place here. I hope I don't never see nothing coz I've a feeling it wouldn't be a pretty sight."

She finished her cheese and sucked her teeth. "But you don't want to hear about my problems, do you?

You want to know about Kelly, don't you?" She pushed her plate away, sat back and folded her arms. "Like I say, I can't tell you much. But she was nice. Down to earth. No side to her. And she was a good worker from the bit I saw – I will give her that."

"Did she talk about her private life at all?"

"She said she had a boyfriend but she didn't sound too gone on him. You know what it's like when you get to the end of a relationship? I reckon that one was on its last legs."

"Did she say why?"

"Just had enough and ready for pastures new, I think. Well, you've got to have a bit of fun, haven't you? That's what's important, isn't it?"

"Do you know if she'd met anyone else?"

"She didn't say. She might have got round to telling me but…there you are. We'll never know now, will we?"

"Did she mention to you that she was going to London?"

"She did." For the first time she smiled. "Dead excited about it, she was."

"What did she say?"

"She didn't say much, actually. She was…what's the word?…cagey, that's right. I was saying how much I missed London and she said she did and then she said she was going there on Monday for the day and I said, 'Oh, that's nice. Shopping trip?' and she said, 'No, it's business,' and I said, 'What sort of business?' and she said, 'Actually Trish, it's confidential.' But she seemed as pleased as anything and I wouldn't be surprised if there was a man involved. That's how it seemed to me."

"A local man, do you think? Or someone from

London?"

"I couldn't say. It's just the impression I got. But depending on how her business meeting went, she was going to move back there."

"Really? She told you that did she?"

"Yes. She'd need to be near her mother, she said."

"Near her mother? Was her mother involved in the business as well?"

"Might have been. Like I say, she was cagey."

"Can you remember exactly what she said about her mother?"

"Exactly? Now you're asking something. Let's think. She was talking about her business meeting and she said depending on how it went she might have to move back home. A girl needs her mother at times like that, she said. Yes, that's right. A girl needs her mother. I've remembered it."

A couple of elderly tourists came in and asked for coffee. With a sigh Trish Goodall dragged herself to her feet and clattered her empty plate across the bar. The two policemen thanked her, asked her to get in touch should anything else occur to her, and taking their aura of London with them, left.

Twenty-Two

"When does a girl need her mother, James?"

"When she's left her partner. They always go home to Mum, don't they?"

"Darren wasn't Kelly's partner. He was just someone to shack up with until she got sick of him and chucked him out. When else might she need her mother?"

"When she's pregnant? But she wasn't, was she?"

"No. But Trish Goodall said that depending on the success of her business meeting she'd need to be near her mother. Knowing Kelly and Liz, what sort of business does that suggest?"

"Prostitution with the mother as maid?"

"Yes, the sex industry would be where it's at for Kelly. And it would explain why Liz wanted to deny all knowledge. Whatever it was, I think she was in charge of arrangements. According to Kelly's phone records the only London number she rang was her mother's. So this business meeting was either set up by word of mouth or someone else's phone was used."

"You think Kelly was meeting a client when she was

murdered?"

"Maybe, but I don't think the client was Raven. You don't travel all the way from the Isle of Wight to meet a punter behind a hedge. No, Kelly must have been on her way to somewhere else. And she had the child with her, remember."

"Yeah. An added attraction."

"God, James, I don't want to think about that possibility."

"What makes you think Kelly would be above pimping out her kid? And though she might have been on her way to somewhere else it doesn't mean the person who murdered her wasn't the one she'd planned to meet."

"You think Raven might be both punter and killer?"

"Exactly. Raven knew Kelly would pass through the park. She or he might even have suggested the route."

Chaudhuri took out his mobile. "We've got to speak to Liz Parker again – today. She might have had a change of heart and be ready to tell us about who Kelly was meeting. I'll put Greene on to it. Have we time for a coffee, as opposed to Trish Goodall's gnat's piss?"

"Loads of time. Stop at the first nice village pub, shall we?"

The hills were round like a child's drawing. They made the perspective odd so that a distant green and yellow tractor looked like a toy you could reach out for. They came to the village of Thorpe Ash and stopped at the Crown Inn; a stream ran through the garden, a white dovecot stood in the middle of the lawn and (in Chaudhuri's opinion the most charming touch) one of the fence posts was carved into the shape of an owl.

The interior was low-beamed and smelt of strong coffee and delicious dishes cooked with garlic. Apart from a party of four having lunch it was empty. Against a sloping wall leaned a dresser black with age and ornate as a nobleman's tomb. The throbbing sound of doves on the windowsill mingled with the hoarse cries of rooks in the nearby churchyard.

They sat at a small table in a shadowy corner. James dunked a biscuit in his coffee. "Sugar for energy. Know what I could do with now? A nice nap. Forty winks in the car."

"Don't tempt me, James." Chaudhuri stretched. His half-closed eyes met the woman's behind the bar. "I don't know if it's this sea air but I could eat a horse and sleep like a log after. Boot up the laptop, mate. Let's have a quick look at Kelly's Facebook contacts."

The tone was innocent at first if not downright cloying, designed to create a favourable impression with each new friend. She informed them she was a single mother 'in a relationship' with Darren. As the friendship progressed a description of her sex life, which nearly put James off his biscuits, alternated with complaints about Darren and eulogies over Jade. Sex, sex, sex. Some Neanderthals lived by it alone. What did they do with their life when they were past it? No mention of London or any meeting there, however.

A long-case clock tolled the quarter hour.

"Ask not for whom the bell tolls because it tolls for us. Come on, James, tear yourself away from Kelly's exalted prose and shake a leg. Alec Johnstone's expecting you."

The road dropped into a valley. A few larch trees,

wild as witches, presented bent backs to the sea. They drove through Shelbury, turning off along a narrow road that seemed to lead nowhere but which eventually brought them to the steep track to Westdown Farm.

When they arrived, a dog that had been sitting in the sun got up and waddled towards them. Not only its tail but its entire back half wagged as it lifted one side of its mouth in a smile.

A man stood on the doorstep. He was broad-shouldered but thin, as if beneath his clothes he would be nothing but bone and tendon. His face was beautiful. With his full, curving mouth and large blue eyes he might have been a blond Adonis. Except that his hair was completely and prematurely grey.

James took out his warrant card. "Mr Johnstone?"

"No, I'm his son-in-law, Peter Rogers." His voice was warm and pleasing but somehow suppressed, as if whatever had whitened his hair had also robbed his spirit of its youth. "You're the police inspectors, I take it? Dad's waiting for you. He's a bit upset to hear about Kelly's death so you'll go easy on him, I hope. He's in the study."

He indicated the way through the hall. The dog's paws tapped on the stone floor as it followed.

Alec stood in front of the hearth. He was what Chaudhuri's father would describe as a gentleman which has nothing to do with money but a considerateness of demeanour. Mild, grey-haired and balding, there nevertheless a vivacity about him, the eyes still lustrous, his red lower lip full if slightly pendulous with age. He wore his shirtsleeves rolled up above the elbow in the way no one but the elderly does nowadays, revealing sinewed forearms covered in black hair. In his maroon tie and grey V-necked sleeveless pullover he seemed locked in the time warp of his youth. Behind him was a pastel portrait of a grave-looking girl, her hair parted at the side and fastened back from her forehead in a round slide. The room apart from a slim computer on a desk was dowdy with 1930s furniture but well kept as if it belonged to a treasured past. Chaudhuri noted it was the sort of furniture James' wife favoured and was now back in fashion. They sat in the springy, broad-armed chairs covered in crazed brown leather.

"Man-traps, my wife used to call them," said Alec. "I daren't risk them any more with my arthritis." He sat on an upright chair next to the desk. "Can I get you a cup of coffee, gentlemen? No? Well, how can I help you? By the way, is it all right if Peter stays?"

James nodded. "Sure, Mr Johnstone, no problem."

Peter sat down next to Alec. Chaudhuri was somewhat surprised to see him hold Alec's hand.

Clearing his throat, James took out his notebook. "Now, as I mentioned when I telephoned, we're investigating the murder of Kelly Houghton and her daughter Jade. I'm sorry if my call shocked you. I took it for granted you'd have heard about their death."

Alec waived away the need for apology. "Normally I'd have seen it in the local paper. But we've been so busy this week, I didn't bother reading it. And what with one thing and another we've been pretty hit and miss with the news."

James nodded understandingly. "I gather Kelly worked for you for some time?"

"She worked for me for five months, at least. And

she was very conscientious. Never missed – every Tuesday and Thursday without fail."

"What sort of a person was she?"

Alec had a mobile face, more often than not smiling even in repose. Now he looked uncertain, perhaps fluctuating between his true opinion and respect for the dead. He spoke with a forced heartiness. "A proper cockney. Lively. And devoted to Jade. Poor little girl. And poor Kelly. She was hardly more than a girl herself."

"She had a boyfriend, Darren, who lived with her. Did she ever talk about him?"

"She mentioned him from time to time but mostly in that disparaging way young women seem to use now. I didn't attach much importance to it."

"Did you get the impression they fought a lot?"

"Fought?" Alec seemed as puzzled as if he didn't know what the word meant. "I really couldn't say. Fought? No, I don't think she would have stayed with him if they did. I don't believe she would have brought up her daughter in such an atmosphere."

"Any friends she talked about?"

"Do you know, it hadn't occurred to me till now but she never mentioned a single one. And thinking about it, I'd have been surprised if she had."

"Why is that?"

Alec paused to choose his words with care – sententious, even pedantic, but a gift to any investigation.

"Kelly wasn't a warm person. She had a fiery temper but that's not the same thing, is it? Friends require an effort of give and take which I can't imagine her making

– she'd be too ready to argue with them over trifles. I can't picture her putting herself out for anyone. Except her daughter, of course. I'd say she needed no other friend but Jade."

"So you don't know of anyone who felt…what's the word?"

Animosity, Chaudhuri wanted to say….

"You don't know if she had any enemies? Did she ever talk about any?" James prompted.

"No." Alec appeared to find the word *enemy* troubling. "No, she never did."

James frowned at his notes. "Do you know why they went to London, Mr Johnstone?"

"I had the impression it was important business – a job interview, perhaps." He seemed glad to be of some definite help at last.

"Did she say what sort of job?"

"No, no, that's just my own assumption. I don't want to mislead you. I assumed it was something like that because amongst other things she said she'd be back the same night. It's a long and expensive journey to London and if it had been to visit her family she'd have told me. And she'd hardly go without Jade. I remember she said she didn't want to be dragging her on and off the underground. All in all a business appointment seemed the most likely. Though what sort of business poor Kelly might be involved in I couldn't say. She didn't volunteer information and I didn't think it my place to ask."

James sat back and crossed his legs. Chaudhuri suspected he was about to steeple his fingers then thought better of it. "Do you think she was an honest person, Mr Johnstone?"

"I've no reason to think otherwise." Which meant he had his doubts.

"Did you know that besides working for you she was claiming social security?"

Alec sighed. "I didn't but I can't say I'm surprised. These days not to be claiming it would be the surprising thing." He hesitated, ruminated on James for a moment, then came to a decision. "There's no point in my pretending. You asked me what I thought of Kelly. I thought she was devoid of any principle whatsoever except the fashionable ones, which is the same as having none. But then I think that of most of her generation. All their morality comes from television. I tried to like her because it's always the easier option, isn't it? But sometimes it's wrong to try."

"Wrong? Why?"

If Alec regretted having said so much it was now too late to retract.

"She allowed Jade to be cruel to Shirley." The dog wagged her tail at the mention of her name. "I suppose it gave her daughter a laugh, to use Kelly's terminology. Perhaps she thought I didn't notice. Or perhaps because I didn't remonstrate she thought I didn't care. I should have remonstrated. Instead of keeping Shirley out of their way I should have made it plain such behaviour was not to be tolerated. We should be careful of what we tolerate. We should be careful of the society we create in its name. The terrible things that happen in the world – the torture and inhumanity – they're perpetrated in my opinion by people like Kelly and Jade. Most of the time all they lack is opportunity."

An unexpected outburst; even Peter looked shocked. Chaudhuri was glad James had the sense to keep silent. Alec shielded his eyes with his large grey-veined hand.

"Don't listen to me. It's guilt talking, guilt trying to justify itself. I've no right to speak of her like this. It's unforgivable, especially since I let her down so badly."

"Guilt?" James edged forward in his chair. "What have you got to feel guilty about, Mr Johnstone?"

Shirley nuzzled Alec with her nose. He took his hand away to look at her. His face was so drawn and livid in colour Chaudhuri wondered if he suffered from something more serious than arthritis.

"When Kelly told me – it must have been the week before last – that she was going to London for the day, she asked me if I would look after Jade. I refused. I said I couldn't because Peter was coming and we would be busy. The truth was I didn't want the child. I regret it. I must learn to live with the fact that but for me she would be alive now."

He drew in breath and folded his lips the way people do when they feel a sudden pain.

"I won't ask you how they died. I haven't the courage. But have you any idea who killed them? I mean, do you think they just happened to come across some psychopath or was their death premeditated or…what?"

James, who'd apparently been expecting a confession, looked as if he'd found a penny and lost a shilling. "We're keeping an open mind. Their bodies were found in a park so it's possible their murder was quite random. But it's also possible they were followed to London by someone from the island. That's why we're here. One thing I need to know – according to Kelly's phone records you spoke to her on the day of her death. Can you tell me what the call was about?"

"I can. It relates to what I said just now." He glanced at his son-in-law. "On reflection, I knew Peter wouldn't mind helping me look after Jade for a few hours. So I rang Kelly early on the Monday morning -I think it was about seven o'clock – to offer to have Jade for the day if she still wanted me to. She didn't. She said she'd decided to take her to London with her after all. Naturally, I was relieved as well as feeling satisfied I'd done my duty. But if I hadn't refused in the first place...well, better not think of it. I'm sorry, that's all I can tell you."

At a glance from Chaudhuri, James stood up. "You've been most helpful. Thank you for your time. If anything else occurs to you about Kelly, I hope you'll let me know."

"I will, of course, Sergeant. Oh, before you go, there is one thing – it might be nothing, but it's just this moment come to me and you mentioned something about Kelly having enemies..."

"Yes, what is it?"

"It's something that happened on the last day I saw her. It was about five o'clock on the Thursday just gone. She'd cleaned for me that day and I was about to take her and Jade to the bus stop when a woman called Naomi Long came by. I don't know whether you're aware of it, but she was murdered the other day on the downs." He took off his glasses and looked from Chaudhuri to James with alarmed eyes. "Good heavens, you don't think there's a link, do you?"

Chaudhuri couldn't restrain himself any longer "What happened that Thursday, Mr Johnstone?"

Alec put his glasses on the desk beside him and pinched where they'd sat on the bridge of his nose. "Naomi stopped for a chat and I introduced Kelly to her and told her she was my cleaner. Naomi asked her if she'd be able to work for her a couple of hours a week. For some reason it made Kelly go berserk. I actually thought she was going to attack Naomi. Most odd, it was. Naomi couldn't understand it."

"Really?" Chaudhuri shot a quick glance at James as if to apologise for muscling in. "She gave no hint of what she thought might have caused it?"

"How could she? There was no cause for it that either of us could see. She didn't know Kelly – never met her before. It was as much a mystery to Naomi as to me."

"She actually said that, did she – that she didn't know Kelly?"

"Yes, I'm sure she did. Of course, I tried to get an explanation out of Kelly but all she did was scream obscenities. I almost made up my mind to tell her not to come back anymore. But on reflection I hadn't the heart – she needed the money and as far as her work was concerned, she was beyond reproach."

Chaudhuri held out his hand. "Mr Johnstone, you've been a marvel. We'll think about what you've said. And if anything else strikes you, you'll let us know, I hope?"

Alec assured them he would. They left him looking preoccupied and stroking Shirley's ears. Peter Rogers walked with them to the gate.

"On holiday, are you, Mr Rogers?" said Chaudhuri.

"Yes, here for another week."

"Lucky you to have your father-in-law living here. Wife with you, I suppose?"

"No, my wife's dead, Inspector." He smiled to show the words no longer hurt him. "That's why I like to be here when I can. It reminds me of her."

"Ah, I see. Yes. Such an atmospheric place, it must make you feel close to her. Tell me, if you've a minute – what was your impression of Kelly Houghton?"

"I'm afraid I don't have one. I never met her."

"You didn't see her on Thursday when she came to clean?"

"She didn't come that day. Dad forgot to mention it but she never came when he had guests – the child was a bit of a handful, as he said."

"That explains it then." Chaudhuri paused at the gate and pointed to the Longstone on the hill above them. "That's like a bit of Stonehenge."

"Yes, not quite as old but almost. There's another stone you can't see from here lying beside it, so it's reasonable to think there may have been more in the past. Some say it's the remains of a long barrow. Must have been gigantic."

"Draws the tourists, I expect?"

"More than just tourists. There are some odd goings-on up there at night, Dad tells me – lights and things, and peculiar sounds. He went up there one morning and the stone was surrounded by pebbles from the beach all painted with signs – broken crosses and one-eyed devils, and what-have-you. He threw them away. Shirley won't go near the place. She's the most gentle dog I know, but I swear she'd bite you if you tried to take her there."

Shading his eyes from the sun, Chaudhuri peered at the dolmen like an enormous ling of Shiva.

"Why not take a closer look, Inspector? You can get back to the road in that direction. And if you walk straight ahead through the woods, you'll come to Dillington Manor. It's well worth seeing, I can tell you. If Sergeant James drives to the road and turns right, he can meet you at the other end of the wood. Won't take you more than twenty minutes if you keep to the track."

Why not? These days out of London had revealed him to be a lover of the country. And he wanted a few moments by himself to think over what Alec had said about Kelly and Naomi. He knew from James' jubilant look there was little chance of that unless he put a gag on him. So, ignoring his exasperated eye-rolling, he bid Peter goodbye and set off towards the Longstone.

The most direct approach was waist-high with gorse. Out of care for his pale grey suit he was obliged to make a detour onto the chalky track branching off in various directions over the downs. As he drew nearer to the Longstone he saw it stood on top of a huge mound. At the base of the upright stone, which was about twelve feet in height, another lay like an altar. Bracken surrounded the mound like a fringe of auburn hair and glowed in the sun as if on fire.

He looked back towards the house. The track to its garden gate was invisible from here. Marooned in loneliness, nothing would have induced him to live there. A cloud covered the sun and left the valley in a flat dull light, the lack of shadow obliterating its features. He watched his car disappear in the distance.

He looked again at the house. Someone came to an upper window then retreated. Knowing he was observed he feigned interest in the Longstone, though close-to it gave him the creeps. Broken crosses and one-eyed devils, eh? He walked round it a couple of times and noted the dark, bronze-coloured notches in it. So minatory was it, on another day he would have climbed it simply to prove himself master. With a last wistful look at the open downland he entered the wood.

It was twilit. The ground was smooth and bare like a sand-strewn floor. The trees hardly looked like trees at all. Pale brown, almost fawn, they grew straight and branchless for many feet before interlocking to form a high roof. Several tracks wound between them and snaked off into the murky distance. But he had been told to follow the one that went straight ahead. Fearful of getting lost he did so.

The track, veined with the roots of trees, ran first uphill then down into a dank, muddy grove – an ancient sunken way. Its banked sides and over-arching foliage formed a tunnel. From foot and hoof prints, this path was much used by both walkers and riders, though it seemed to him too uneven and narrow for any pony. He hesitated. No birdsong. He might suddenly have gone deaf.

A bract fungus like dead lips burst from the side of a tree, another from the mulchy earth like a pair of black wings. Rotting leaves made the ground so boggy he had to look for a stick to stop himself slipping. Had he not done so he would have missed whatever it was behind him, crossing the mouth of the tunnel at terrific speed. The colour of meat fat and naked; the back bent double as if creeping, yet the thin shanks high-stepping like a horse, its wedge-shaped face turned to him. He experienced that terror which concentrates all life in the present, and afterwards – if there is an afterwards – demonstrates how rarely we live there. Only in extremity. This was what they meant when they talked about being rooted to the spot with fear. He couldn't move. Then on a level with his eyes something blocked out the sun setting through the branches. Whatever the horror was, it was watching him. He could smell it, but like nothing he'd ever smelled before. Could a smell infect not only the body but the soul? If it could, then he knew it was this. He fled, the hair on the back of his neck rising as if dragged towards the presence that kept pace with him on the bank.

His mobile rang and he almost cried out with terror. He was sure it would be no earthly voice. Greene's number. Was it really Greene? Still running, he listened without speaking. A Yorkshire accent – surely the best, most human sound in the world? It was Greene. He shouted to prove he was not alone.

"Ben! How's it going? Yes, I'm OK, just jogging off a hangover. Did you manage to see Liz Parker? Did she tell you anything new? Come on, let's hear what you've been up to. I hope you've got something positive for me."

"I think she's done a runner, sir."

"What? Don't tell me that, Ben. I definitely don't want to hear it."

The mist of foliage thinned and knew he must be near the end of the wood.

"Either that," said Greene, "or she's lying low in the

flat and refusing to answer the door or the phone. I don't think so, though. The place seemed deserted. Clare Mayhew got no joy when she called. And the neighbours haven't seen anyone for a couple of days."

"Did you check her work place?"

"Yeah. She's not been there since Sunday. She had Monday off, of course, but hasn't been back since. They've heard nothing from her. I called on the boyfriend Brian at the factory and he says they had an argument on Tuesday night and he moved out. He's dossing on his brother's floor for the moment."

"Does he know where Liz has gone?"

"He spent quite a bit of time convincing me he couldn't give a monkey's. Then he said she might have gone to stay with her mother on Teesside. He couldn't think of anywhere else she might go at short notice."

"Did he give you an address?"

"Said he didn't know. Just that the mother lives at Hartlepool. He couldn't give a name, either, but assumes it's Parker."

"Hartlepool? That's near your part of the world, isn't it? Fancy a trip back home?"

"I wouldn't mind."

"Great stuff. I want to know who Kelly was meeting on Monday. Liz knows, so keep at her. Take DC Mortimer with you."

He could stroll now. Ahead of him was a stile and the curve of the silent road on which cars might never have travelled and an old Norman church over-looking a deserted village green. On a bench under an oak tree James sat, smoking a cigarette.

"Come and look at this," he called. "It's like a

picture off a chocolate box."

Chaudhuri looked at Dillington Manor, the doves resting on its steep roof. In shape it was no more elaborate than a barn. Yet it seemed the most beautiful building in the world. Its stone was the same as the dolmen on the hill. So was the stone of the church. He sat beside James on the bench.

"You did well back there, mate."

James looked pleased.

"Yes, concise and controlled. A really great interview."

"Thanks, Tom."

"What did you make of Alec Johnstone? Not much love lost between him and Kelly, wouldn't you say?"

"I'd have been disappointed in him if there was. Doesn't mean he murdered her, though."

"But he didn't just dislike her. It sounded as if he loathed her."

James ground his cigarette out. "So what? I expect most people loathed her. But very few people, especially people like Alec, make that a motive for murder. And he wasn't anywhere near the mainland at the time. Unless Peter's covering for him, of course. The CCTV on the ferry will tell us if they're lying. Alec looks nothing like Raven, though – too old and frail."

"True. OK, who's next on Kelly's calendar? The MacArthurs at Ryde. Come on, get off your arse, we've wasted enough time. Let's get going."

"I thought we were going to have lunch? There's a lovely old pub along there. I saw the sign to it."

"Christ, you're a greedy sod. What about all those biscuits you guzzled not long since?"

"But what's the point? The MacArthurs aren't in, are they? If they were, they'd answer the phone."

"This break from London's gone to your head, James. What makes you assume because they don't answer the phone that they're not in? Pull yourself together. We'll get fish and chips on the way back. Satisfied? OK, give me a cigarette, will you?"

"No, you've given up."

"I've started again. No cigarette, no fish and chips." He took one and inhaled deeply. "So, what did you make of that business of Kelly going berserk at Naomi?"

"Yeah, it was weird, that."

"Would you go berserk for no apparent reason with someone you'd never met before? It just doesn't happen, does it? No matter what they told Alec Johnstone Kelly and Naomi knew each other, I'm certain."

James shook his head. "Not necessarily, not then. Naomi was just the woman at the post office who sometimes gave Kelly her Jobseeker's Allowance. Then she finds out that Kelly works for Alec. Kelly probably expected her to report her – the game was up. That's what made her go berserk."

"It establishes a connection between them, though. It's a basis for establishing a connection between their murders."

"No it's not, sir. It a basis for establishing Kelly as a suspect for Naomi's murder, which I'm sure Trent'll be glad to hear about. But I don't see how it gets us any nearer to solving Kelly's. And that's what we're here for. Though if you ask me, we'd be better off in London, grilling Liz."

"Bollocks to London. London's incidental. The cause of everything is here. OK, say for the sake of argument that Kelly kills Naomi. And the next day, by pure coincidence, she gets murdered by someone else. Do you know how far-fetched that is? A rational person would see immediately that both of them being murdered by the same person – in this case Raven – is the most likely scenario. And that means someone from this island."

"You just want to stay here a bit longer, that's what it is. You'll be looking for holiday cottages next."

He had to laugh. But would he? Could he live alone here? In the day it was like fairyland. But at night?

"Do you think there are any deer in that wood, James?"

"What wood, the one you just walked through?"

"Yes. I thought I saw something running between the trees. Do you think it could have been a deer?"

James shrugged. "I doubt it. Doesn't look as if there's any grazing land. And I've a feeling there aren't any deer on the island – something I heard."

No deer? Impossible. Grazing land? What did James know about grazing land? It must have been a deer. How could it be anything else?

He took out his mobile. "I'm going to ask Trent to sort out a warrant. It's time to turn Kelly's flat upside-down."

Twenty-Three

It might have been a spring morning except the blackbird sang no more. A red squirrel with tufted ears swung from a feeder in the cypress only to disappear into the tree's darkness like a wind-blown plume as Verity opened her daughter's bedroom window. The lawn under the apple tree was scattered with the first fallen fruit. She remembered how a very small Ophelia would collect apples in her blue plastic basket. If she closed her eyes and concentrated she could still hear those little feet on the stairs, running to bring her the rosiest apple. It all seemed to have happened to other people in another life.

Ophelia's alarm clock went off and made her jump. For the past two days Ophelia had been going to school. Deep in sleep she no longer smelt the same as the baby who used to smile and hold out her arms to be picked up on waking. Now she smelt of staleness and cigarettes, on her way to death; already decaying. It seemed incredible. Fighting an urge to grasp her child in her arms and kiss her and hold her to make everything right, instead she just shook her shoulder.

"Time for school, darling. I've brought you a cup of coffee."

A grunt from under the duvet was her only answer so she left the cup covered with its saucer to keep it warm and took her own coffee to drink while she had her bath. The saucer was still in place when she came back to tell Ophelia her bath was ready. She gave her a few more minutes.

Unless the weather was cold Verity always ate breakfast in the little lean-to conservatory her father had built. Pink Busy Lizzies on the windowsill grew as sturdy as miniature trees. While eating Ryvita and marmalade she read some essays by H.G. Wells from an old book now long out of print. Her father, a train driver, working class, had devoured such literature eagerly. He saw it as his right to be as educated and cultured as anyone else. What would he have made of a granddaughter whose learning seemed stuck in infancy? He would have said it was not simply her right but her duty to be educated and then he'd have dragged her to school if necessary. But if Verity were to try that the teachers would prosecute and probably give Ophelia counselling. Tell that to her father and he'd think himself in a lunatic asylum. She put the book down and ran upstairs.

She leant over the bed and shook her daughter's shoulder for the second time that morning.

"Breakfast's ready. Come on, darling, you don't want to be late."

An arm appeared from the duvet and lashed her across the temple. She hadn't been hit for nearly a week and with that one blow despondency flooded back bringing with it a familiar painful fluttering in her chest.

Ophelia reared up, hair tousled, face contorted.

"Just fuck off, will you?"

Verity's eye throbbed but she resisted the urge to rub it. On top of the pain she felt stupid for letting her guard down and allowing herself to be hurt yet again. The only way she could keep her dignity was by pretending it hadn't happened.

"Am I to take it you've given up on school again?"

"Yes, I have, OK?"

"Well, I've never known such good intentions so short-lived." It was always safest to argue while she was in bed because she hated to get out of it. "Come on, have a quick bath and I'll walk to school with you. I've got an appointment with the hairdresser. It's on the way."

"Will you piss off and let me get some sleep?"

She burrowed back under the duvet like a ferocious mole. One more word, one more touch and she'd tear the room apart. There had been no miracle cure. Remission, that was all, and now it was over. Verity went to dress.

She was no longer took pleasure in choosing what to wear because Ophelia had drummed into her that her clothes sense was ridiculous but she felt especially self-conscious when going to the hairdresser, where appearances were the only thing. Those silly shallow girls with their judgemental glances and false professional chat, *Going anywhere nice for your holidays?* in their singsong voices, and preening over her head. Once they would have looked at her reflection next to their own with envy. Now it was the other way round. Like the loss of Ophelia's love she couldn't remember when that had happened, either. But she never looked good anymore. She might tell herself that in her heyday these average girls would have been eclipsed by her. What did that matter? She was no longer young, there was the rub. Could there be such a thing as beautiful and old? Ask a man to choose between her and the plainest of young women and she'd lose out every time. Still, she had to get dressed so she might as well do it carefully as not. She finally decided on her new charity shop jeans, a tight black charity shop T-shirt and leopard-skin pumps (charity shop) suitable for walking the two miles to the town. A liberal spray of 'Obsession' (Superdrug) and she was ready. She folded her suede jacket into her bronze bag and stuck her head round Ophelia's door.

"I'm going to the hairdresser now. I'll be gone no more than a couple of hours. But if you're still here when I get back I'm going to phone your teacher. Did you hear me? Your breakfast's on the table, waiting for you."

Ophelia's snore didn't miss a beat. What did it matter? Would a few days at school make any difference to what was bound to come? Yet what if she was wrong? Surely the police should have been here by now? In that event, she had a plan of sorts. Should they show the slightest suspicion of Ophelia she'd tell them she herself had murdered a blackmailing Naomi. She told herself a lifetime in prison held no fears after these last few hellish years, but deep down she knew she was terrified. In the meantime they must both appear as innocent as possible, which included Ophelia going to school at least a couple of times a week. Remembering the recycling at the last minute, she left the house.

Abigail's had been a hairdresser's for as long as she could remember though it had changed hands and names several times in those years. These days it looked like a laboratory, all white and chrome. Even the hair dryers were chrome like surgical instruments and there were several rooms off a corridor where mysterious treatments took place. Hairdressing had come to take itself very seriously. They'd be giving degrees in it soon.

Behind a semi-circular desk sat Megan, the receptionist. Her white overall was fastened at the side of her neck like a dentist's. Her hair was highlighted and low-lighted in zebra stripes and drawn into a pony-tail that made slits of her eyes. She'd shaved one eyebrow in a dotted line. She looked at Verity without the hint of a smile, with no more recognition than she'd given to the appointments book a second before. It made Verity defiantly bright.

"Good morning, Megan. Isn't it a heavenly day? I've an appointment at ten o'clock with Abby. I'm a bit early, I think."

"Abby isn't here today." Megan's voice was the expected nasal singsong.

"Oh, but…"

"She's cancelled all her appointments. You can see someone else but it won't be till this afternoon." She pursed her lips and frowned at the book. "Laura's free at two-thirty."

"A bit late, I'm afraid. And I like Abby to do my hair. She knows how I prefer it. I'll leave it, I think. I hope Abby's not unwell?"

"Dunno."

"Will she be here tomorrow?"

"That's up to her, isn't it?"

"You're so right, it is. And if it were up to me you

wouldn't be working here any longer than it took you to get your coat."

She slammed the door behind her and caught sight of Megan sniggering with another stylist.

What was the matter with the young nowadays? Were they all in varying degrees versions of Ophelia? Would *she* grow up to be like Megan? No. As things stood, even ending up like charmlessly nasal Megan was a prospect beyond poor Ophelia's reach.

Poor baby Ophelia who'd been read Shakespeare and who used to listen rapt when her grandfather practised *The Messiah*.

How could things have come to this? Whichever way she looked at it, she knew she'd been a bad mother. She'd left Ophelia so often and then, against her own mother's advice, tried to assuage guilt for it by indulging the child. And now the two of them were reaping the results. Well, no more. It was time to get the bus home and make Ophelia go to school without any more of the morning being lost.

And if she was hit, she'd hit back. Yes, hit, and not before time. No one not prepared to stand up to violence could exert any sort of authority. Hadn't that been the case throughout history? Wasn't that the very reason women no longer wanted to be dependent on men? Well, then, the worm would turn. She hitched her bag more firmly on her shoulder and strode with determination towards the bus stop.

She'd got as far as the car park when she saw Abby standing amongst the cars looking as if she'd forgotten where she was. Verity didn't really want to stop and risk her resolution over Ophelia faltering. Despite this she decided to practise her new personality and take control. She called out making the other woman jump.

"Sorry, darling, did I startle you? You were miles away, weren't you?"

Abby couldn't have looked more alarmed if a bomb had gone off. "I thought you were him." She gave her the look of a wary animal. "Is he with you?" She stared wide-eyed over Verity's shoulder. "Has he sent you to find me?"

"Him? I don't know whom you mean. No one's with me." Irritated and intrigued, Verity glanced round to make sure. "What on earth's the matter?"

Abby fumbled in her bag and brought out car keys. "I've got to go before he hears about it. They could be telling him this very minute. I've got to get away." She tried to unlock the car, dropped the keys and with a cry that made people look, covered her face. Verity picked the keys up.

"Let me do that." She checked whether her bus had arrived. "Come on, let's sit in the car for a minute and relax. There, that's better, isn't it? Now, why not tell me what's upset you?"

Abby closed her eyes. Her lids fluttered and there was a frown between her brows. With guilty satisfaction Verity noticed she didn't look beautiful anymore.

"I've been to the police station."

"The police station?"

"Yes. If I hadn't, they'd have come to the salon and he'd have killed me. He'll kill me anyway. I know that's what he means to do. I think he killed his first."

"Who'll kill you?" All this death, it was like Armageddon.

"They think I murdered her." She whispered and stared wildly. "They didn't say it but I know they think it. But I paid her the money so why should I kill her after that? They think I broke into her house, too. They asked if I wanted to find the photos before they did. But I was at the salon all day. And at night I didn't go anywhere. She was killed on the downs. I never went near the downs."

Verity understood at last and her heart leapt at the hope someone else might end up taking the blame. "Naomi Long? They think you murdered Naomi Long? But why?"

"She was blackmailing me. She took photos of me…with a man. She said she'd send them to Dougie if I didn't give her a thousand pounds."

"Blackmailing you? And the police know about it? How?"

"They found the photos in her cottage."

If there was evidence about Abby there may be evidence about herself. Hope was swiftly overwhelmed and her chest tightened with palpitations again. The bus she'd meant to catch drew in to the station and left. She'd catch the next one.

"Abby, why should the police think Naomi a blackmailer just because of a few photos? There must have been something else, surely? A written list or something? Did the police mention that? Try to think. Was there a list of Naomi's other victims?" She did a few breathing exercises to try and calm down as she waited for the reply.

"Other victims?" Abby looked, as Ophelia might have said, gobsmacked. "They didn't say anything about other victims. But do you think there were others?"

"I think it's likely, don't you? If Naomi had the nerve to do it once, she could do it countless times. Yes, I think there were others. In fact, I'm certain of it. So if they suspect you, they must suspect them, too. They haven't charged you with anything, have they?"

"No." She had the dazed look of someone who'd escaped disaster by a hair's breadth. Verity wished she could feel the same way. "I went to them of my own accord. Darius warned me they'd been to see him and that they'd come to the salon today. I had to stop it. I couldn't risk one of the girls bumping into Dougie and saying something. So I went to the police station myself this morning."

Dougie *and* Darius. Two men. *Two?*

"Dougie's your violent husband, I take it?" It gave her some satisfaction to see Abby look ashamed.

"And Darius is the one in the photos, is he? Well, he must help you."

"But he has, Verity." She sounded like a daughter trying to endear her boyfriend to a strict mother. "He paid Naomi the money. If he hadn't, I don't know what I'd have done. Dougie keeps all our money in a joint account. I'd never have been able to take out a thousand pounds without him noticing."

Of course he'd paid. Someone like Abby would always have a man ready to pay for them.

"Paying's the easy part," she snapped. "But if he really cared for you, he'd find you a place of refuge. Leaving you to face a violent husband alone, it's disgraceful." Even to her own ears she sounded like a frumpy, grudging old aunt, the kind no man would ever pay a thousand pounds for.

"Oh, please, don't say bad things about him, Verity. He's already found me somewhere to live." Abby's hair fell like thick black silk as she hung her head. "The only trouble is, he'd want to move in."

"Well, what's wrong with that? You love him, I suppose?"

"Yes. That's why I don't want him to find out I'm an alcoholic."

From her unsure, sidelong glance, Verity could tell she'd never admitted it before.

"I can't ever live with another man. Only Dougie. He sees it as one of his greatest achievements."

Verity felt a prickling of the scalp, almost like a fear of the supernatural, as despite herself she finally saw the woman in front of her as a fellow abuse victim.

"Oh, Abby, how did things get into such a state?"

Abby shrugged. "They've always been like it. At least since the time I told him …oh, God, it was such an insignificant remark, I don't even remember making it. Though I probably did because it's true. But why should it make him hate me? And if he hates me, why won't he let me leave him?"

Let her leave? Verity knew there'd never be any of that. She took hold of her hand.

"Tell me about it. You never know, I may be able to help."

Twenty-Four

Funny, how beauty depends on the state of mind. Prettiness is always prettiness no matter what the facial expression, just blood and skin and the particular formation of certain bones. But beauty is a way of looking out at the world. At twenty-five, Abby was tall with the slim figure and large breasts men are supposed to prefer. Her black hair reached almost to her waist. She was one of the prettiest women Verity had ever seen. But in these few hours her beauty had gone. She clung to Verity's hand and looked out over the parked cars as if her past hovered there like a ghost.

"Dougie says I was a spoilt child. He was around for most of my childhood so he should know, I suppose. Mum was forty-nine when she had me. She'd given up hope of getting pregnant so it's not surprising when I arrived she loved me to distraction. But it made me loving as well, Verity." She sounded apologetic, as if it were too much to be believed. "I may have been spoilt but I've a lot of love to give. I can't bear to hurt anyone."

"I know you can't. You're sensitive to others. I've

noticed that."

She looked disconcerted for a moment and Verity wondered if being praised was so rare an occurrence Abby didn't know how to respond to it.

"We lived in Appulchurch. Dougie was our neighbour. He'd only been married a year when his first wife killed herself. I was five at the time but I can remember Mum and Dad discussing it and saying how sorry they were for him. They used to invite him in for meals. They didn't have many friends and I think they were flattered someone younger wanted to be with them. He was twenty-six and handsome. Mum and Dad used to say I had a crush on him."

She moved as if the thought made her restless.

"When I think about it now I can hardly believe they didn't see through him. But they were of a generation that tried not to think bad of anyone. We're not like that anymore, are we? But Mum and Dad saw something good in everyone they met. And I think Dougie was as fond of them as someone like him can be. It didn't go very deep and the minute he felt they were in his way he wanted rid of them. But at the time they were useful to him and there was no need to show what he was really like.

"He became part of the family, practically. When I went to the grammar school he even came to see me in the school plays. I wanted to be an actress, did I ever tell you? I always played the leading parts at school. But Dougie said the life was too precarious and Mum and Dad agreed."

She brought out a packet of cigarettes and offered them as tentatively as if they were heroin. Had domestic abuse made her like this, fearful even in a crisis of offending everyone's slightest sensibilities? Was she, Verity, like it too? She didn't smoke but she took a cigarette anyway. Abby leaned her head back and blew smoke through her nose.

"After A-levels I went to college in Portsmouth. I'd decided to be a beautician. I had a few boyfriends but nothing serious – no one I ever took home. To be honest, I didn't want Mum and Dad to think I preferred anyone to them. I was always shy in front of them about the subject of boyfriends."

Yes, Verity could believe it. Though Abby looked like a sex bomb, the more she spoke it became clear she was by inclination what used to be called a spinster. The sort of woman who never wanted to grow up and leave home and was seldom encouraged to do so by her parents. She would have boyfriends and treat them like gentlemen callers. Eventually the boyfriends would marry but the spinster would remain with her parents, dressing carefully to go shopping with mother, never abandoning the style of clothes of her youth and becoming more eccentric with every year. The chances were that unlike her parents, she'd die alone. But then didn't all love end in some degree of tragedy?

"I used to fantasize about becoming a makeup artist for films and marrying one of the stars and travelling the world." Of course she had, spinsters always had unfulfilled dreams. "Instead, the day I finished college I came back to get a job on the island. Dad had found out he didn't have long to live. I wanted to be with him in whatever time was left.

"Well, I must have been home no more than a

week when Dougie came in one morning and told us he'd bought a beauty salon in Newport. He wanted me to be in charge. We were so grateful that when he asked if I'd marry him, actually going to Dad first like something out of an old novel, I couldn't see any reason to say no. I knew I didn't love him but I already had so much love in my life I didn't think I needed more. Dougie was quite fanciable and I thought that was enough in a husband. And I could see Dad thought it would be a good thing for me. He'd die happy."

Verity noticed that two lines between her brows remained even when her frown was smoothed away. They would probably be there now till she died.

"As they got older my parents blamed themselves for having me late in life. They didn't have much money or a house to leave me. Dad had been a farm labourer until he'd retired and Mum never worked. We lived in a council house. It worried them sick that they'd die and the house would be repossessed before I was independent. Most parents don't have that worry, do they? By the time they start thinking about death their children are middle-aged and settled. Anyway, in their eyes Dougie was rich. He had two shops. He was a special constable as well, which must have made him seem a pillar of the community. Dad said it was a load off his mind knowing I had someone who'd take care of me.

"I didn't dislike him, Verity." She stubbed out her cigarette in the ashtray, tapping and tapping it into a concertina. "I found him attractive though you'd hardly recognise him now. I suppose he's suffered too. But it was the way I loved Mum and Dad that was the cause of everything.

"The trouble started not long after we'd been married. He'd let his house in Appulchurch and bought a cottage for us in Athercombe. He said he wanted a romantic house without memories of his first wife. I didn't mind. It was still close enough for me to visit Mum and Dad several times a week.

"He was a clinging husband. He was always asking if I loved him. He used to make me sit close to him so he could wrap me in his arms. It embarrassed me when he did it in front of Mum and Dad. In bed he'd pin me down with his legs while he slept till I could hardly move.

"One night we were sitting entwined on the sofa talking about our marriage, as usual. He said he couldn't believe it...he couldn't believe someone like me who – these are his words – could have whoever she wanted should settle for someone like him. He looked smug. He said it was proof I really loved him. In fact, I'd never once said I loved him. But that night we were relaxed and comfortable with each other and I was beginning to think I might come to love him and I suppose I let my guard down. So I said – and now that I've been talking about it I remember saying this one thing that started everything – I said that it was Mum and Dad he ought to thank for our marriage, that my only aim in life was to make them happy. A bit tactless, wasn't it? But not something a normal person couldn't get over. I behaved as if I loved him and that's the important thing, isn't it? Many people say they love but make their partner's life hell, don't they? But from that night he decided I had to be punished. He didn't say anything. He didn't make any threats. He waited.

"The following evening I went to see Dad. He was close to the end and it was the worst time I'd ever known. I got back to the cottage later than usual. Dougie was sitting with a sort of transfixed look, waiting for me. I hadn't even taken my coat off. He jumped up, got hold of me and dragged me upstairs. Then he flung me on the bed and tied my wrists and ankles to it with a tow-rope he kept in the car. When he bent his bloated face over me I thought he was going to bite me. He said I was never to visit Mum and Dad again, that I was his wife and must start behaving like one, that if I thought I could spend my life trampling over people I was wrong, there was nothing special about me as I'd soon find out if he turfed me onto the streets. He hit me and went downstairs. Five minutes later he ran back up and started again. It went on like that all night. At one point he got so angry I thought he'd beat me to death.

"After that I used to visit Mum and Dad in secret. I took time off work to see them. But he always knew when I'd been. Don't ask me how, but he did. But I wouldn't stop, no matter what he did to me. I loved them more than myself. Many a time I thought of not going back to him, of just staying with Mum and Dad and letting things be the way they used to be. But when it came to it, I couldn't bring myself to tell them. I knew Dad would have blamed himself, so I tried to pretend I was happy. But I started to get irritable and bad-tempered when I was with them. The remorse of that was terrible. Every time I told myself I wouldn't lose my temper but every time I did. I came to associate them with punishment, you see."

She lit another cigarette.

"Dad died eight months after my marriage. I was so depressed I hardly left the house except sometimes to sneak out to see Mum. It didn't register that she never suggested visiting me, but she must have guessed how things were and stayed away for my sake. I know she was worried about something happening to her and me having no one but Doug, because one day she showed me a letter from her brother in Yorkshire. He'd retired and was coming to live on the island. She was going to move in with him. She was immensely relieved about that."

Her hand shook as she held the cigarette to her lips.

"In the meantime she was by herself. I never imagined with me in the world that she'd become a lonely old woman. When I was little just the thought was enough to make me cry. I used to promise myself I'd never let it happen. But Dougie wouldn't allow her to live with us. He was furious that I'd asked, furious that I might even be thinking about it. Things got very bad and I didn't go as much."

She looked at Verity, expressionless.

"She died alone, Verity. I found her in her chair and at first I thought she was asleep. I bent over to kiss her but she was dead. She died alone.

"I have to drink myself stupid every night to forget for a bit but it'll never go away and I'll never get over it, not if I live till I'm a hundred. And if I didn't have the guts to leave him when she was alive, why should I do it now? I deserted her to make things easier for myself. I could have divorced him and had half of what he owns and bought a house for Mum and me. I could have made the rest of her life happy. It sounds an immoral thing to do and I think it is, no matter what other people say. But that's not what stopped me. It was cowardice. I was frightened of what he'd do, so I just put up with it like a slave and let Mummy die alone. I deserve to be punished. I want to be punished. I deserve it."

Verity took out a tissue and dabbed at Abby's scrunched-up face.

"Darling, stop crying for a minute and listen to me. For your parents' sake, who wanted nothing but the best for you, you must leave Dougie immediately. You know that, don't you? Wouldn't they tell you the same if they were here? Did they give birth to you so that you could be no more than Dougie's punch bag? No, like all of us, you made mistakes. So what? Even murderers don't expect to be punished for the rest of their life. Right then, why not stay with me tonight? You can stay as long as you like. At least you'll be safe until you can decide what to do."

Abby tried to smile through her tears. The bravery of that attempt nearly started Verity off.

"Thanks, but there's no need for you to put yourself out like that. I'll stay with my uncle. He wants me to. I didn't want to involve him if I could help it. But things are different now. Doug's sure to find out about what's happened today. If I go back, the only way I'll leave him is dead."

"Does your uncle know about his violence?"

Abby nodded and blew her nose.

"And will he be able to deal with Doug if he comes looking for you?"

"We'll lock the door. We won't open it to him."

"Then go at once. It's the right thing to do. And as for this business of the murder, forget it. You've done nothing wrong, as the police probably already know. The wretched, evil woman was blackmailing lots of people. I know because I was one of them. So you see, you're not alone."

She laughed at Abby's astonished face.

"I'll tell you all about it some time but not yet. All you must think about is getting safely to your uncle's. Do you want me to come with you? You won't feel tempted to go home for a second, not even to pick up a toothbrush? Right, here's my phone number. Ring me any time. I've got a few things to see to, so I'll leave you for now. But you mustn't worry. Everything will work out perfectly. Just go."

She got out of the car and took a deep breath of the smokeless air, so fresh she was sure she could smell the sea. She watched and waved as Abby drove away. Then she went into the public lavatory to tidy her unstyled hair as best she could.

As she put on a fresh layer of lip gloss she thought about what Abby had told her, especially about the cottage where she lived with her husband. Verity had forgotten, if she'd ever known, that they lived in Athercombe.

Could she make something of it? One thing certain – it was just a matter of time before the police came knocking on her door. Like Abby, she'd pre-empt it. And if she could deflect them, if she could cast suspicion onto the man she'd seen that night, not only might the nightmare be over for Abby, it might be over for Ophelia and herself.

With a last glance at her reflection she made her way to the police station.

Twenty-Five

For the third time Chaudhuri rang the MacArthurs' doorbell. At a window opposite someone pulled the curtains aside and looked out at them.

"They might be deaf," said James. "You can tell from the state of the house that they're old. Funny how you can, isn't it? Try the knocker instead."

Chaudhuri rapped with the black-painted door-knocker shaped like a mermaid. When this fetched no one he crouched down and peered through the letterbox: a dark, dingy hall that hadn't been decorated for years. James was right – too old to bother. And a faint smell, ominous but familiar. Impossible though for it to be what he thought.

"Can I help you?"

It was the woman from the house opposite. She was elderly and scrawny with a scored face, her hair cut in a short back and sides, the top brushed in a fringe over her forehead. It was dyed a youthful brown and in the sunlight had a greenish tinge.

"We're trying to get in touch with Mr and Mrs MacArthur." Chaudhuri smiled as he always did at old ladies, though he needn't have bothered with this one.

"Mr and *Miss*." She made the word into a hissing sound. "They're brother and sister."

"Ah, right. Thank you. And you are...?" Before she could tell him to mind his own business he showed her his warrant card.

"Oh, goodness, the police." The hand she brought to her mouth was chunkier than the rest of her – a strong hand with ribbed nails and a short thick thumb. "So there's something wrong, then?"

"No, no, not at all. We simply wanted to speak to Mr and Ms MacArthur about a certain matter. You don't know where they've gone, I suppose?"

"They went to London on Monday, I do know that. I waved to them as they left – just happened to be looking out. Giving some sort of special talk somewhere, she was. But no one's seen them since. There was a crowd outside the door last night waiting to be let in but in the end they gave up and went home."

"A crowd?"

"Yes. The Wednesday congregation," said a bit impatiently, as if he should know. "Miss Mac's a medium. She has a chapel up there in one of them bedrooms for her weekly meetings. Stood out here for ages they all were and a bit disgruntled at being left in the lurch. Well, it's not nice, is it? Gives an unreliable impression. Not that Spiritualism impresses me one way or the other. Leave the dead in peace, I say. It's not right. Do you think it's right?" Looking at him through narrowed eyes like an inquisitor.

"I've never really thought about it, but I can see your point. So as far as you're aware, no one saw the

MacArthurs come back from London on Monday?"

"Well, I know I didn't. Not that I'd be on the watch for them." She folded her arms with self-satisfaction. "I like to keep myself to myself."

"Quite right. But you say you saw them leave. What time would that have been?"

She put her head on one side and pressed her forefinger to her cheek. "Ooh, let's think, now. It was after breakfast but before lunch. Say nine o'clock?"

"They used public transport, I suppose?"

"Oh, no, drove, they did. That's their car there."

"The blue ford Fiesta? That's their car? So they're back from London?"

She must have thought his tone accusing. Or maybe she just hated to be wrong-footed. She looked disconcerted and avoided his eye. "Well their car's there, that's all I know. I'm just saying I haven't seen *them*."

"Is it usual not to see them for several days?"

She shrugged elaborately.

"And these Wednesday meetings Ms MacArthur holds – is it usual for her not to be there when people are coming to one of them?"

She'd had enough of what she'd decided was criticism.

"How should I know, people like that? They might do anything. All that religion and superstition – shouldn't be allowed in this day and age. Religion should be banned, my old man used to say. An atheist, he was," she added superfluously. "All I know is, *I haven't* seen them. I didn't have to come and talk to you, you know." The more she thought about it, the angrier she became. "And if this is the thanks I get I'll think twice about trying to help anyone in future."

"You misunderstand me, Mrs...? Mrs Robinson. I'm extremely grateful for the information you've given us."

She looked away huffily, hugged herself closer then looked back.

"Well, are you going to break the door down or not? No point just standing there. They could be in there, you know. Old, they are. Could be ill."

"We'll see to it, don't you worry. All in hand, now." He half pushed, half escorted her through the gate. "Thanks for your help. We won't keep you any longer."

They watched her cross the road, a miffed look on her face as she let herself into the house.

Chaudhuri peered through the letterbox again.

"I don't like it, James. There's an odd smell. I'm going to ask Trent to send someone from uniform. In the meantime we'll try to have a look at the back of the house. Go round the corner and do a quick recce, will you?"

He finished his call to Trent as James hurried back.

"There's another terrace of houses parallel to this one. Looks as if their back gardens overlook one another. We could try next door. If they let us into their garden we could climb over their wall into the MacArthurs'."

No one answered at the house on the right so they tried the one on the left. A woman, eastern European or Russian, answered the door. She spoke no English and looked at them in terror. She seemed desperate to oblige, maybe having experience of police tactics wherever she came from. With obsequious gestures she invited them in, smiling and almost doing obeisance as they made their way to her garden and thence to the one next door.

It was long and narrow, divided in the middle by a flagstoned path. On one side was a wooden shed, a greenhouse full of tomato plants on the other. This side of the path was given over to vegetables, the shed side to lawn.

In front of the house was a bit of patio, a couple of aluminium watering cans flanking the brown back door. It was locked. They looked through the kitchen window between a gap in the closed curtains. The budgie in its cage fluttered from perch to perch.

Twenty-Six

The coroner's officer removed the MacArthurs' bodies while their parched little budgie, still full of life, was taken to Ryde police station to await a new home. The crime scene investigators in their white suits moved round the old house like giant pupae, grubs of death crawling into every crevice and drain.

While they waited for an incident room to be set up, Trent, Chaudhuri, James and DI Stott sat for a few minutes in the sitting room overlooking the cordoned-off front garden.

Beige, olive and brown. How many people chose to live in a world of beige and brown? Even the brass vases on the mantelpiece were brown from lack of polish. Kelly had been a perfunctory cleaner here. A dark wooden Napoleon clock ticked between the vases. Above it in a mahogany oval frame hung a large sepia photograph of a blonde smiling child – a little girl no more than two years old in a gauzy dress of the 1920s. A blessing not to know what our end will be. Had Emily MacArthur known hers? Had the spirits she communed with watched her progression towards it, a bead on the string of fate shuttled to this conclusion?

Trent spoke.

"Right, bearing in mind we haven't had the post mortem findings yet, estimated time of death is sometime on Monday night between nine o'clock and midnight. According to Dr Lewis the weapon was a large blade, probably with a smooth edge and about four centimetres at its widest point. The perpetrator was alone. Due to the position of the bodies, Mr MacArthur fell first and therefore was possibly attacked first. Looks as if the poor old girl might have tried to cover him with her body. There's hundreds of fingerprints all over the place as you'd expect with so many people coming and going to meetings. But there are footprints in the blood apart from those made by the victims. It's the sole of a size ten shoe with a wide, deep tread. They continue from the kitchen out into the hall. According to you, Tom, they resemble footprints found in London at the scene where Kelly Houghton was murdered and which your Forensic conclude to be the tread of a rubber Wellington boot, in your case a Dunlop. The manner of killing, the size and shape of the wounds, is also in your opinion similar in both cases. So though we'll keep an open mind, it's far from unreasonable to suspect the two crimes were committed by the same person.

"As for the killing of Naomi Long, there are too many differences. For example, whoever killed her wore trainers – that's difference number one. The size of the feet – size six and seven – that's difference number two. The manner of killing – kicking – that's difference number three. And of course number four – the fact that in Naomi's case there were two of them. So it looks as if we've three murderers, one unconnected with the other two but all from the island.

"Now, as a working hypothesis, let's think about this – that Kelly and Jade's murderer is also likely to be the MacArthurs' murderer, for the reasons we've already discussed. To make things easier we'll keep the name you gave, Tom – Raven.

"Why do we assume Raven is from the island and not London? Because after killing Kelly and her child, Raven travelled here at a time of night when there are few ferries and none at all after midnight. You don't travel all that way to murder someone knowing you might get stranded afterwards. And if she's a Londoner – let's be PC for once and face the possibility Raven could be a woman – why should she have any connection with the MacArthurs? According to the neighbours they hardly left the house except to shop at Somerfield on Saturday mornings.

"All right, then, Raven is from the island. She murders Kelly and Jade in London, travels home on the ferry and almost without pause stops off here and murders the MacArthurs. I grant you, in a tiny place like Ryde it's the sort of thing you'd rather do at night, but the *same* night? That doesn't seem like forward planning. That seems to me like someone who makes a decision on the spur of the moment and daren't wait. Why? Because I believe that on the ferry the MacArthurs recognised her."

Trent took centre stage in front of the fireplace and leaned on the mantelpiece, his elbow dangerously close to the Napoleon clock.

"Think about this – Raven catches an evening ferry,

this time probably without either of the disguises she used in London. She knows they'd make her stand out like a sore thumb on the ferry CCTV. She knows we'd be watching for the car driven away by someone wearing a cap and overcoat. So she has a third disguise, one especially for the ferry. So far, so good. But on the ferry coming back are the MacArthurs. It was the Lymington one, by the way, we found the ticket in Emily's bag. Either they recognise Raven or she *thinks* they recognise her. Whatever, she panics. They're bound to hear about Kelly and Jade being murdered in London. And they'll remember seeing her on the ferry that night. Already a nervous wreck, Raven daren't risk them putting two and two together. Did she know Kelly cleaned for them? Maybe. Anyway, she follows them home, calls at the house on some pretext, puts on the wellies and stuff to protect her from the blood and does the deed."

Chaudhuri nodded. "I think you're right. I couldn't work out why my guy at Portsmouth hadn't picked Raven out at any of the railway stations or ferry terminals. I thought she must have driven to the coast, crossed to the island by private boat and collected her car the following day."

"In that case she wouldn't have bumped into the MacArthurs."

"Exactly. So she must have been on the ferry but in another disguise. I said she was a master of it, didn't I, James? Do we know where the MacArthurs' meeting in London was?"

"We think so. There was a cheque in Emily's bag dated for Monday and a complimentary slip from the

British Spiritualist Association in Belgrave Square. That's a first line of enquiry for you, Stott. Find out if they've a list of the people attending the meeting and the time it took place and ended. Another is house to house here. We'll start with Mrs Robinson over the way. I'll pop over now myself. It might be useful for you to come along as well, Tom. Better rustle up an interpreter for the woman next door, Stott."

"Do you know," said Chaudhuri, "something's just occurred to me. It's to do with those size ten wellies. When Raven was on her way to the crime scene at Ravenscourt Park she had an odd, shuffling walk. It struck me at the time, didn't it, James? Yet when she left she appeared to be walking normally. Is it possible that the wellies were too big? They're probably a man's wellies. But could they have been borrowed for the purpose by someone with a smaller foot? A woman?"

"Interesting. Someone with a size six or seven foot like one of the people who killed Naomi? Did one of them carry out the killings of both Kelly and the MacArthurs while the other broke into Naomi's cottage? That brings us back to two perpetrators instead of three. We've gone round in a circle and come back to square one." He ran his fingers through his hair and made a piece stand up like a cockatoo's crest. "I tell you what, Tom, it's time we did a proper search of Kelly's flat. Chase up that warrant Stott, we want it double quick. We've still got Naomi's blackmail victims to question. Which reminds me, apparently one of them came into the station this morning while I was at Yarmouth and gave a statement – Darius Field's bit on the side. I'll be speaking to her later."

James cleared his throat. "There couldn't be a supernatural angle to all this, could there?"

DI Stott gave him a look as if to say *It speaks,* though he seemed to find what it said risible.

"I mean she had second sight, didn't she, Ms MacArthur? Suppose she knew something about Raven – been given a spirit message or whatever? And Raven knew she knew?"

Trent looked impressed. "That's definitely a possibility, James. We need to find out who came to these meetings of hers and what happened at them. Did she go into a trance, for example? Did she remember afterwards what she said?"

"Maybe Naomi Long could have told you."

"Good God, James, you're right. Did Naomi come here for her séances? And if she did, is it significant? Is it significant that Kelly came here to clean? Is the common denominator in all these deaths the MacArthurs, or rather something to do with their spiritualism?" He rubbed his hands with relish. "Right, Stott, solve all that, will you, while we have a chat with the old girl over the way? Mrs Robinson, is it, Tom? Do you think she'll offer us a cup of tea and maybe a bite to eat? I've had nothing all day."

Twenty-Seven

Mrs Robinson belonged to that generation of English women who prefer baking to cooking. She thought nothing (she informed Trent) of having meat and vegetables out of a tin but would have died before she'd buy a shop-made cake or pie. Sometimes she even made her own toffee.

The eyes of the three policemen lit up at the plate of butterfly cakes she put on the coffee table – a table with a Perspex top covering a photo of a tropical beach in exaggerated colours.

"Tuck in while I bring the teapot." She hurried to the kitchen. It delighted her when she came back to see the cakes had all gone. Some women rely on their looks to impress men. It appeared Mrs Robinson relied on her baking. With a smug expression she went off again for a coffee and walnut log.

"That your husband, Mrs Robinson?" Trent's voice was muffled by cake. He nodded towards a photo on the china cabinet next to a vase of silk daffodils and hydrangeas.

"Yes, that's him. Dead for years but never a day

passes without I miss him. A special constable at Ryde police station, he was. That's his uniform he's got on."

"And very smart he looks in it, as well."

"Yes, he always looked good in a uniform. I think it was his naval rig-out that clinched our marriage. Always looked dashing in it, he did. Not so dashing out of it." She roared with laughter and showed dentures like joke teeth as enormous in her fleshless face as teeth in a skull. "Have the rest of the cake?" She'd decided Trent was her favourite and concentrated on him to the detriment of Chaudhuri and James.

Trent shook his head. "Not for me, thanks. Enough's as good as a feast. But that's the best cake I've had since my gran was alive." He quelled a burp with the back of his hand. "Now, Mrs Robinson – business. Tell us about this Wednesday-night crowd at the MacArthurs'. A lot of people, were there?"

She cast Chaudhuri a glance as if to say this was the way to gain her co-operation and put her finger on her cheek to show she was thinking.

"A lot came and went. Seven o'clock they start those meetings, but I've seen Bert open the door to folk time without number from half past six on – a stream of people. Not this Wednesday, though. As I told your colleague," she gestured towards Chaudhuri, "there was no sign of either Bert or Emily. That's funny, I thought. Umpteen people knocked but there was no answer. Some went off but a few waited and chatted amongst themselves. About twenty of them, there were. I expect they thought the MacArthurs were out somewhere and would be coming back shortly. But gradually they drifted away and by half past seven they'd all gone."

"Did you recognise any of them?"

"Oh, yes, same lot as come every week."

"Do you know their names?"

"Oh, no. I don't know them to speak to. Like I told this coloured gentleman, I don't hold with religion and stuff. I just mean that I see them every week – from the window, like. I can't say for certain if Dougie was there but he might have come and gone while I was getting myself a cup of tea."

"Dougie?"

"Dougie Benson. A regular over there, he is. Now I can say without a word of a lie that I know *him* because he used to be a special constable with my husband – they call them something different, now – you'll know. A lot younger than my Roger, Dougie was, of course. But mad as a hatter even then. He told my Roger that he summoned Alexander the Great from his grave one night. Came clattering down Appulchurch seafront on his horse, according to Dougie, and stared at him through his living-room window. I ask you! Oh, they had a good laugh at Dougie many a time down at Ryde nick."

"I bet they did." Trent looked at Chaudhuri from the corner of his eyes. "But you're certain you didn't see this Dougie Benson on Wednesday night?"

She put her head on one side and looked prim. "No, I didn't see him and I won't lie to you and say I did. But I'd swear on my Roger's ashes – that's them in the cabinet, there. Nice urn, isn't it? Got a clause in my will that they'll be scattered with mine from Blackgang Chine when the time comes."

"Very touching. What is it you'd swear to?"

"Pardon?"

"You said you'd swear to something on Roger's ashes?"

"Oh, yes. Drat it all, what were we talking about?"

"Dougie Benson. You were saying how you couldn't swear to seeing him on Wednesday night."

"Oh, yes, that's right." She gave James a sharp look. "No need to roll your eyes like that, young man."

"What?" James was dumbfounded.

"Yes, I saw you. Not much gets past me. But the time'll come when *you* forget things. And when it does, you'll think of me and regret how you showed me that sarcastic expression."

She gazed before her with a martyred air and James, receiving severe glances from Trent and Chaudhuri, was forced to waste quite a bit of time assuring her that sarcasm couldn't have been further from his mind. She resumed her account but with less enthusiasm then before.

"No, I couldn't swear to seeing Dougie on Wednesday and not being one to tell lies, as you must have discovered about me by now, I won't. But I might be able to swear to seeing him on Monday."

"Monday?" Trent leaned towards her with his arms on his knees. "You saw him on Monday? Tell me about it, Mrs Robinson. This could be very important."

As soon as he'd said those last few words he knew he'd made a mistake to show his eagerness. She paused and pursed her mouth, savouring her power not to give him the satisfaction. Eventually, with the air of someone who cannot help doing her duty, she said:

"Yes, Monday night. Late, it was. The ten o'clock

news had been on for a bit. It was the week for the garden waste to be collected – you know, rose clippings and that – and I nearly forgot and the bin's already full and I didn't want it standing around till next month. A disgrace it is, them doing just monthly collections. Don't you think it's a disgrace, young man?"

James nodded.

"Should be weekly, wouldn't you say?"

With not even a suggestion of rolling the eyes, James agreed. She was triumphant.

"Anyway, as I was saying about Dougie – I went out to the back garden and wheeled the bin round the side into the front garden, ready for collection first thing next morning. And that's when I saw someone in the MacArthurs' garden. I had a good look in case it was them just got back from London. I was going to give Bert a shout and remind him about the bin because he gets the weeks mixed up. But it was Dougie."

"Mrs Robinson, are you sure? It was dark."

Still offended, she snapped. "Of course I'm sure. Bert's house is never dark. The street light's right outside. Anyway, if you knew Dougie as I do, which you don't, you'd know he's unmistakeable – great big fat thing with greasy hair nearly down to his shoulders." She shuddered.

"Did you speak to him?"

"What? You must be joking. Never speak to strange men, I don't, and definitely not at night. And Dougie's strange, all right, in the worst sense of the word."

"He was going into the MacArthurs' or coming out?"

"Coming out, I think. Looked as if he'd just left. Facing the gate, he was. The door was shut and there were no lights on. Funny, now I come to think about it. Oh, and he had a carrier bag with him – one of those plastic ones."

"That's all, only a carrier bag? Did it seem full?"

"Now you're asking something. No, it's no good. Age is catching up with me," she stole another glance to check on James' reaction to her words. "I can't remember."

Trent's phone rang. He sat back in his chair to answer it. Chaudhuri asked for the rest of the cake and forced James to eat half. It put Mrs Robinson in a good mood again. Trent finished his call and stood up.

"A new development, so we'll have to go, I'm afraid. But I can't tell you how helpful you've been. A true policeman's widow, you are, Mrs Robinson. We're extremely grateful."

"I don't want your gratitude young man, I'm just doing my duty as a good citizen."

"Of course you are. If you need to contact me about anything further just give me a ring on this number on my card. And thanks for those delicious cakes. Practically saved our lives, didn't she?"

Chaudhuri and James agreed she practically had. They gave several waves and nods as they left. It was a while before she closed the door.

"Come on, back to Newport as quick as we can." Trent strode to his car.

"Where are we off to? To pick up Dougie

Benson?"

"Not yet. There's a lady waiting to see us – a Miss Verity Shaw. Thinks she saw the person who murdered Naomi Long and insists on speaking to who she calls the officer in charge. Verity Shaw – V.S. Remember those initials in Naomi's diary? OK, let's hear what *VS* has to say."

Twenty-Eight

"Sorry we kept you waiting, Ms Shaw."

"It's Bob, isn't it?" She jumped up and held out her hand. "It never occurred to me you were the Inspector Trent they were talking about. It's marvellous to see you. It must be more than twenty years."

"Yes, a long time. Take a seat, will you?"

She had one of those faces that showed what she was feeling. He could see the coldness of his welcome had disappointed her. Then she smiled to let him know she understood – he was being professional. Forcing herself to look serious she sat down.

He'd once had what amounted to an obsession for her. She'd been the most beautiful and brilliant creature he'd ever known. He used to give her a lift home from the school dramatic society in his mother's Fiat 500. One night he could bear it no longer and begged to kiss her. She'd laughed – not unkindly – but had refused. That night was as vivid as if it were yesterday. He noted with pleasure and pain that her looks had faded considerably.

"You don't mind if Inspector Chaudhuri listens to

what you have to say? He's from the Metropolitan
Police and he's helping us with the investigation into
Naomi Long's murder."

"I don't mind a bit."

She crossed her legs and pointed one foot in its
leopard skin shoe like a ballerina. He riffled through
some papers on his desk as if they were of far more
interest.

"So you think you saw the person who broke into
Miss Long's cottage?"

"Yes. I think I did."

"What time did you see this person?"

"It was nine-thirty on Monday night."

"Nine-thirty? Really? You were a good friend of
Miss Long's, I take it?"

"We were extremely close – almost like sisters."

"I ask because nine-thirty seems late to go visiting.
You live in Maryford, I believe?"

"Yes, still the same old house," again the smile,
suggesting amusement at his pretence not to know.

"So you must have driven to Athercombe?"

"Driven?" He'd forgotten that laugh – a slight lifting
of the shoulders and sideways tilt of the head. "I'm one
of those people who can't control a car. I've sat my test
five times. Now I've decided to leave driving to you
men."

She was too old to play the coquette and he was too
old to be impressed by it.

"So you got the bus?"

"Yes. That's why I arrived at Naomi's so late. I
waited a full forty-five minutes for it. It didn't come
until nine o'clock, would you believe?"

"Yes, they're very unreliable at that time of night. Why did you go to see her?"

"I thought she might be unwell. I didn't see her at our meeting on the previous Thursday. Normally she never misses."

"Meeting?"

"Our spiritualist meeting in Ryde."

His heart sank. "That would be Miss MacArthur, I take it?"

"Yes. A brilliant woman. Do you know her, Inspector?"

So, she was guilty, he'd suspected it before he walked through the door, but of how much? Of one thing he was certain – she was the *VS* in Naomi's little black book and he was going to make her admit it. Ignoring her question about Miss MacArthur, he said, "If you were worried about Naomi, why didn't you just phone her?"

She hesitated. He'd caught her off guard.

"I didn't have her number, I'm afraid."

"You mean you'd lost it? Forgotten it?"

His abruptness startled her. "To be honest, she never gave it to me." There was rebuke in her look as if she thought he was taking the professional act too far. No act.

"And yet you were as close as sisters?"

"Make allowances for the exaggeration of an actress, Inspector."

"I'd rather not have to bother, Ms Shaw." She was like a child when a game in the playground turns into a fight. He felt ashamed of himself. And gratified. "If you were worried about Naomi on Thursday, why did you leave it till the following Monday to visit her? More importantly, why did you wait until now to tell me you'd witnessed the break-in?"

She blinked. "Terribly busy. I'm a ballet teacher, as you possibly know, and…I simply didn't have a spare minute before."

He could see she wanted to cry. He leaned back in his chair.

"All right. Tell us what you saw on Monday night."

He saw her take a breath. He knew this was the bit she'd rehearsed. She'd had plenty of time.

"I arrived at Athercombe on the bus, as I told you. It was rather dark when it had gone. Those villages have hardly any street lights, do they? I spent a few minutes getting my bearings. I was still standing at the bus stop when I heard footsteps – quick footsteps. I looked up and there was a man running out of a garden gate. And instantly I knew there was something not quite right about him – something furtive."

"Why? What did he do?"

"He didn't do anything except hurry away. But…and this is what I think significant…every now and then he'd break into a run and then stop and walk as if trying to appear calm. And he looked from side to side, like this, as if to check no one was watching." She gave a dramatic re-enactment and Trent saw Chaudhuri suppress a smile. He wanted to hit him.

"Then what happened?"

"He started to search his pockets. It looked like he was trying to find his keys. Oh, and he was carrying something – something like a box, which he changed from his right hand to his left while he was searching."

"Did you notice if he was wearing gloves?"

"I didn't, I'm afraid."

"Right. Go on, Ms Shaw."

"He went into one of the gardens on the other side of the road. It's a few doors away from Naomi's and has a high privet. I couldn't see him go into the house but I heard him close the door – slam it, almost, as if he was relieved to be home. I stood still and waited. But the lights went on and he didn't come out again, so I assumed he lived there."

"Then what did you do?"

"I started to look for Naomi's cottage. I knew it was called *Holly Cottage*. Well, I'd reached the gate the man had come out of, when I almost collapsed. It was Naomi's cottage, the one I was looking for. He'd been to see Naomi. And the place was in darkness. I suppose he could have been a quite innocent caller but somehow from the way he was behaving I didn't think so. I don't know how I could tell exactly, maybe my training in observing human nature has made me rather acute about these things. Also I noticed her car drawn up on the grass verge which ought to mean she was at home. It made the absence of lights doubly eerie. Well, I ran to the door and rang the bell with all my might. I rang and rang but there was no reply. I tried not to let my imagination get the better of me and told myself that perhaps the bell wasn't working, so I knocked. Then I thought if she was in one of the back rooms she might not hear. So very cautiously I followed the path round to the back of the house."

"It was the first time you'd been to the cottage?"

"What?"

He knew she'd heard him.

"You and Naomi were as close as sisters yet you'd never been to the cottage before? You were unfamiliar with it?"

"No. I'd never been before." She looked down.

"Go on, Ms Shaw. Sorry for interrupting."

She raised her eyes to his. "The door had been forced open. The wood was splintered next to the lock. I felt the hair rise on my head. I couldn't go in. I called to her and the sound of my own voice made me go cold. I ran for dear life. There was a bus coming and though it was going in the wrong direction I got on it. I was terrified the man had heard me knocking and was coming after me. As the bus passed his cottage I ducked down in my seat. That's why I didn't come to you before. I was afraid. But when I heard you suspected Abigail Benson of the break-in…"

"Ah, yes, Abigail Benson. How do you come to know of her involvement in the case?"

She was now angry and her mouth hardened in irritation.

"I explained it all to your officer on the desk. Don't try to tell me he didn't brief you before you came in here. But if you need to hear it again I'll repeat it. Abby told me about her interview with you when I saw her this morning. She was supposed to be doing my hair – that's why I'm such a mess, I'm afraid – but naturally she was far too upset to do anything but talk. And when she told me you'd questioned her about breaking into Naomi's cottage…"

"Did she say why?"

If looks could kill. "She said something about some

photos but the reason is irrelevant. The point is I couldn't stay silent any longer. I had to come and tell you what I'd seen. And that's what I'm doing to the best of my ability. Though I can describe him, I don't know who the person was that broke in to Naomi's. I only know it wasn't Abby."

She glared at him and he returned to his papers.

"Is it really because you were afraid of this man that you didn't come to us before, Ms Shaw? Don't get me wrong, I'm grateful that you're here especially in the cause of a friend. It does you credit. But isn't the reason you hesitated because you were afraid we'd find out Naomi Long was blackmailing you?"

She turned her head to the window. On the third floor there was nothing visible from where she sat but the sky, grey and white cumulus sailing across the blue of her eyes towards the sea. She looked back at him.

"You're a very shrewd man, Inspector, and I'm sorry for wasting your time. I might have known someone like you would have already discovered it. But I clung to just the tiniest hope that you hadn't. Will you have to prosecute me?"

Dread made him hoarse. "What for?"

"For drawing my mother's pension after her death."

He didn't know whether to laugh or cry. What a bloody awful thing life was. He and his mates had hated her because she was too good for them. She'd seemed made for great things. But after all, she'd been made for this. He cleared his throat.

"It might have escaped your notice but I've more serious things to think about than pensions."

He got up and shouted through the door for

someone to bring a cup of tea and a packet of biscuits. He opened the packet and put it beside her.

"Here, have something to eat since you've been waiting so long. And while you're eating tell me about this blackmail business."

Her posture had slipped. She took a sip of tea.

"It was three weeks ago, a Wednesday. I went to a meeting at Miss MacArthur's. It was my first time and I'd no idea who would be present. In fact it wasn't until the end when Naomi came up to me that I knew she was there. She often cashed Mummy's pension for me at the post office. But at the meeting she'd heard me say Mummy had been dead for three months. That's what gave her the idea of blackmail, I suppose. She offered me a lift home and then threatened to report me if I didn't give her the pension every week. She said if they heard about it, they'd put my daughter in care. I was so frightened for Ophelia that I paid Naomi for a couple of weeks. Then last Thursday I went to another spiritualist meeting – I went on the Thursday because I knew Naomi always went on a Wednesday – and I got the most disturbing message from Mummy, saying she couldn't rest because of what I was doing. So next morning I got in touch with the social security and told them everything. They're sending someone to see me next week." She took a bite of biscuit and finished her tea as if parched. "I wish I'd left it at that. I don't know why I went to Naomi's on Monday night – well, I wanted to tell her that I wouldn't pay her anymore but I needn't have bothered, she'd have found out soon enough. But I wanted to confront her. Does that make sense? Suddenly I couldn't rest until I'd told her to her face and got it over and done with. I didn't kill her, though. I'd already confessed to the social security so I'd no reason. She had no hold over me anymore. You can see that, can't you?"

Of course he could see it. It irritated him that Chaudhuri, butting in, should look and sound so sceptical.

"Did Miss Long ever allude to other of her blackmail victims? We know about Abby Benson. But did she ever mention someone of the name of Kelly Houghton?"

"Kelly Houghton? Isn't she the one who was found murdered in London last week?"

"That's right. Was she acquainted with Miss Long as far as you know?"

"Goodness, I really couldn't say. As you've probably already gathered, I actually hardly knew Naomi. But if she knew Kelly Houghton, she never mentioned it to me."

"Did you know her, Miss Shaw?"

"Who? Kelly Houghton? As a matter of fact her daughter used to come to my ballet class. Only for a couple of lessons – she was so badly behaved I had to tell Kelly not to bring her anymore."

"And how did Kelly react to that?"

"With almost as much rudeness as her daughter. But I was adamant – the other mothers had complained about…Jade, I think her name was…bullying and attacking the other children. She used to bite, if you can believe it. Poor little girl, she died as well, didn't she? But, anyway, I had to stand firm. I saw nothing of either of them afterwards."

Chaudhuri crossed a leg and brushed imaginary fluff from his thigh. "On Monday night when you caught the wrong bus to get away from Naomi's, where did it take you?"

"Oh, goodness me, talk about a round trip. It was the coastal bus. It took me all the way to Sandown. I had to change there and luckily caught the last bus back to Athercombe."

"What time did you get home?"

"It was nearly half past eleven. Ophelia thought I'd got lost."

"And last night did you go to the spiritualist meeting as usual?"

"No, not last night."

"Why was that?"

"Somehow I couldn't face it after Naomi's death. Not that I liked the woman, as you can imagine. But it just didn't seem appropriate."

"You'll not have heard about the MacArthurs' murder, then?"

"The MacArthurs' murder?"

"Yes, we found their bodies today. Though it's likely they'd been dead some time."

"Why on earth would anyone want to murder them? Why?" This time she really did cry. "Do you know who did it? Have you caught whoever it is?"

"Early days. Would you tell me where you were on Monday afternoon?"

She looked at him vaguely. "Monday? I was at home. I always do the washing and housework on Monday."

"You were at home all day until you went out at just after eight o'clock to see Naomi?"

"Yes."

"Were you alone?"

"No, Ophelia was with me. I know she should have been at school but she'd had a bit of an accident, so I let her stay home to recover."

"Nothing serious, I hope?"

"No, no. A few scratches – been raiding someone's orchard, the naughty girl. She was just a bit shocked. And they're so vain at that age, aren't they?"

"On her face, were they?"

"Actually, yes, they were."

"And this must have happened on Sunday?"

She hesitated.

"Where were you on Sunday?"

"I was at home most of the day. Well, all day until I went to church in the evening."

"What time was that?"

"Evensong starts at half past six."

"Was Ophelia at church with you?"

"No, I'm afraid she's going through the rebellious stage."

"But until you went to church in the evening, she was at home with you all day?"

She nodded.

"Apart from the time when she was raiding someone's orchard?"

"Oh, yes, I'm sorry, I forgot about that."

"Was Ophelia aware of Naomi's threat to have her put into care?"

The stillness of panic, the distracted look of rapid thought. "Let me see. No, Naomi's threats all took place in her car when she gave me a lift home. No, Ophelia knew nothing about it."

"Does she know about Naomi's blackmail?"

"No, she hasn't a clue. It's not the sort of thing you'd discuss with a twelve-year-old girl."

She picked up her cup and brought it to her lips. It was empty.

Trent decided she'd had enough. "Can you give us a description of the man you saw coming out of Miss Long's garden?" Was it his imagination that she looked at him with gratitude?

"I get the feeling he was elderly. I don't know why I want to say that because most burglars are young, aren't they? Yet that's my impression."

"What sort of build?"

"Tall and well built, I think. Large framed."

"Fair or dark?"

"I don't know. He was wearing a hat – a trilby hat. Maybe that's why he seemed to be older."

"And you think you know where he lives? Can you describe the house?"

"Not offhand. It was just a glimpse. I'd remember if I saw it again, though."

"That's just what I was about to suggest. Inspector Chaudhuri and I have to get over to the incident room at Athercombe. Would you mind coming with us and pointing out the house? That's all we'd want you to do. No need even to get out of the car. Someone would drive you home."

She pushed her teacup aside and leaned her forearms on the desk.

"Could I tell you something else, first, Inspector? Tell you my thoughts, as it were?"

"By all means. Feel free to say whatever you like."

"I don't know whether it's an offence to cast suspicion on someone who hasn't been charged with anything but I'm wondering if the man I saw coming out of Naomi's garden could have been Abby Benson's husband."

"Go on, Ms Shaw. All theories welcome at this stage."

"Well, Abby told me she came to see you this morning because she didn't want her husband to know she was involved in the investigation, which he would have done if you'd gone to her salon. She was terrified he'd find out about the photos. But supposing he already knew about them? Wouldn't that give him a motive for killing Naomi? And why shouldn't he be the man who broke into her cottage? He wanted the photos, not to save Abby's reputation, but to destroy any evidence which might appear to involve him in the murder. He didn't find them, of course, because Abby said *you* had them."

"I'm not sure that theory holds water. If he's the violent type you imply, wouldn't knowledge of the photos make Abby rather than Naomi the more likely victim? Surely his anger would be towards her, at least initially?"

"Yes, I see what you mean. It would." She bit her lip then brightened. "But suppose he was another of Naomi's blackmail victims? The man I saw leaving Naomi's cottage had found something. The object I saw him carrying – could it be something connected not with Abby but with himself? One thing I know, he wasn't innocent. If he were, when he found the cottage broken into he'd have phoned the police. And he didn't, did he? I can tell from the way you listened as I talked about him that you knew nothing of this man before."

"As a theory, it makes good sense. Shall we set off now and put it to the test?"

"Just one more thing, Inspector. It's disturbed me more than I can say which is why I want you to hear it. Abby is this Dougie Benson's second wife. Apparently his first wife committed suicide just a year after their marriage. Abby says she thinks he killed her, which I'm sure is hysteria on her part. But she thinks he means too kill her, too, and in that case I fear she could be right. She's terrified of him. That's why it's important I take up a little more of your time and tell you all I can about him."

"Plenty of time. No hurry."

"Well, the other day I heard a rather unpleasant story. It could be fabrication but it's best you know. Years ago a woman hanged herself in woods somewhere on the island. And the person who found her saw Naomi Long in the woods. She was watching the woman as she died."

She looked at him, hoping he would share her horror. He shook his head in disgust.

"Could the woman who killed herself in the woods have been Dougie Benson's first wife? Could he have somehow got to know about Naomi being there and taken his revenge? I know it was a long time after the event but it's worth thinking about, isn't it?"

"Who told you this, Ms Shaw?"

"It was Mr Smythe-Pryce, the churchwarden at St Mary's in Maryford. He heard it from someone else."

"He gave no name of the person who allegedly saw Naomi in the woods the day this woman died? No name of the woman?"

"No, I don't think he knew."

"It's just that it's the sort of thing you'd expect to be reported to us. You'd report it wouldn't you? I mean, how did the person who claims to have seen Naomi there know that she hadn't a hand in the woman's death? And there were no such reports about Naomi. In a murder enquiry we look into every bit of the victim's background and I can tell you categorically that there were none."

"Yes. I see. You think it's all made up then?"

"I don't quite know what to think yet. One thing at a time." He stood up. "Let's drive to Athercombe and have you point out that house for me."

She sat on the back seat beside him. Her perfume drifted towards him every time she moved her head. The church at Redvers St Cross rose on the horizon. He remembered a school lesson in brass rubbing when he'd knelt close to her on the floor of the nave, her long fair hair hiding her face.

Too quickly they arrived at Athercombe. The car drew up onto the grass verge.

"Now, can you remember which house you saw the man go into?"

"It's that last one – the one at the end, where the road turns."

"Thank you. If you'll wait here, I'll get someone to drive you back to Maryford. We'll need you to pop into the station in the next couple of days and leave a signed statement. And since you were in the vicinity of a crime scene we'll need a DNA sample. Just a formality. It'll be destroyed at the end of the investigation. Nothing to worry about."

"Shall I ask for you?"

"You can if you like. I'm not always there, of course."

"No, you must be very busy."

"I'll go and find you a driver, Ms Shaw." He shook her hand. "Thank you for your time."

Twenty-Nine

There was no doubt about it – Trent was disgruntled. It was one of those moments in a new relationship when an argument can sour it for good. If possible Chaudhuri wished to avoid it.

"Fascinating woman, that Ms Shaw. Strange, but I've a feeling I've seen her before somewhere."

"Seen her?" From Trent's tone you'd have thought Chaudhuri had spoken of maybe recognising the Queen. It was a useful cover for his irritation. "Of course you'll have seen her. She was always on the TV a while back doing adverts for some famous perfume or cosmetics company or other."

"Ah! Now that does ring a bell. Yes, I'm sure you're right. She must have been very beautiful."

Trent was mollified. "Been in West End musicals. *Local Girl Makes Good* is what the paper used to say about her. Gave it all up when her mother got ill. Pity to think she's fallen on hard times."

He turned his back as though Chaudhuri intruded, and watched the car out of sight.

"I'll check, of course, that she really did own up to the

social security and on the day she claims. But on the face of it, it rules her out as our murderer, wouldn't you say? I mean, if she'd already confessed to them on Friday why murder Naomi on Sunday? As she herself pointed out, Naomi had no hold over her anymore."

Chaudhuri said nothing. Trent gave him an angry glance.

"Anyway, Naomi was murdered by two people. And both with much bigger feet than Verity, if I'm any judge. I noticed she has very dainty feet – typical dancer."

Throwing down the gauntlet, that's what he was doing. Testing to see how much nonsense Chaudhuri would let pass. Well, better have the argument and clear the air.

"What about Ophelia as accomplice, Bob? All right, roll your eyes if you want. But if Naomi was threatening to have me put into care – and no matter what Verity says to the contrary I'm certain Ophelia knew about it – I'd be pretty cheesed-off."

"But it wouldn't happen, would it?" His bellow made Chaudhuri wince. "You don't put a kid in care for bunking off school. Half the country would be in care at that rate."

"Neither Ophelia nor Verity might know that. And what if it wasn't for just bunking off school? What if there was more to it than that, something quite serious?"

"Like what?"

"I don't know yet. But Ophelia hardly sounds a model daughter. Scrumping apples, my arse. If she got her face scratched on Sunday it definitely wasn't in the Enid Blyton pastime of robbing someone's orchard."

Trent folded his arms and looked at Chaudhuri as if seeing him for the first time.

"Are you seriously saying you can picture Verity Shaw

kicking someone to death? You really think she's capable of that?"

"What I think is neither here nor there."

"You're right. It's not. It's fucking fiddlesticks."

He stormed off, stopped, and stormed back.

"And the break-in at the cottage? Are you saying she's guilty of that too? It would be a pretty senseless thing to lie about since we're on the point of putting what she's told us to the test."

"Maybe she hasn't much sense." Heresy that. Again Trent turned on his heel but this time Chaudhuri kept with him. "Maybe she's like most other criminals and thinks we can't sort out the truth from a lie. And why was she at the cottage at all? That business about going to tell Naomi she wouldn't pay her anymore won't wash, Bob. Why bother? Isn't it more likely she herself broke in? Or that she went there with that intention and found someone had got there before her?"

"But why, why, why?" Trent struck his forehead on each 'why'. "She'd already confessed to the social about the pension two days before Naomi was murdered."

"It wasn't the pension that worried her. It was something else. Something to do with Ophelia."

Trent threw up his hands.

"All right. She's guilty. Then why come to us and deliberately put herself in the frame? She came of her own accord, remember."

"Because she knew we'd found evidence that Naomi was a blackmailer. Abby Benson had already told her. She knew we'd get to her eventually. She thought it better to pre-empt it and try to have the interview on her own terms."

"But she'd know we'd want DNA. She confessed to being at the scene of a burglary. She'd know we'd be able to compare it to the scene of the murder."

"I doubt very much that such thoughts occurred to her. Most of the public haven't a clue about procedure. Even serial offenders leave such a trail behind them I'm surprised they don't save us time and money and turn themselves in straight after."

Trent hesitated. He looked gloomy.

"I must say, Tom, I was surprised at her reaction when she realised we knew about the blackmail. I had a funny feeling she was relieved – almost as if it was the least of her worries."

"Really? That's odd. I thought exactly the same. Do you know what I think? She was there because she wanted to be close to the investigation. How many times have we come across that from guilty parties? It's a compulsion with some of them."

Trent stuffed his hands in his pockets and gave his shoes a stare. "You think she killed Naomi?"

"I'm saying it's possible – she, or Ophelia, or both. At least you've got an excuse to take DNA when she comes to sign a statement. We didn't get any from Ravenscourt Park to compare it to, unfortunately. But she'll know London well, I should think, being an actress. Probably spent half her life there."

Trent looked at him from the corner of his eyes. "What's that got to do with it?"

"She's a tall, slim woman. About the height of Raven. Used to playing parts and dressing up. And as you say, with the dainty feet that would struggle in a pair of size ten wellies."

"You're not thinking she killed Kelly as well? Haven't we already established Naomi's killer is unlikely to be also Kelly's killer?"

"No. But if we have, we'll have to un-establish it. By her own admission Verity knew Kelly. And Kelly's dead. She knew Naomi. Also dead. Ditto the MacArthurs."

Trent slumped down on a garden wall, squashing a late clump of aubrietia.

"I don't believe this. You're saying Verity kills Naomi on Sunday, calmly goes to church in the evening, travels all the way to London on Monday – and she doesn't drive, bear that in mind – kills Kelly, hares back here, attempts to rob Naomi's cottage, then gets the bus to Ryde and murders the MacArthurs? Is that what you're saying? Because if it is, she must have the strength of Superwoman. She must have wings."

"Why should she have had wings? An ordinary car would do. I think we'll find she hired one."

"But she can't drive."

"She's lying. Think about it, Bob, just as a hypothesis and you'll see it's not so fantastical. Verity knew and was involved with all our victims and had reason for killing at least one of them. Naomi was killed by two people – Verity and Ophelia. Kelly was supposed to be meeting two people. Was one of them Ophelia? Was she too injured in the killing of Naomi to be able to travel to London the next day? Dare you dismiss this out of hand? You know we have to be ready to believe anything of murderers. The ordinary rules definitely don't apply. Anyway, I want to question both Verity and Ophelia about their movements on Monday."

Trent ran his hands through his hair till it resembled a

clown's.

"And where do you fit Dougie Benson into all this? Or have you conveniently forgotten he was seen at the MacArthurs' the night of their murder?"

"I haven't forgotten him, Bob. I'm simply taking one suspect at a time." It was the way he and James always worked and took pleasure in. He missed it. "I would just point out that as for Verity seeing Dougie leave Naomi's cottage, at the moment we've only her word for it."

Trent stood up and dusted the seat of his trousers.

"If you think back, Tom, she didn't claim the man she saw leaving Naomi's was Dougie."

"She certainly implied it, even going as far as showing us where he lives."

"She hasn't showed us where he lives."

"Of course she has. All right, she didn't say in so many words she knew Dougie lives in that house, but that was the gist."

"But Dougie doesn't live there. I don't know which one of these cottages is his, but it's not that one. If Verity thinks that, she's way off the mark."

"Dougie doesn't live there?"

Trent squeezed him round the shoulders so hard Chaudhuri feared dislocation.

"It perks me up no end to see that smart Alec expression wiped off your face. No, that's not where Dougie lives. That's where the churchwarden lives."

"Churchwarden?"

"Yes. Ted Britten – the one who found Naomi's body on Monday evening, remember? Exciting, isn't it? Gives you butterflies." He let go of Chaudhuri's shoulder. "Come on."

Thirty

From a diamond-paned window with a pane of blue glass in one corner a bar of light shone between curtains onto a brick path. This was edged with lavender bushes, straggly now, the last blooms scenting the evening air. Trent used the brass door-knocker shaped like a fox's head and was answered by a dog's gruff bark. He knocked again. The curtains at the window parted and a forbidding face stared out. At the sight of Trent it broke into a smile.

"Sorry if I made you feel unwelcome." Ted Britten held the door wide. "I thought it was someone else – kids, you know, playing tricks. I'll give it to them if I catch them. Come in, gents, come in."

They went down two stone steps into a sitting room, low with a beamed ceiling. Chaudhuri, used to the cramped and often squalid dwellings of London, was as fascinated by these country cottages as if he'd stepped into a book of fairy tales. The old uneven walls were whitewashed, the furniture upholstered in blue and white striped covers, faded and reminding him of the sea. On the mantelpiece of the brick fireplace stood blue and white bowls and jars and cherry-coloured curtains were drawn against the night.

Ted Britten must have been in his seventies but still had thick sandy hair. His was the sort of colouring always associated with green. His V-necked jumper was leaf-coloured over a fawn and white checked shirt and cinnamon tie.

"How about a drink? I was going to have something."

Trent shook his head. "Nothing for us, thanks. But you go ahead. This is my colleague, Inspector Chaudhuri, by the way. We just want to recap what you told us yesterday. Shouldn't take long."

Ted sat down with his whisky in a cut-glass tumbler. The dog, a black Labrador with amber eyes, curled up at his feet and went to sleep.

"I was telling Inspector Chaudhuri that you were the gentleman who found Miss Long's body on Monday."

"It was Dusky, really." Ted smiled at the dog who opened its eyes at the mention of its name.

Chaudhuri said, "That was at five thirty, I believe?"

"About then. Maybe a little later. I was on the home stretch of my walk. I'd been as far as the Pepperpot and was on my way back. Say twenty to six, to be accurate."

How alike people were. When they lied about the big things they stressed the truth of trifles.

"Miss Long often took the same walk, did she, Mr Britten?"

"She did. She was more of a morning person, though, especially at this time of the year. I've often met her walking early before she went to work. But she never went that way on dark nights. Well, no one does, I should think. Black as your hat up there." Chaudhuri, feeling like the Witchfinder General, recognised the sudden anxious look of someone worried they'd inadvertently made a racist remark. "You seem to have known her well."

"I did. Or I knew her ways, at least."

"Would you say she was the sort of woman to make enemies?"

Ted scorned such a melodramatic idea. "Never went anywhere to make them, as far as I can see. The post office and the church were her limits. How can you make enemies there?"

"Who do you think might be responsible for her death, then?"

"A nut case. A mental patient on the loose. They hang out in lonely places, don't they, just waiting for the first vulnerable woman to come along? She often took that walk, as I said. Maybe someone got his eye on her and decided to wait for an opportunity. That's *care in the community* for you. I don't know who it is they're supposed to be caring for but I know it's not us sane ones. We've just got to take our chance." He took a gulp of whisky.

Trent said, "When I spoke to you yesterday morning I informed you her cottage had been broken into. Would you tell us again for Inspector Chaudhuri's benefit what your reaction to that information was?"

"Of course." Ted turned himself in his chair to face Chaudhuri. "My initial reaction, well, my certain knowledge was that it must have taken place after her death. And I'll tell you why. I'm churchwarden at St Andrews. Miss Long had been a staunch member of the congregation for years. Now Sunday was our Harvest Festival. We had a morning and an evening service. She wasn't generally a morning worshipper but when she didn't come to evening service I was a bit surprised since it was a special event. Thinking she might be ill Mrs Prentiss and I called on her afterwards. That would be about eight o'clock. She wasn't at home and her car was in its usual place. However, everything was as normal. Certainly no break-in. Mrs Prentiss will back me up on that. At a little after ten that night I tried again with the same result. I assumed Miss Long had gone away for the weekend and for some reason hadn't needed to take her car."

He paused and took another sip of whisky, keeping his eye on Chaudhuri to make sure his attention didn't wander.

"Next morning after breakfast – say quarter to eight – I called again. Dusky and I were going for our first walk and I thought I'd catch Miss Long before she left for work. Mrs Prentiss was with me. She's a bit of a busybody but good-hearted. She happened to be out sweeping her path and when I told her I was going to call on Naomi she came with me. Again there was no reply but still nothing looked amiss. Well, I had various matters at the church to see to, distributing the harvest fruit and so forth, so I didn't get much of a chance to dwell on her absence. But at five that evening on our way to the Pepperpot Dusky and I called again. Still no answer. It wasn't long of course before we discovered why. She was by that time…" he stopped and rubbed his forehead with the flat of his hand. "Well, the rest you know, gentlemen. That was where you came in, as the Yanks put it."

Chaudhuri said, "So the last time you went to Miss Long's cottage was about five on Monday evening? And everything was as normal?"

Ted nodded.

"And by the time we ourselves got there at eleven," said Trent, "the break-in had occurred. Do you think that's accurate, Mr Britten – to put it at between five and eleven o'clock?"

"Definitely after five."

"Maybe more definitely between five and nine-thirty?"

Ted looked wary. He sat very still. "Nine-thirty? You think that, do you? Well, you could be right."

"We don't think it, Mr Britten. We know it. We have a witness to the fact that by nine-thirty the cottage had already been ransacked. We also have a witness to the fact of your leaving it at that time."

Ted's face took on a vacant expression, giving away nothing. He reached down to fondle Dusky's grey-flecked muzzle.

"Why did you break into Miss Long's cottage, Mr Britten?"

"Leave him alone."

A woman burst through the doorway that opened onto the built-in stairs, ran up to Ted and threw her arms round his neck. "He's done nothing except try to help me." She glared at Chaudhuri and Trent like a Fury. "Don't you dare blame him."

She wore a man's tartan dressing gown and her long dark hair was damp as if she'd recently washed it. Though Chaudhuri had seen only a shadowy photograph of her he'd have known Abigail Benson anywhere. For reasons he couldn't account for, he felt desolate to see her in what his father would have termed an *unsavoury situation*. Ted Britten was old enough to be her grandfather.

"Calm down, Abby, calm down." Ted stroked her face. "These policemen have to do their job, haven't they? This little firebrand is my niece, gentlemen." He looked at her with what Chaudhuri could only call adoration.

"He didn't kill Naomi." She spoke with a faint country accent. "He found her body on the downs but he didn't kill her. After he'd spoken to you – the police, I mean – he phoned me to tell me about it. He was in shock. He needed someone to talk to. But when I heard she was dead, I was frantic. I knew you'd find the photos. So I told him everything…about the blackmail and…everything. And I said I'd have to search her cottage that night and find the photos before you did. But he wouldn't let me. He knew I was afraid about leaving the house – my husband was out and I didn't know when he'd be back. So he went himself."

Her great soulful eyes reminded Chaudhuri of a portrait, *The Awakening Conscience*, he'd seen in a book about the Pre-Raphaelites that his father had left lying around at home.

Trent turned to Ted. "Is this true?"

"Yes." He showed no signs of unease at being found out. "As you saw, I went through the place with a fine-tooth comb. But in the end I came to the conclusion there was nothing to find. Maybe there were no more photos. I took an address book and a diary from

Naomi's handbag in case Abby was mentioned in them. There was a camera on the dresser and I took that too, just to be on the safe side. Then I left."

He reached up to take Abby's hand.

"It's not the police we were afraid of. It's her husband. In fact, that's why I was so unwelcoming when you knocked just now – I thought it was him. He ill-treats her."

A grimace of pain flickered across his face, quickly turned into a brave grin.

"It's strange but as I left Naomi's cottage I felt I was being watched. I couldn't see anyone but I could feel them. I expect you'll want the address books, won't you? Would you get them, Abby? They're in the top drawer of the desk. The camera's in the left-hand cupboard."

Trent said, "I'm afraid we'll also want you to come to the incident room with us, Mr Britten. We'll have to charge you with breaking and entering, you realise that?"

Ted stood up and threw out his chest. "Charge me with what you like but I don't leave this house without Abby. You think I'll leave her to the clutches of that wretch who calls himself a husband? Not as long as I've breath in my body. The sweetest little girl that ever was, who wouldn't hurt a fly? She wouldn't even eat her jelly babies when she was little, for fear of hurting them. Dougie and that Naomi, they're not fit to be in the same room as her."

He rubbed the sleeve of his cardigan across his eyes then gave then another ferocious look. "We'll go with you together. She's not staying by herself for that…that…person to get at. It's either that or I'll bring charges against him now, this very minute, and you'll have to arrest him."

"All right, Mr Britten. No problem. We'll wait while you get yourselves ready."

"Will you be locking us up? It's Dusky I'm thinking of."

"That's most unlikely. You'll have to appear before the magistrate tomorrow, but you'll be home on bail tonight. Don't worry it's just a short walk to the church hall. Dusky will be all right for an hour or so."

Abby went upstairs. She came down after a few minutes dressed in a long black coat, its fur trimmed hood covering her damp hair. She appeared to notice no one but her uncle, focusing on him with such intensity as if fearing he was about to disappear. Chaudhuri would have died for such a look. But for the first time in his life he felt a woman's complete indifference.

They had locked the front door and were walking in a single file along the narrow path when Ted, who was ahead of them, stopped. A man stood at the gate, his hand on the latch as if about to open it. He was tall, his light brown hair brushed flat from his forehead and clinging to the collar of his jacket in greasy tendrils. His heavy jowls made his little round nose and curving mouth look as though they belonged to a baby. Between the edges of his tweed jacket a pullover ballooned over his enormous girth. The delicate hand on the gate seemed to belong to someone else, perhaps a woman. There was a large carnelian ring in what looked like a snake-setting on his wedding finger. He had eyes for none but Abby. As if they were alone he smiled at her, a grin showing a lot of dingy but well-shaped teeth. He had grey-flecked eyes like birds' eggs.

"I wondered where you'd got to." His accent was northern, a thin nasal tenor. "What's going on then? Off on the razzle somewhere?" A frown formed between his scanty brows and he struggled to keep the smile in place. It incensed Ted Britten.

"I'll throttle you, I will. I'll wring your fat neck for you."

He tried to shake Abby off his arm. She stumbled against Chaudhuri and struck his chin with her head, leaving him in as much bliss as if she'd kissed him. Ted slipped off the path on the side of his foot, trod on the lavender bushes and cupped his mouth to hold in his false teeth. Trent caught hold of him to stop him falling.

"Easy, now, Mr Britten, easy, we don't want any more trouble. Best get off home, Dougie. Leave things to simmer down a bit, eh?"

Dougie watched Ted with contempt. "Fine by me. Just popped by to make sure the lady wife's all right. I expect she's told you about our little tiff? I'm giving her a few days to cool off, isn't that right, darling? Married couples, eh?"

"Not for much longer." This was Ted. "She's slept under your roof for the last time, let me tell you. You'll have to get past me – a man – before you get to her. And I'll give you such a hiding there'll be no skin on your backside. I'll kick it off. I wouldn't use my hand."

"Come along, now, Mr Britten, no threats, please. Go home, Dougie. I'll be along for a word in a few minutes."

"But what's happening?" Dougie's hand moved to the latch again. "Where are you taking her? Don't want me to worry and have a sleepless night, do you?"

"I'll give you sleepless nights." Ted shook his fist over Trent's shoulder. "You'll need sleeping tablets before I've finished with you."

"Mr Britten, *please*. Cut along, Dougie, you can see you're doing no good here. I've a few questions to ask Mr Britten after which I'll call at your cottage. Which one is it? All right, I'll speak to you later. Go on, now, lad."

Smiling to himself, Dougie went. He had a rolling walk, his legs moving not from the hips but the knees, his small feet turned out like a ballet dancer. Chaudhuri resisted the temptation to join with Ted in kicking his fat arse. People from all sides looked through their curtains as the four of them set off along the lane to the incident room.

Thirty-One

They left Abby and Ted with the custody sergeant and went back along the lane to Dougie's cottage. The new thatch looked like a youthful blond head among its grey neighbours. A cat-slide roof at one end came within three feet of the ground. On the chimney a weathervane of a witch at a cauldron stood against the evening sky. The garden had been gravelled over to form a drive on which was parked an old brown Mercedes, lugubrious as a hearse.

Dougie was in no hurry to let them in. He opened the door slowly, like the butler at Dracula's castle. He still wore his jacket, though half an hour had passed.

Behind him the hall carpet was black. There was not a speck of dust or a crumb on it. Still, the impression was unpleasant, as if a hundred moles had been skinned to make it, perhaps by one of the battle-axes or swords that hung at regular intervals on the white walls.

"Well, well, I thought you'd forgotten all about me. Going to tell me what's happening at last?" He spoke with a sort of disaffected smugness. Like all who think the worst of humanity, he belittled it while demanding from it unreasonably high standards. That way he derived satisfaction when it failed. "Come through to the lounge."

More black carpet. Two red satin sofas in carved frames glistened like gashes in flesh. A brass model of Lucifer, the size of a child, squatted and grinned on a pedestal in a corner, incense sticks smoking between his hooves. The effect, while it gave an unsettling glimpse into Dougie's mind, was so over-stated as to be comical. Chaudhuri noticed Trent's mouth twitching.

"Cup of tea? No? Sit down, then."

Above the fireplace hung a head and shoulders photo of an elderly man in a pin-stripe suit. At first glance a straightforward portrait, closer inspection revealed a troubling quality. The jaw hung loose like a marionette's and the eyes were opaque, as if covered by a dark cataract. Dougie saw Chaudhuri looking and cocked his thumb towards it.

"That's a ghost." He was matter-of-fact, refusing to countenance non-believers.

"What?"

He beamed, Chaudhuri's confusion having the desired effect. "Photo of a ghost, that is. Friend of mine took it." He reached up and polished the glass with his sleeve. "Got a CD as well. Ever heard a ghost talking? Well, you will on this CD. Want me to play it?"

With what for him was probably eagerness, he sauntered towards a black gothic cabinet. Trent groaned.

"Cut the crap, Dougie, because there's no time. We want to know where you were on Monday night."

An artist versus a philistine, Dougie contemplated Trent with his head on one side and shook it a bit as though despairing of him.

"Something up, is there? Well, I like to be helpful to an old colleague." He made it sound exactly the opposite. "Any particular bit of Monday night?"

"Late. Say nine to midnight."

Dougie pursed his little mouth till it resembled a cat's rectum.

"Let's see, now. I'd been to London that day. Set off mid-morning. Caught the eleven o'clock car ferry."

"From Yarmouth?"

"No, Ryde. Got to London in time for a spot of lunch prior to my lesson."

"And what lesson would that be?"

"Spiritual healing. Not faith healing, mind – you don't need faith anymore. Just have to want something and you'll get it."

"Sounds perfect for this day and age."

"Yes." Dougie gave the smile that was more like the baring of teeth. "We've a good following. There's money in it."

"Any other people at this lesson with you?"

"Just the tutor, Sam Pearman. I prefer one-to-one sessions. Pay extra for them. Have a three-hour session every month."

"And where does all this take place?"

"The British Spiritualist Association." Whether he realised it or not, his Yorkshire accent became a bit refined. "In Belgravia, it is."

"Very posh. Must cost a packet. Thinking of changing your trade, are you?"

"I am, as it happens. Got my sights on a nice little premises in Newport. Spiritual healing, clairvoyance, exorcisms, that sort of thing. Might even go in for a bit of hypnotism. Should do well on this island." He turned to Chaudhuri. "Do you know it's the most haunted place in the world? You *should* know it – you've got the gift."

Trent gave an ostentatious yawn. "What time did your lesson finish?"

"Started at two and finished at five."

"Left London straight after, did you?"

"Now what sort of mug would drive at that time?" He spoke as though Trent had shown himself the biggest fool in the world. It would be a favourite tactic of his, trying to make people feel small. "I had something to eat in the cafeteria and chatted for half an hour to a few like-minded friends. Set off at seven o'clock sharp."

"What time did you get back to the island?"

"Bit before eleven."

"Came straight home, did you?"

"Course I did."

"That's strange, because we have witnesses who saw you in Ryde at half past ten. At the house of Bert and Emily MacArthur, to be precise."

"Witnesses?" Dougie narrowed his eyes. "Funny choice of word. If you're questioning me about something, I've a right to know what it is, haven't I? But," he nodded and smiled like one of those toy dogs seen in the back of cars, "I've a feeling I already know. Yes, I remember now – I did call at the MacArthurs' on my way home."

"Why?"

"Had something to give to Bert – a hat. This one."

He opened a built-in cupboard next to the fireplace, took out a carrier bag and dangled it in front of Trent's face.

"Bert left that at the BSA on Monday. The president asked me to take it to him. I told her it was no trouble. I had to pass through Ryde on my way home." He sat down in the chair next to Lucifer and stretched out his legs, thighs like chicken drumsticks.

Trent examined the black trilby, an old man's hat. "The MacArthurs were at the BSA on Monday?"

"Yes. Giving a psychometry demonstration. That's receiving spirit messages through objects. Went down very well, I gather."

"Why have you still got the hat?"

"They must have gone to bed when I called. The house was in darkness. I didn't knock, in case they were asleep."

"Very considerate. But they weren't asleep. They were dead."

Dougie widened his eyes like someone receiving good news. He seemed to take pride in his abnormal response, another way of making people feel uncomfortable.

"Now, isn't that peculiar. I had a look through the letter box to see if there was a light on in the kitchen, and I saw them." With a deprecating gesture he flapped his weak hand in its heavy ring. "Now don't get excited, I don't mean I saw *them*, their *bodies*. I saw their spirits. Violent death, was it? Yes, I saw them floating back and forth in the dark of the stairwell. Looked a bit distressed. Mind, I couldn't be sure if it was a sign they'd already died or were going to in the near future. Difficult to tell sometimes. But isn't that interesting? Seems I've got the gift in a big way." He gazed at the carpet between his splayed feet and shook his head in wonder. For the first time his smile showed genuine pleasure.

"You had a premonition they were dead, yet you didn't come to us?"

Trent's tone made him frown. Without the smile it was possible to see the malice of his mind.

"Don't be daft, man. I've already told you it didn't mean they were dead that minute. I can see Death peeping over your shoulder now." Unscrupulous as a witchdoctor playing on fear, he gave what he perhaps thought was an unnerving stare. "You might still have a few months, though. Couple of years, even."

"That's odd, because I can see him over yours and I don't feel optimistic enough to give you that long."

Proud of his rejoinder, Trent sat back and crossed his legs.

"Now, let's move on to Wednesday night. That's the night you went to the MacArthurs' house for a meeting and according to my witness couldn't get in. Didn't it occur to you even then that something might be wrong?"

"Oh, yes, it occurred to me. In fact, I knew they were long gone. But if I'd come to you what would you have done? First, put me down as a nutter, the way you used to. Second, when you'd discovered what I said was right, accused me of their murder. Oh, calm down." He flapped his hand again as if Trent, who sat impassive, threatened to get over-excited. "You think you've tricked me into a confession because I know they were murdered? I've already told you how I know and it'll take someone a bit sharper than you to prove otherwise."

"And if you were more sparing with your insults they might carry more weight. Now, when you called with the hat on Monday night, did you see anyone hanging around? Live people are the only ones I'm interested in, by the way."

"Nope. Saw a woman opposite putting her bin out but apart from that there was no one."

Trent stood up. "We'll want a statement. And fingerprints. You know the procedure. Got your ferry ticket, have you?"

"It's probably still in the car."

"Bring it with you when you come to give that statement."

He turned to leave. Dougie waggled his fingers at his back. "Hey, hold your horses. You haven't told me what's going on with my wife."

"You need me to tell you? Looks like she's left you, Dougie."

"Did she call you out, then?"

"No. I wish she had. It was her uncle we wanted to speak to."

"And what's he been up to? Something to do with Naomi Long?"

"Naomi Long?" Trent paused at the door. "What makes you say that?"

"Famous discoverer of dead bodies, he is, didn't you know? Giving interviews to the media left, right and centre about how he alerted the police. I don't suppose it's occurred to any of you that I'm the sort you should be consulting in a murder case. Untold help I could be with my psychic gift."

"I don't suppose you need to be psychic to tell us where you were last Sunday afternoon?"

"Last Sunday? In bed." He stretched as if he relished the memory. There was something indecent in the way he arched his back and thrust his belly out. "Normally have a clairaudience meeting on Sunday, but last week I fancied giving it a miss. Yes, in bed. Went there after lunch and stayed until maybe six o'clock. The wife was there." He rested his chin on his forefinger in a parody of cogitation. "Wonder if it was when she was going down on me for the third time that Naomi was killed? Could have been, couldn't it?" He giggled as Chaudhuri turned away.

"What makes you think Naomi was killed on Sunday?"

"You did, mate, by asking me that question. You might have forgotten I was in the force, the way you go on." He stretched again and looked at Trent through the slits of his eyes. "You keeping Ted in the nick tonight, by the way?"

"Definitely not. But in any case, steer clear of Abby unless you want a case of domestic violence brought."

"Did she say that's what she intends to do?"

"No. It's what I'm going to advise her to do. And it's what I'd advise you to accept. Otherwise I might be forced to remember all those unprovoked attacks on prisoners when you were on duty at Ryde nick – as long as they were wearing handcuffs, of course."

In a movement that made Chaudhuri think he should intervene, Trent strode across and landed a kick on the side of Dougie's chair, nearly toppling it.

"Leave the lady alone unless you want an injunction against you. And don't waste any time over that statement."

He marched out. Dougie's shocked expression was the most human Chaudhuri had seen on him that night.

Thirty-Two

"I shouldn't have done that, Tom." Trent stood at the gate, watching a pipistrelle fly from a tree like a windblown leaf. "I shouldn't have lost my temper with the bastard. He's the type to make something of it."

"Yes, he's probably putting a curse on you as we speak."

Trent laughed but not with ease. "You don't think he's capable of that, do you?"

"I know he's not. If he were, he'd have done it years ago."

"Do you know what I feel like, Tom? I feel like a battered old box-file that'll burst if it has one more bit of information stuffed into it. I have to sit down and think."

"Fine by me. Fancy a cup of tea at the incident room?"

"Christ, no, we'll never get a second's peace. The Trout Inn is just along here. Let's have a drink. If anyone needs us they'll get in touch."

"But don't you think we should talk to Abby Benson first. I mean oughtn't we to see if she can confirm

Doug's alibi for Sunday?"

"It'll keep. Have you got those diaries Ted Britten gave us? Good. We'll flick through them while we're at it, see if there's anything of interest. Here's the pub. Might have a bite to eat, eh?"

The Trout Inn, once the haunt of many a smuggler, was ancient at its core. But being a *family pub* with so many extensions and play areas having been added, it looked no more historic than a Burger King restaurant. In fact, that had probably been its inspiration. Inside, the dividing walls had been removed to allow one themed area to lead into another.

At this time of the year it was almost empty. In the bit that looked like a trendy metropolitan café Chaudhuri and Trent sat in leather armchairs close to the 'real' gas fire, open on two sides to give a glimpse through the chimney breast into the room beyond. Trent took a menu from the railway-sleeper mantelpiece. A bright photo of each meal accompanied a drooling description.

"Fancy a lean minute steak pan-fried in herb butter, served on a crisply-toasted ciabatta with a tomato, green chilli and red onion salsa?"

"If I was a meat-eater I would. Anything in the fish line?"

"Sorry, mate, I keep forgetting. OK, how about fresh local scampi, that'll be local to Taiwan, in a lemon batter, served in a basket with roasted baby sweet corn cobs and a tossed mixed salad?"

"That'll do."

"A pint of the local?"

"Better make it a half for me. I could fall asleep as it

is. Want some money?"

"No, it's my treat, this one. Shan't be a tick."

So far, every treat had been his. Chaudhuri watched the gigantic, amiable figure lumber to the bar. The landlord or manager gave a shout of welcome and went over for a chat. It looked as if he'd have a few minutes to himself. He wasted no time in turning his thoughts to Abby.

How many people can say they've met their ideal? How often does it happen in any lifetime? Like most people, he had learned to love from what was on offer. But seeing Abby was almost a supernatural experience. It wasn't going too far to say it was like seeing God. Would he give up all other women for one night with her? Yes, as a martyr gives up his life for his faith. There could be no more women, no more life after her. He wanted to beat Dougie to a pulp for ever having touched her, beat him until he begged on his knees for her pardon. Darius Field he couldn't think about. But he was sure Field's love would be nothing compared with his own. Was it possible she was a murderer? Dougie had given her as well as himself an alibi for Sunday afternoon. Supposing she'd somehow managed to get away from him for an hour? Would her husband lie for her now that she'd left him? And how could she find the courage to kill but not to leave a husband she hated? What would be the point? Someone might kill to keep a man's love. Someone might kill to keep a man's money. But he knew Abby didn't care about money. And he'd seen with his own eyes how she felt about Dougie. Supposing it had happened, though, who was her accomplice? Ted Britten? Why would he kill to help his niece remain with an abusive husband? Surely Ted would just do what he'd already done – take her to live safely with him. Chaudhuri felt a rush of affection towards the elderly man for his kindly nature. He reminded him of his own father.

And if Abby could murder, would she be afraid to break into Naomi's cottage and look for the photos? More implausible, would she have forgotten to take the keys from the body? Of course not. Nor, knowing Naomi to be dead, would she have left it until Monday night. She was innocent.

And Dougie? He'd meant to question him about his movements on Monday to see if he could place him at Ravenscourt Park. As it was, he'd been filled with such revulsion he hadn't been able to get out of the house quick enough. He'd leave it till they'd confirmed his story with his spiritualist cronies in London. But if wishing was enough, Dougie should already be in solitary for life.

He closed his ears to the tinned music and took out Naomi's address book and diary. The address book was pretty – royal blue leather stamped with gold *fleur de lys*. It was something he wouldn't have associated with her, having seen the state of her house. Perhaps it had been a present, though he couldn't imagine that, either. Poor woman. The book's edges were gilded and indented below each letter of the alphabet. Automatically, he turned to the letter 'H'. And now his heart pounded. It pounded nearly as much as when he thought about Abby. There, staring at him was the name, address and telephone number of Kelly Houghton. The connection between her and Naomi and the connection that would lead him to Raven was established beyond doubt.

Trent came back with their beer and a couple of raffle tickets as receipt for their meal.

"Any luck with those books?"

"Yes." His grin would have made the Cheshire cat look sulky. "Kelly and Naomi knew each other, Bob. Look, Kelly's address is in this one. And I've just found something even more interesting in the diary. See that entry? It's a note Naomi made to herself to babysit Jade. And look at the date – it's the day Jade and Kelly were murdered."

Trent downed half his pint and exhaled with a loud "Ah". The froth on his upper lip clung like a blond Viking moustache.

"This is more like it. Now we're getting somewhere. OK, let's go through all the permutations. Let's forget for a moment all previous assumptions about the killers of Naomi and Kelly. Since Naomi was killed first, start with who might have wanted her dead and see if there's a link to Kelly.

"First, Abby Benson. Do you know what occurred to me while I was stood at the bar? It occurred to me that Dougie could be lying about her spending Sunday in bed with him. But she had to have an accomplice for Naomi's murder and it couldn't be Darius Field because he can prove he was in London all day Sunday. Her uncle, Ted Britten? Out of the question, I'd say. But what about this, Tom – could her accomplice by any stretch of the imagination be Dougie himself? Or put another way, could Abby be his?"

Dougie as an accomplice? He hadn't thought of that. His heart pounded again but this time from panic. Let

Dougie be innocent, as pure as the driven snow, rather than Abby share his guilt.

"But it doesn't make sense, Bob. The only reason Abby would have for killing Naomi is that Dougie shouldn't find out about her affair with Field."

"Suppose he had and this was some sort of punishment? He's a sadistic, twisted bastard, as I happen to know. He couldn't kill Abby without being the obvious suspect. But he could kill Naomi. Or suppose, as Verity Shaw intimated, he had his own separate reasons for wanting Naomi dead and forced Abby on pain of her own death to help him? I tell you, it's exactly the sort of thing I can see Dougie revelling in."

"But Verity's assumption was based on the belief that it was Dougie who broke into the cottage. And we now know it was Ted."

"Doesn't alter the theory that Naomi might have known something about Dougie that he'd prefer to keep secret – maybe something she discovered at one of their spiritualist meetings. Maybe the MacArthurs knew it as well. Didn't James suggest there might be a supernatural element?"

There was something all wrong with this argument but in his present state he couldn't grasp it. He downed some of his bitter and forced himself to think.

"OK, but if Abby was Dougie's accomplice why should she get Ted to try to steal the photos afterwards? Why should she come to the station this morning and own up to being blackmailed? Why should the thought of Dougie finding out about it make her run away from him?" Yes, that was it. "It was merely evidence of an affair he already knew about, by your argument."

Trent struck his forehead for the fourth time that night.

"You're right. I'm letting my aversion for Dougie make a monkey out of me. Abby can't have been his accomplice, for the reasons you state. Also, if she and someone other than Dougie did the killing, she'd have tried to get the photos immediately, not knowing how long the body would lie undiscovered. OK, on the face of it, it looks unlikely that she killed Naomi. We know she was at the salon all day Monday, so she couldn't have killed Kelly. And she was waiting for Ted Britten to bring her the photos when the MacArthurs were murdered on Monday night. So we'll cross her off for a while."

Chaudhuri downed his drink. A waitress in a black waistcoat and a white apron that reached her ankles brought their meal. Trent swooped on his sandwich like a bird of prey and munched in silence for a few minutes. An owl straining on a shrew, he swallowed and wiped his mouth on a paper napkin.

"Now – Darius Field. Though he has a motive, for him to have killed Naomi is an impossibility. We know he was in London. However, depending on his whereabouts in London on Monday he could have killed Kelly. But since we've no reason to believe he knew her, we've no reason to believe he killed her. The only strange coincidence is the fact of them both being from the island and both being in a contiguous part of London on the same day."

"Contiguous? Have they given you a few pages of the dictionary with that steak?"

Trent grinned. "Good word, eh? Don't know where

it came from. Just popped into my head. Anyway, we know Field got back to the island on Monday night in time to kill the MacArthurs. But, again, we've no reason in the world for believing he did. So cross him off as well."

A drop of salsa fell on his tie and he suctioned it up.

"Who have we got who could have murdered all five people – Naomi, Kelly, Jade and the MacArthurs? We've got two – Dougie Benson and as you so coherently pointed out earlier this evening, Verity Shaw." He smiled wryly at Chaudhuri.

"I was simply surmising, Bob – I didn't mean..."

"That's all right, you were reminding me to stay professional and I appreciate it. Impossible to be otherwise, of course, since we'll be taking DNA from both of them. We've two different blood samples from the downs, so no problem convicting Naomi's murderer once we get a match. In the case of the MacArthurs, we just have to hope for a DNA match of the right sort anywhere near the kitchen. A hair in the chapel won't do. We know both Dougie and Verity went there often. But whoever we charge with killing the MacArthurs, we also charge – circumstantially at the moment – with Kelly's murder. I just can't help praying it won't be Verity."

"An old flame, is she, Bob?"

"I wish." He took another gulp of beer. "So, one murderer, that's what we're concentrating on. One murderer with, in the killing of Naomi, an accomplice. And an islander, not a Londoner. All right, back to sluggy Dougie.

"We've yet to check his whereabouts. But if he's

lying about spending Sunday afternoon with Abby, I think she'll tell us, don't you? I had a look earlier at the statement she made this morning. In it she said he was at home with her all day. But she could have said that out of fear. If he's lying, I'm sure she'll tell us now."

"And his accomplice?"

"No idea. It could be his fucking spirit guide for all I care. Speaking of which, he needn't have been at that spiritualist place in London all the time he claims. He could have spent some of it in your park waiting for Kelly and Jade. He's suspect number one in my book. It could be the answer for why you couldn't spot Raven on any of the ferries – it was Dougie all along, travelling quite openly from Ryde with what he considers a cast-iron alibi."

"His motive for killing the MacArthurs couldn't have been because they'd seen him on the ferry, then."

"Nope, looks like I was wrong about that, unless he's lying when he says he travelled from Ryde. We'll soon know, anyway. You're getting nowhere with those prawns. All right, are they? Eat up, then." He took another bite of steak.

"Next, Verity Shaw. I can't deny Tom, that she has links to all five victims. We can see she and her daughter might have had a reason, albeit a tenuous one, for killing Naomi – she threatened to have the daughter put into care for bunking off school. Verity strikes me as too intelligent to give credence to that, but it's only my opinion. As for Kelly and the MacArthurs, the fact that we can't see a reason for her killing them doesn't mean there wasn't one. But the time factor worries me. We know Verity doesn't drive. All right, she says she doesn't, and it's something else for someone to check. But if she's telling the truth, to have travelled such distances by public transport is unfeasible."

"But not impossible?"

Trent looked down, remembered his pint and finished it. "No, it's not impossible. Illogical, though, unless there was a particular reason why London had to be the place and that day the day. Not so illogical for Dougie since he was already there. Which reminds me – I didn't ask him if he took his car to London. I just assumed he did. Something else to check."

They fell silent. Chaudhuri picked up the diary and studied it. And then he saw them – the two faces. The face of culprit turned away to present the face of victim.

"Bob, what about this for a theory? We have evidence from the entries in this book that Naomi and Kelly knew each other. But at the interview I had this morning with Alec Johnstone, he told me he was certain that the day they bumped into each other at his farm, they'd never met before. Naomi herself told him they hadn't, which was why she was so mystified by Kelly's instant dislike. Yet hardly a week later, according to this diary, Naomi was to babysit Jade. What I'm thinking is this – suppose, after that chance meeting, Kelly became another victim of Naomi's blackmail?"

"What for? And why are her initials not in Naomi's blackmail book? There's Only *VS* and *AB* in there."

"Because Naomi was meticulous about her book-keeping and Kelly hadn't got round to paying. Before payment was due, both she and Naomi were dead. Now we know Kelly was on benefit and therefore was working for Alec Johnstone illegally. Well, that must have occurred to Naomi Long the day she saw her at Alec's farm. As in the case of Verity Shaw, she would have turned the knowledge to what she thought was her advantage. She'd have blackmailed Kelly. But before she could collect her first payment and make a methodical note of it in her blackmail book, she was kicked to death. By Kelly and our mysterious accomplice?"

Trent screwed up his napkin and threw it on his plate. "Bloody hell, we're back to three murderers again. OK, if Kelly killed Naomi, the accomplice must be the boyfriend, Darren Frost."

"Exactly. Did he kill Kelly too? The manager of the zoo where he worked didn't recall seeing him, but seems to think Darren's signature in the work register was proof of his presence on Monday. But anyone could have forged that semi-literate scrawl."

Trent looked doubtful. "And the MacArthurs? Darren has an alibi for Monday night, remember."

"Alibi? Some alibi. Only Hayley Ashley's word. Her type'll say anything."

Trent's phone rang. With a groan he rummaged for it in his pocket. It was Sergeant Stott, reporting on the search of Kelly's flat. Chaudhuri gathered enough of its import to force down a bit of salad.

"Two pairs of bloody trainers, size six and size seven, found in the boot of Darren's car."

"Christ, I never thought to ask if he had a car."

"Why would you? The lazy bugger never parks it in the car port in front of the house, just leaves it on the street. Of course it wouldn't occur to you. It only occurred to Stott because he saw him driving from work in it. He says the front seats and the floor are smeared with blood despite evidence of cleaning. Waste-pipe in the kitchen and bathroom still with traces of blood. They've taken him to Newport nick. Don't look like that, you're still a genius, my son. Come on, better not keep the charmer waiting."

Thirty-Three

As if he were in a television police drama – probably imagining he *was* in one – Darren answered 'No comment' to every enquiry, even when asked his name and address and looked as if he felt a burning ambition had been accomplished at last. But either he didn't have the hang of the plot or felt it lacked impact: to the consternation of his solicitor he went on calmly to accuse Kelly of the murder of Naomi Long. Of course he denied taking the slightest part in it himself and seemed to think while he did so, nothing, not even evidence of his footprint on Naomi's face, could convict him. It weren't his.

Naomi, he explained, had tried to blackmail Kelly over moonlighting while she was on Jobseeker's Allowance. Well, Kelly wasn't having any. That Sunday afternoon they were on their way to her house so Kelly could have it out with her when they saw her up on the downs. They parked the car at the viewpoint, locked Jade inside, went up there and Kelly killed her. That's all there was to it. If there was blood on his car seat it must have come from Kelly. That's how it must have got on his jeans and T-shirt. As for the blood on his trainers, he couldn't help it if he'd stepped in it, could he? He hadn't done nothing, though, he stressed. Kelly done it all.

"What fucking cretins." Trent and Chaudhuri sat in the canteen while Darren was on one of the many breaks demanded by his solicitor.

"Most murderers are cretins," Chaudhuri agreed through a mouthful of sandwich. "No, correction, all of them are. Fucking cretinous bastards."

"Fancy keeping those trainers, though. They couldn't even be bothered to wash them."

"Because they don't take it seriously. In their book they've done nothing wrong. They only think something's wrong if they get punished for it, right? Well, that toerag's never been punished for all the robbery, and arson, and God knows what else he's perpetrated since he started to walk. He's only ever been given a warning. I'd like to give him a beating. No, I'm not speaking out of vindictiveness, Bob. If that's the only way to deter him, then it's a just punishment. The fear of physical pain can make even the most moral person do what they know to be wrong. Are you telling me the same fear can't make arseholes like him do what is right?"

"That's just in theory, though, Tom. But there are plenty of countries where the police force is brutal but crime is still out of control, far worse than here."

"That's because they're Third World countries. They need to commit crime to live, so the prospect of a police beating is hardly going to deter them." He opened the wedge-shaped pack of his third sandwich. He'd got his appetite back. "Anyway, I'm not talking about the police, I'm talking about the Law. If, after you've mugged your old lady for fifty pence the courts decide fifty lashes is in order, I reckon I'm looking at one mugger who'll decide it's about time he turned over a new leaf."

Trent was in stitches. "One penny equals one lash, eh? I wonder how many you'd give to our Darren? Because as things stand, he'll never think what he did was wrong. He'll regret being caught but he'll still think Naomi had it coming to her. She crossed him, didn't she? She crossed Kelly. A capital offence that is, man. Did you see his face when he said Naomi had asked for money? You'd think she'd asked for a pound of flesh."

"I wish to God I could pin Kelly and Jade's murder on him."

"Yeah. Hard luck, that. But there's no way he was in London on the day. No way he was in Ryde on Monday night, either. Still, look at it like this – at least one murderer's been executed, if not by the law. And you'll find Kelly's executioner, mate, don't you worry."

He looked at his watch.

"Four o'clock. I'm going to charge Darren now, and then maybe we can get out of this place for a few hours. You still intend to go back to the smoke tomorrow?"

"Unfortunately. I want to go over everything at that end again – concentrate on Dougie's little day out in London. Apart from that, the Super's playing up as if I've gone AWOL. But I've a funny feeling I'll be back before long."

Trent put his hand on Chaudhuri's arm. "I couldn't have cracked this one without you, you know."

"Oh, come on…."

"No, if you hadn't put us on to Darren, we'd have had to wait for him to get nicked for something else before we'd have got a DNA match. Could have been years. I appreciate it, Tom."

Chaudhuri stood up and stretched. "Well, I'll be off and pick up James. He's still mooching and ferreting around in Kelly's flat. Might pop in tomorrow to say goodbye – today, rather – for a few minutes if I get the chance."

"Great. You take care, now. And don't worry – any further developments at this end and I'll be in touch immediately. I've high hopes for Dougie's DNA results. Wouldn't be surprised if we didn't uncover Raven's hooded coat at the back of his wardrobe. Perfect garment for summoning Satan." He reached out and took Chaudhuri in a bear hug. "All the best, Tom. Remember me to James."

The short journey in the lift was lonely. Already his time on the island seemed behind him, an episode that could have no role in his future, as separate from his real life as a dream. He felt unsatisfied, eager to waste no more emotion but be gone. In the foyer he exchanged a few words with the duty sergeant for the last time.

The streets of Newport were deserted but brightly lit, as if at any moment they expected to be thronged with people. He drove east out of the town and on a whim turned into Burnt House Lane. Here in the eighteenth century had lived the woodcutter Michael Morey, one of the island's most notorious murderers. On conviction of murdering his nephew for money, his hovel had been burnt down, hence the name of the lane. His ghost was said to haunt it. It was winding, banked up by hedgerow and wide enough for only one vehicle. The headlights beamed a few feet in front. In the rear-view mirror all was black. Against the sky on either side rose the ramparts of the downs. At the crossroads was the burial mound where Morey's corpse had rotted on the gibbet.

Chaudhuri stopped on Wilfridstone Down, one of the highest spots of the island. The Solent was on his left, the Channel on his right. Sea and sky merged so that the lights of ferries and fishing boats might have been comets. Beneath this same sky and surrounded by this very sea, Abigail Benson slept. He knew how her hair would fall on the pillow; as if in another, better life, he'd seen it. But not in this one. He set off for Wilfridstone, past Trish Goodall's haunted pub, to the shabby suburbia of Sandown.

James was alone in Kelly's flat. He sat at an open window in the dismal living room, smoking a cigarette. The mess made in the search hadn't been cleared up, and probably never would be till the next tenants did it themselves. Chaudhuri handed him a sandwich and a can of coke he'd brought from the canteen. "They've charged our Darren."

"That's great." James stubbed out his cigarette on the windowsill, picked up a small Barbie photograph album, and handed it to Chaudhuri. "Found it in the doll's house just now, tucked up in the doll's bed. There's quite a few snaps in it – mostly of Jade – but a few other people as well. There's one of Jade with a man and a woman. Looks as if they're at a stately home. Maybe they took her out for the day. Yes, that's the one. There's nothing written on the back. Like you said the other day, she wasn't one for words, Kelly. There's nothing either written or printed in the whole flat."

"It doesn't matter, James." He was too tired to feel excitement, only a sleepy sort of contentment. "As they say, a picture paints a thousand words. And they're not at a stately home. They're at Corve Manor. This is Darius Field. You know – the one Bob and I went to talk to? The one in the photos Naomi Long took?"

"Christ, so it is." James looked at the picture over Chaudhuri's shoulder. "Sorry, he looks so different squinting into the sun that I didn't recognise him. Who's the woman? Nice pair of tits."

"She's his wife. When I asked him if he knew Kelly Houghton, he said he didn't. No hesitation. And do you know where he was on the day of her murder? He was in Hammersmith. It's not exactly a million miles away from Ravenscourt Park, is it?" He looked into James' exhausted face and realised his own probably looked as bad. "Have we cracked it, James? Have we?"

"I think we're well on the way."

"So do I. Shall we call it a day? Come on, let's get out of here, it stinks. I'll drive. You can eat your sandwich on the way."

Thirty-Four

It was six o'clock. A rosy dawn glowed through what looked like a torn sky of worn black silk and the old staircase in the Painted Plough creaked as Chaudhuri crept to his room without pausing at the landlady's door. The night before last (had it only been such a short time ago?) he'd stayed with her till morning. He dreaded the possibility she might be waiting for him even now, exhausted but wakeful to be taken in his arms. With any luck she'd be fast asleep. He'd hardly closed his door when he heard hers open. Imagining reproach in her every step as she passed his room, he lay down on his bed and listened to the sound of her running a bath.

He slept for two hours. At nine o'clock, after a substantial breakfast, he kissed her. He blamed himself for the puzzled look on her once confident face. He promised to stay with her if he returned. He and James threw their luggage in the boot of the car and left.

The road to Corve Manor was becoming familiar. In the liquid English light, where the distant horizon is clear even on a dull day, each tree and farm stood out as if painted on canvas. As they turned through the manor gates Chaudhuri noticed what it had been too dark to see on his last visit – a deserted church on a hill beyond the grounds.

The gnarled knotted door to the manor was opened by a woman wearing black leggings and a long white T-shirt with some sort of yachting logo on the front. She glanced at his warrant card and gave the door-knob a swift polish with the duster she carried.

"Mr Field's away on business," she said.

"Is Mrs Field available?"

"I'll go and see."

Some moments later she reappeared.

"Come in. Would you mind closing the door behind you? Mrs Field's in there." She pointed to the room then hurried away as if to show she had no intention of eavesdropping.

Like the room in which Field had received them, it was panelled. But the paintings on it were brighter and more intact, the lilies on a woman's gown swirling in its folds. The window looked onto a formal garden, parterred like a miniature maze. Beyond it a sweep of lawn ran to a plantation of yews in the distance.

In a corner of the room stood a heavy candelabrum the size of a small tree. The sofa was black and embroidered with pagodas. Karina Field reclined on it – there was no other word for it.

She wore a dark blue silk kimono and her vivid hair was piled high on her head in a haphazard way that Chaudhuri guessed had probably taken hours. Her feet were bare. Her toenails painted the colour of blackcurrant ice cream. She'd been reading a newspaper, one of the broadsheets, which she'd let fall to the floor next to the black and white dog. Snuggled in its basket, it lifted its muzzle in warning.

"And what can I do for you gentlemen?" Her voice was mellifluous, without doubt a drawback for anyone wanting to work as an actress nowadays. "No, no, I don't need to see your ID I remember you from the other night." Her eyes lingered on Chaudhuri. "Tell me your name again."

"I'm Inspector Chaudhuri. And this is Sergeant James."

"That's right. Sit down, Inspector. And you too, Sergeant. Is it about the woman who was murdered on the downs? If you've come to show me those snaps from her family album, I must tell you here and now that I'm not interested. Darius obviously saw great merit in them considering how much he paid for them, but I find other people's photographs interminably boring, don't you?"

Though naturally poised, her provocativeness was overdone. Was it because she knew she was not as beautiful as Abigail Benson and they, having seen the photographs, knew it also? Or did she hope they wondered how Darius could ever look at another woman?

Chaudhuri sat on the sofa at the opposite end of the enormous hearth.

"No, we're not investigating the murder of Naomi Long. I presume that's whom you refer to? We're here about the murder in London of a woman known as Kelly Houghton."

She neither moved nor spoke. Could he sense an awareness of danger in her stillness?

"But," he continued, "I do have a photograph to show you, as it happens." He handed her the picture James had found in Jade's doll's house. "The child pictured here with you and your husband – would you tell me what you know of her?"

She frowned as she took it and her lower lip hung slack. She looked older. It was possible to see how she would look when she was very old. A quick glance and she handed it back to him.

"Don't infer too much from that picture. It seems more significant than it is."

"In what way?"

She shrugged – a roll of delicate shoulders, head thrown slightly back. "You asked me what I knew of the child. Well, hardly anything. The same goes for Darius. It looks as if we both adored her, doesn't it? In fact Darius had never seen her until that day. I'd seen her several times, and each time liked her less."

She was composed again, curled in what she probably hoped was a sex-kitten pose. Her elbow rested on the back of the sofa. She wove a lock of hair in and out of her long fingers with their blackcurrant nails. It was a habit more common in teenage girls.

"Why didn't you like her?"

She thought for a moment then said what he'd never have expected to hear from her.

"She had no tenderness – not for a single living thing. It was depressing. No, worrying. Children aren't often like that, are they? Especially very young children. And she can't have been more than two when that photograph was taken. Jade. I find it an amusing name. Jade by name and jade by nature. Though the mother

310

was too illiterate to have intended it. Yes, she was well named." Her eyes twinkled and she smiled at him.

"Was the photo taken on a special occasion?"

"I doubt it. There was no special occasion for Kelly – she was always photographing her offspring. She used to clean for me during the week, always with the jade in tow. But since Darius is in the photo it must have been a weekend. Maybe we were having a dinner party, and I'd asked her to help in the kitchen."

"She used to clean for you?"

"Why else would she be here? Yes, she was my cleaner. I suppose it lasted for about six months."

"Was this recently?"

"Oh, no. She hasn't been here for nearly a year."

"Why?"

"I asked her to leave."

"Was her work unsatisfactory?"

"No. But she was."

"In what way?"

Her eyes were greeny-blue, intelligent but as shallow as glass. She looked down at her tanned legs revealed as far as the thigh by the opening of her kimono. With coquettish slowness she drew one of its edges across.

"Have you any children, Inspector?"

"No." He knew James was stifling a grin. He ignored him.

"Neither have I. Apparently I'm not destined to reproduce myself. There's something in my genes, evolution thinks it would be better off without. I marvel at its discrimination. If I had a child it would never be ignorant and vulgar and cruel and a bane to humankind from its birth to its death. Most children born nowadays are exactly like that. But perhaps it's evolution's way of bringing us all to a speedy end. What do you say, inspector? If the world's been badly run in the past, can you imagine the future?"

She spoke lightly, as if what she said had nothing to do with her at all. The dog shuffled in its basket and she reached down to pat its head.

"I've had several courses of IVF. They've all failed. I began the last one while Kelly was working for me. Naturally, two women together, I told her about it. She looked on me with pity. As a fertile woman she could achieve no more than the very lowest of the animals, yet she saw it as the greatest of talents that I obviously lacked. When I miscarried, the sight of her and her child was almost more than I could bear. She knew it and flaunted the homunculus. She was quite simply the biggest bitch I've ever known.

"Well, one morning, out of the blue, she asked me if I'd considered surrogacy. She knew all about it, she said, because she'd been a surrogate mother herself. She looked as if she thought she'd sprouted a halo. It was before Jade was born, she told me. She'd been living in London and already had her first child – a little boy. She wanted, as she put it, to share her good fortune with less lucky women. She wanted to help them have babies. Smug cows like her never say *children*, have you noticed? It's always *babies*.

"Anyway, she'd got her name on the list of an agency that puts surrogates in touch with infertile women and one couple chose her to give birth for them. She preened when she told me they'd paid her eight thousand pounds – expenses, she called it."

She leaped up and paced the room, her arms wrapped around her waist as if to hold in emotion. She tore the bobble from her hair and the bright curls flared like flames across her back. She clutched them and ran her hands through them. Then she threw herself on the sofa and spoke as quietly as before.

"She got pregnant with this couple's child. She revelled being in charge of the happiness or misery of two people. And being Kelly, inflicting misery was infinitely more pleasurable. When the child was born she decided to keep it. If she hadn't intended to do it all along knowing someone else desperately wanted it would be enough to make her change her mind."

She looked beyond Chaudhuri at the yews in the distance, her pale eyes as empty as if in a trance. "She'd have no pity – the more the poor mother begged and pleaded the more resolute she'd become. The baby, a little girl, lived for a year. One of her boyfriends shook it to death to stop it crying. He went to prison and she got off scot-free.

"Christ, her stupid, sentimental, illiterate face when she told me she'd put a bunch of flowers outside the door of her flat with a card saying 'Why?' We know fucking why, don't we? Because of her. It was because of her that her little boy died not long after. She asked her mother to babysit one night while she went to bingo. The mother took care of him as much as she had of Kelly I suppose, which was not at all. She went out and left him with her boyfriend for his dog to attack him. He was eaten alive."

She looked at Chaudhuri, daring him to be shocked by her choice of words.

"When she told me, she was conventionally sorry, as if it had happened to an unknown child she'd read about in the paper. It was then I asked her to leave. I gave her a handful of money – it must have been more than she was entitled to, she'd have complained otherwise – and told her to get out. I'm glad she's dead. I hope before she died, she suffered. Did she?" Her eyes glittered. She hadn't asked what had become of Jade. Because she didn't care? Or because she knew what had happened to her?

Chaudhuri said, "Mrs Field, where were you on Monday?"

"You know where I was. Darius told you."

"I'd like to hear your own account."

She sighed and raised her eyes to the ceiling. "For any particular part of the day?"

"Say, from two o'clock onwards."

"I was on my way to the Wanda West Academy in Hammersmith. It's a stage school. My niece had an audition there. It took place at three and it was after five when we left."

"Your husband was with you? He stayed with you all the time?"

"Of course."

"Why, then, when I spoke to the school secretary this morning, should she say he left the building at three o'clock?"

She frowned. "I don't know why she should say it. She's mistaken, that's all. Oh, hang on, he did go out. Yes, I remember now." She smiled at him but said no more. He had to prompt her.

"Where did he go?"

"He went to move the car. We were illegally parked. There wasn't a meter for miles, so he had to park where he could and keep an eye open in case a warden was on the prowl. He saw one coming, so he went out to park somewhere else."

"And it took him over two hours? The secretary remembers the time he left, because he asked her how long the audition was likely to last and to give you a message to wait for him if he was late. That was just after you and your niece had gone into the audition at three o'clock. He didn't arrive back until quarter past five. She remembers you waiting for him in the porch because twice she came out to ask if you'd prefer to come in from the rain."

"So?" She rolled her shoulders again. "He waited till he'd be sure we were finished."

"But what did he do in that time? He didn't return to the school."

"He sat in the car and read. He was parked streets away – again illegally – so he thought he'd wait and be ready to drive off if necessary. And I can prove it because he got a ticket. Stay there. I'm going to get it." She jumped up and ran out of the room. The dog watched them. A few minutes later she returned and waved the ticket under Chaudhuri's nose. He looked at it then passed it to James, who made a note of the details.

"Forgive me, but this implies your husband was not in his car at the time. The ticket was issued at just gone ten to five. What happened? Are you saying he simply didn't see the traffic warden until this ticket was slapped on the windscreen?"

"I could if I wanted." She was playful – playing for time, he was sure. "I could say he fell asleep, couldn't I? But you're right, he wasn't in the car when he got the ticket. There was an estate agent's on the corner, and the rain had let up a bit, so he went to ask for information about any property auctions they were having. He was gone no more than five minutes but by the time he got back some unkempt African who'd be a dictator in his own country was issuing a fine. But what does it matter? It proves he was there, doesn't it? The estate agents will certainly remember him. You can check. They put his name on their mailing list."

He had no doubt to see Darius Field once was to remember him. Would he have the nerve to pop into an estate agent's on his way from a murder? In the pouring rain he would have been soaked through. He may have been stained with blood. Unfortunately, when he'd picked his wife up at a quarter past five he'd remained in the car. The secretary had not seen him again to notice his clothes. The niece would be able to say, but either by accident or design was confined to her bed with tonsillitis and a raging temperature. Her father would allow no one to see or speak to her until she was better. He thought of Field's tall elegance. Raven in the hooded coat hadn't looked particularly elegant on her arrival at the crime scene, shuffling and stooping. But on leaving, her posture had been quite different.

"This couple for whom Kelly was a surrogate mother – did she tell you their name?"

"No, she was absurdly secretive even over the most unnecessary things. She enjoyed keeping things back. Probably lived in a permanent state of constipation."

"She didn't mention the clinic where it took place?"

"Not even a hint."

"Which clinic did you attend for your IVF, Mrs Field?"

"The Lytton, in north London."

He stood up. The dog flattened its ears and gave a low growl.

"Would you tell us where we can find your husband?"

"Try Milan. That's where he should be till tomorrow night."

"You expect him home then?"

"Possibly."

"All right, we'll be in touch. Thank you for talking to us. I'm sorry we took up so much of your time."

"Oh, are you going?" She pouted in disappointment.

"Yes, we've a ferry to catch. Back to London, I'm afraid."

She wrinkled her nose. "It's an awful hole, isn't it? Getting worse, too. All those foreigners wanting to grab the assets and change the culture. It used to be called colonialism but apparently we're only allowed to call it that when the English do it. So we'll be seeing you again?"

"You can put money on it. Goodbye, Mrs Field."

She didn't get up but gave a luxurious stretch and waggled her fingers in farewell.

Thirty-Five

At last, after nearly five hours, DS Greene and DC Mortimer were near the end of their journey north. The white horse on the hillside at Kilburn faded into the dusk as on either hand dale and moor became part of the night. The lights of Richmond shone out like a constellation, a black rectangle in their midst denoting what Greene said was the largest market square in England. For a moment the town was hidden by an arch of trees that enclosed the lane to the ruined abbey. Then around the next bend it was there, the castle rising above the gorge of the River Swale while Frenchgate with its cobbled street – the street where Greene lived – ran downhill to meet it.

"Here we are." He stopped at the traffic lights and gazed at the floodlit castle keep. "Home."

A Londoner, this was not what DC Mortimer had expected from *the north*. She'd never been to an English country town before and felt so out of place, she regretted accepting Greene's offer of a room for the night. Bed and breakfast at Hartlepool was more in her line. They drew up outside a long, low house with a sagging red-tiled roof.

The door, the perfect height for a midget, was opened by a woman she guessed was Greene's mother. Like her son she had auburn hair, but it resembled the fur of a red squirrel, having lost its glossiness. According to Greene she was an artist with her own gallery in the town. In her shapeless clothes she reminded Mortimer of a spinster in an old English film – Joyce Grenfell, maybe. Nothing like her own mother who favoured lycra mini dresses. She watched as the woman put her arms round Greene's neck and held him. Mortimer and her family never showed emotion unless they were pissed. This woman laughed and looked as if she wanted to cry at the same time.

"Come in, darling." Hanging onto Greene's arm, she led them into a square oak hall. In the middle a carved table was piled high with shoe boxes. More were stacked underneath it.

"What's all this, Mum?" Mortimer thought Greene sounded like a little kid.

"I'll tell you in a minute. By the way, Dad'll be late. He's got a concert at Darlington. But we won't wait for him, we'll have our supper now. Let me take your jacket, Helen. It is Helen, isn't it? Yes, I thought that's what Ben said. I'm Marion. Did you have a good journey?"

From habit Mortimer was about to moan but there was something about Marion that made her crank herself into positive mode – like a wind-up gramophone that takes time to get going. "So-so. Yeah. It was OK actually, I suppose."

"I don't mind it myself. I think it's a pretty

motorway – the views, I mean. But they all are in England, aren't they? Oh, before I forget, the loo's at the top of the stairs on the left, in case you're desperate. Now," she opened the door of what Mortimer assumed was a lounge, "sit down and relax while I bring some supper. Would you like a drink? A hot drink or a proper drink?"

Mortimer asked for a glass of water. She drank a lot of water. She was never without a bottle in her bag. She sat awkwardly on the edge of her chair while Greene went off to help his mother. She listened to their voices, Marion's animated, his quieter but laughing, while she looked round the room.

No fitted carpets, that was good. But she would have covered the polished boards in beech wood flooring if it had been hers. She coveted the real fire, not as something homely, but as a background to passion. She imagined herself seductive on a white fur rug while flames flickered in her eyes.

The pictures on the walls were unfamiliar which meant they must be originals. The whole place stank of money and that was all right, she wasn't envious. She didn't begrudge lottery winners. She didn't begrudge Posh and Becks. They were enough like her to make their success accessible. What she objected to was this elitism, this being better than others: the open piano with a sheet of music propped ready; the walls lined with books; Marion's accent, posher even than Greene's, and hinting at private education, which shouldn't be allowed. She hated it all. By the time Marion brought her a supper of lasagne and salad on a tray, she was indignant enough to accept it with indifference. She went to bed early. Marion and Greene were going to sort out the rest of the shoe boxes, which were to be filled with Christmas gifts for Romanian and Bosnian orphans. Patronising.

But she slept well and knowing she and Greene would be on their way after breakfast was passably civil at breakfast next morning. Greene took the country roads to Hartlepool. As on the journey of the day before, he called her attention to sights along the way, dwelling with pride on the sign telling of the world's first passenger train. She wasn't interested. She detested everything. Arriving at the town was a relief. It was urban and acceptable, though she looked in vain for a black face.

They drove to a council estate on the outskirts. No big city high-rise here, but semi-detached, pebble-dashed, painted cream, and most with broken fences and gardens used as a dump. Elsie Parker's was without the discarded fridge and wheel-less bicycle but there was plenty of litter, some of it sodden. Under the window a rectangle of earth set in concrete sprouted a few hummocks of grass.

A man halfway into his jacket answered the door. He had a pasty, early-morning look and a surprised expression, as if everything were strange to him. Greene showed his warrant card.

"Mr Parker?"

"There's no Mr Parker here, son. The lodger, that's me."

"Right. Mrs Parker at home? She's expecting us."

The man jerked his head towards an inner room. Then, leaving the door ajar, he went off without a word.

They knocked again. A woman appeared. She was scraggy and lined. Her stiffly set hair had an enamel sheen and seemed not to belong to her. Her upper lip was much creased, something Mortimer dreaded happening to herself. Elsie Parker could have been sixty or eighty. Like the man, her blue eyes had an empty look. Though they turned towards Greene's warrant card, it was difficult to say if they saw it.

"Come in."

They followed her inside. She walked with the minimum of movement, head slightly forward and arms still. The bones of her ankles and wrists looked enormous against her skinny limbs. She went to a chair next to a table strewn with breakfast things. She was like a bird returning to its perch. Mortimer noticed Greene already looked snooty. No consideration. He probably thought only posh people suffered when their relatives got murdered. He cleared his throat.

"I'm sorry to trouble you at such a sad time, but we need to speak to your daughter, Liz Parker. She's expecting us, I believe?"

"She's in bed." Elsie's eyes drifted here and there. Nothing could hold her attention.

"Would you tell her we're here?"

She got up and walked like a zombie to the door. They listened to her climbing the stairs slowly and then to the yelled obscenities coming from a room directly above. In the silence that followed she returned and took her place at the table.

"She's coming."

Without being asked, Greene sat on the vinyl sofa.

Mortimer sat on the arm. The room was a sitting room and dining room combined, a hatch in one wall to the kitchen. It was tidy, superficially clean, but ugly, decorated cheaply in the popular colours of twenty years ago. Mortimer liked things to be *contemporary*. And spotlessly clean. There was a faint unpleasant smell, a suggestion of an unemptied rubbish bin, or discarded socks. Mortimer was comparing it to Greene's house when he caught her eye and smiled. Did he think she was in cahoots with him against these people? She pursed her lips and turned away.

A toilet flushed. There was a rush of footsteps and Liz Parker appeared in a washed-out pink towelling dressing gown scarred with cigarette burns. Her face was puffy and her bleached hair hung in lank sections.

"What do youse lot fucking want? I've come here to get a bit of fucking peace."

"I'm sorry." Greene didn't sound sorry. "There are some important questions we must ask you."

"Like what? I've told you all I fucking know, haven't I? I can't tell you no more, can I? Fucking Jesus!"

She lit a fag from a packet on the mantelpiece, threw herself into a vinyl armchair and like a sulky child rested her cheek on her fist. Mortimer, who was already homesick, was disappointed to notice that in just four days Liz's London accent had disappeared. She was pure Teesside. Still, you had to fit in.

Greene picked up his briefcase and opened it. "The other night, when Inspector Chaudhuri spoke to you at your home in London, you stated that on the day of her death Kelly was meeting more than one person."

"I didn't say nothing like that."

"Yes, you did." He took out the copy of a transcript. "When Inspector Chaudhuri suggested Kelly's murderer might be someone known to her, you said, 'It can't have been the people she was going to meet, then. I know for a fact she never set eyes on them before.' How do you know that for a fact, Ms Parker?"

Liz glared at the transcript as if it was a typical example of police underhandedness, and chewed the inside of her lip. Mortimer leaned towards her with her forearms on her knees.

"No one's getting at you, Liz." She put an extra singsong quality into her voice. "We know you're just as much a victim as Kelly and Jade."

"Where's my counselling, then?"

"You can have counselling whenever you like. Now we know where you are we can arrange it – and for your mother, if she wants it. All we want is to catch Kelly's killer, right? It's what we all want, isn't it?"

"Yeah, yeah, yeah, whatever. Except I've a funny feeling you might try to pin some of the blame on me in the process."

Greene pounced on this. "Why should we want to do that?"

"Coz it's what you do." Liz gave him a pop-eyed glare. "I just want to get away from it all." She pouted as if she was about to cry and put on a whiney voice. "I can't do nothing to change things, can I?"

Mortimer shuffled closer. "We've got CCTV footage of a woman who was at the scene round about the time of Kelly's death. Would you come with us to the police station and see if you can identify her?"

Liz, who'd been flopping about in her chair, sat very still. "You got footage of the woman?" She was obviously trying to sound uninterested and failing badly.

"Yes. And we'd like you to look at it."

"Just the woman?" She stubbed out her fag. "There weren't no man with her?"

"She was alone."

"You arrested her yet?"

"No, but we hope to speak to her very soon."

Liz looked sly and this time chewed the side of her thumb.

"I don't need to look at no CCTV. I know who she is. Her name's Leanne Turnbull. But she's a liar. She'll try to tell you I took money from her, but I never. I never had one penny from her. She might have sent some to Kell but it was expenses, not payment. Payment's against the law, as everyone knows. You make a note of what I say, so if she tells you different you'll know she's a liar."

"Why did she give money to Kelly?" This was Greene.

"Kell was going to have a baby for her."

It seemed reasonable enough to Mortimer. But Greene reacted as if it was some sort of perversion.

"Have a baby for her? What...a surrogate, you mean?"

"Yeah, a surrogate. I told Kell not to, coz it can lead to trouble but she had her own ideas. But I didn't want her to do it. If Leanne says different it's a pack of lies."

Mortimer reached across Greene and placed a hand on Liz's arm. "Lets just get something cleared up, shall we? You say Kelly had never met this Leanne Turnbull, yet she was going to have a baby for her?"

"They was going to meet and discuss it, that's all."

"Did you set up the meeting? Was Leanne a friend of yours?"

Liz shrugged.

"Why did you arrange for them to meet at Ravenscourt Park?"

"I didn't arrange nothing. It was all Kell's idea. She thought it looked more official like."

"To meet in the park?" Greene again, giving a sneery sort of laugh guaranteed to get up Liz's nose.

"They was gonna meet in the Masonic hospital, in the restaurant. All right? Satisfied, now?"

"Why didn't you tell this to Inspector Chaudhuri?"

"Coz I don't want things being raked up again, right? I don't want no one to know I was connected to Kell. Like I said, I can't change nothing, I can't bring her back, so what's the point in sticking me neck out?"

"What things don't you want raked up again?"

Liz's face seemed to swell in an effort to hold back the words. "Them things what happened last time."

"You mean when Kelly's first daughter was killed?" Greene looked at his notes. "Latisha, wasn't it?"

"No." Liz paused to light another fag. "Everyone was really, really understanding about Latisha coz they saw it on the TV. It was when Todd got killed they turned nasty." Her lower lip quivered. "It weren't my fault. It weren't even my dog. He'd been told not to touch it. But I got all the blame. I couldn't go out nowhere. The bastards put me windows out and shat on me doorstep."

Greene was giving Liz a very judgemental look. "What about his father?"

"What? Tod's father? What about him?"

"Was he upset at his son's death? Enough to want to get back at Kelly, maybe?"

"I dunno what you're on about, mate. He never even knew he'd been born, never mind died. My Kell wanted nothing from him. She was very independent."

"And Zia Haq? Did you or Kelly have any contact with his family after the death of Latisha?"

Liz got restive again. "See? You see why I had to get away? You're raking things up, like I said. I don't want to think about them things. I want a bit of peace."

That pissed Greene off. "Answer the question, Liz." His pale skin had gone beetroot.

"I didn't never have no contact with them Haqs," she yelled. "I wouldn't know them if I passed them in the street. Same with Kell. Why are you hounding me? I ain't done nothing."

"How can we get in touch with Leanne Turnbull?"

"You're a copper and you're asking me? Why don't you try the phone book?"

"London?"

"Course."

"You don't know her address?"

She thrashed around a bit more. "If I tell you will you fucking go?"

She jumped up and rummaged in a big black patent handbag on top of a china cabinet. She brought out a piece of paper and threw it at him. Mortimer grabbed hold of a corner of it. On it was written a Maze Hill address and telephone number.

"Thanks." Greene was up and making for the door. "You've been very helpful."

Mortimer squeezed Liz's arm in encouragement. When she caught up with Greene at the bottom of the barren garden, he was already on the phone to Chaudhuri.

Thirty-Six

Chaudhuri had hardly glimpsed the sign to Minstead before it was gone. He'd planned to stop and visit the grave of his hero on the journey back to London. But like so much of life it was an opportunity missed. He watched the woodland road to the village wind away from him as for the umpteenth time his mobile rang. From then on he was so preoccupied, the next sign he noticed was for Virginia Water. The country was ending. He threw his mobile on the back seat and undid his tie.

"I've just been speaking to Crawford. Leanne Turnbull's not at home and hasn't been seen by the neighbours all week. It's unusual, apparently, since she doesn't work. The husband's home in the evenings, so we'll drop in on him later. Crawford's got the house under surveillance and if Leanne shows he'll ring us. For now, we're left with the Imperial Masons' Hospital at Ravenscourt Park. Liz refused to answer any more questions or even open the door, so I've told Greene to stand by for a bit in case we need a warrant. I've got Ellis trying to trace Kelly's GP and get a look at her medical records. But this hospital has a private IVF clinic, so it must be where she was treated as a surrogate, surely? Why would she arrange to meet Leanne there otherwise? If so, they'll be able to tell us the name of the couple she gave birth for. And I wouldn't be surprised if it turned out to be someone we've recently met."

It was one o'clock when they parked in the grounds of the Imperial Masons' Hospital. Built in the 1930's, it looked like a cruise ship, a terrace girdling each storey like a passenger deck. Its gardens, mostly lawn and beds of annuals, were as boring as the park they overlooked. Not a soul was to be seen. The circular entrance hall had a domed ceiling from where the Masonic emblem hung, the same design repeated in the inlay of the parquet floor. Against the walls urns of silk flowers topped classical pedestals. A lone woman slumped in one of the green leather chairs.

Behind the reception desk sat a large, powerful man in security guard's uniform, a shabby tiger tamed by his sedentary occupation. Chaudhuri presented his warrant card.

"Good afternoon. I'd like to speak to someone in charge of the IVF clinic, please."

The guard looked up and pushed his glasses more firmly onto his nose. "The Churchill?" He had a Geordie accent, soft and plaintive. "It's not open, sir. There's no one there."

"I see. When will it be open?"

The guard looked at his watch. "Should be open at two. I say 'should be', but sometimes it's more like three when they haven't any egg collections. Depends on when their first appointment is, see."

"All right, is there someone else in the hospital who

can help? I need to access the clinic's records as quickly as possible."

The guard shook his head. "There's no one here who can do that for you. The clinic's a separate concern, see? Nothing to do with the rest of the hospital."

"Who's the senior person in charge of the Churchill Clinic?"

"That'll be Professor Gregson. He's based at Hammersmith Hospital."

"Phone him, will you – yes, do it now – and tell him I need to see someone with access to the records immediately. Inspector Chaudhuri's the name."

The guard did so; informing Chaudhuri in his soothing old-fashioned voice that someone would be with him as soon as possible. Chaudhuri thanked him.

"In the meantime, you may be able to help me. Have you ever seen this person?" He took out a photograph. "Her name's Kelly Parker."

The guard examined it with interest. "Looks a bit like the poor woman who got murdered here a couple of days back. I remember the picture in the paper. Parker wasn't her name, though, if memory serves me."

"You're right. She was known more recently as Kelly Houghton. We believe she was on her way to see someone here at the hospital the day she met her death. Have you had anyone asking about her?"

The guard opened his mouth and drew breath. "Don't tell me that's who she's been waiting for all this time. Don't tell me she's been waiting for the one who was murdered."

"Who are you talking about?"

"That lady over there." He indicated the woman in

the chair, who stood up and gave them an anxious look. The guard lowered his voice. "She's been here every day this week. Leanne Turnbull her name is. She tells me that every morning, though I'm not likely to forget. She walks in in a daze, reminds me if anyone asks for her she's over there by the coffee machine, and sits in that chair for the rest of the day. Still there when I knock off at five."

"Who does she say she's waiting for?"

"Somebody called Kelly Field. Crikey," he struck the top of the desk, "the same Christian name. It's quite common, though, so I didn't connect it with the woman in the park."

"No reason at all why you should. I'll just have a quick word with this lady."

"She doesn't cause any trouble." He seemed concerned he might have made some for her. "She just sits there staring into space and watching the door. No trouble at all, though."

"I'm sure she isn't. Thanks for your help. Give me a shout when the person from Hammersmith arrives, will you?"

He went over to the woman, holding out his warrant card for inspection.

"Mrs Leanne Turnbull?"

"Yes."

"I believe you're waiting for someone called Kelly Field?"

"What's happened?" She looked at him with a mixture of apprehension and hope. "I was supposed to meet her here. I been here every day since Monday. What's happened? Is she coming?"

She was over weight, almost obese, her dark hair scraped back in a ponytail. Her broad peasant face glowed with rosy cheeks. She wore trainers, pedal-pusher trousers, and a hooded tracksuit top.

"I think it would be better if we talked privately," said Chaudhuri. He called to the guard, "Is there somewhere we could go?"

"There's the patients' day room down there on the left. There's seldom anybody in there."

The day room had french windows opening onto the gardens. It was at once comfortable and depressing, with beige walls, brown carpet and olive green chairs. In recesses glazed bookcases contained what looked like novels mostly about the Wild West, suitable reading for elderly masons recovering from treatment.

Chaudhuri indicated one of the green chairs.

"Let's sit down, shall we, Mrs Turnbull? I'd like you, if you would, to tell me and Sergeant James here all you can about Kelly Field. Firstly, I'd like you to tell me the purpose of your meeting with her."

"I never met her," she contradicted. Already she was in tears. "She was supposed to come on Monday, but she never showed. What's going on? I can't think of nuffink till I know where I stand. It's driving me round the twist."

"Yes, I can appreciate that. That's why I want you to tell me about it. I can't help you till you do."

Leanne wiped her tears away with a stubby thumb.

"We was to meet her in the restaurant on the terrace. Four thirty was the time agreed. Three hours, we waited. We got here at half past three and never moved from that terrace till half six, even though it was pouring with rain. It's covered, but it wouldn't have made no difference to us even if it wasn't. We never moved, apart from going out to put more money in the parking meter and ask at the reception now and then if she'd come. A couple of times they put a message out for her over the loudspeaker, coz I was worried we was waiting in the wrong place, though I'd written it down. But she never came."

"You said 'we'. There was someone else with you?"

"Yes. My partner, Duane."

"I see. You were both expecting to meet Kelly? Why?"

"She was a surrogate mother." She said it in the way she might say teacher or bus driver or any other everyday occupation. "She was going to have a baby for us. We can't have none of our own."

"You'd met her before, had you?"

"No. But I spoke to her on the phone. Really, really nice, she sounded. Understanding."

"How did you find out about her? Through an advertisement?"

"Oh, no. Nuffink like that. It was through a woman at bingo. Liz Parker, she's called."

She swallowed and adjusted herself in the chair. He could tell she was looking forward to giving him a full account.

"We was talking one time about babies, and I was saying how devastated I was not having any, and someone said I should try IVF, and I said I had, and it hadn't worked, and then Liz said I should try surrogacy. She said she personally knew of someone who'd helped a couple have a baby, and she'd transformed their lives.

She was like a saint, she said, giving people what they most wanted."

It energised her, this subject of her sterility. Her cheeks shone.

"Well, I couldn't stop thinking about it, and the next week I asked her to tell me more. We went for a quiet cup of coffee, and she said if I was really, really like interested, not just messing about, she might be able to speak to this woman for me. I said I was really, really serious like, and she promised to phone her the next night and let me know."

Her thick lower lip jutted out like a child's, ready to cry.

"It weren't good news. The woman didn't want to put herself through it again, she said. She really like felt for me, but she'd ended up out of pocket the last time, and it wouldn't be fair to rob her own child again, would it? I said I'd pay her well, and Liz got the hump, and said they wasn't allowed to take payment, they was benefactors. Expenses they could take but payment never. I said I'd pay expenses and asked how much they'd come to, and she said they could sometimes be up to ten grand, to cover loss of earnings. But no matter what the amount, the woman didn't want to know, Liz said. She'd been through enough last time, what with medical tests, and questionnaires, and forms and what have you. A private arrangement, just between her and the couple, she might one day consider, but not in the near future."

She turned her head to the window and gave the garden a grumpy look.

"Well, I asked what a private arrangement meant.

Did it mean she'd have to sleep with the husband? Liz laughed and said it wasn't even necessary to see the husband. Artificial inseminy…what's the word? Insemiation was what she was talking about."

She lifted her round dark eyes to Chaudhuri then dropped them. She rubbed the back of her left hand with her right. They were the hands of a fat child, the nails short and embedded.

"Well, I thought about it, and me and Duane discussed it, and it seemed silly not to take advantage of something. Why shouldn't we have a baby if there's a way? People's always being surrogates, aren't they? You hear about it all the time on breakfast TV. And if *they* have them, why shouldn't we?"

She stared at him, waiting for his response. He nodded and smiled. It seemed to encourage her.

"Anyway, next week at bingo Liz called me aside. She said she might be able to help. I said, had the woman agreed to have a baby for us? And she said not to get me hopes up, but to have a chat with her. Her name was Kelly Field. I gave Liz me phone number, and Kelly rang me next day."

She gave a maudlin smile. "She sounded really, really nice. She had a fun loving, bubbly personality. She told me if we was to meet for a talk, she'd need me to send her three hundred quid coz she lived on the Isle of Wight. I sent it to her in cash care of Liz Parker, like she asked, and we made an appointment for two weeks away – that was Monday."

She wiped her tears with her thumb again, opening her mouth as if saying 'Ah' at the doctor's.

"I was glad we was meeting at a hospital. It made it

more professional like. But, like I say, she never showed. I didn't have her phone number – I hadn't rung 1471 after she'd phoned me, I hadn't seen the need – so I went to bingo the next night to have it out with Liz. But she never showed, neither. The women said her daughter and her grand daughter had just got murdered, so I didn't like to bother her that night, but I rang the next morning and there were no answer. So I come here every day in case I got the day wrong, or Kelly got delayed for some reason. It's driving Duane mad, he says I should give over coz we've been ripped off, but I thought maybe she had an accident. Is that why you're here?" Self-obsessed, she seemed to find nothing incongruous in the suggestion, though in different circumstances she would complain about the police wasting time over trivialities. "Have you come to tell me she's had an accident?"

"Kelly's dead, Mrs Turnbull. We found her body in the park on Monday. Didn't you hear about it? Surely this place must have been buzzing with it?"

"I never noticed." She frowned in disbelief or incomprehension. "I got me own troubles, like I told you. So," she looked at him in confusion, "she's not coming, then?"

"No, she's not coming. If I were you, I'd go home and forget about it."

"Forget about it?" She dwelt on this for a second. "But what about me three hundred quid? Do I get it back?"

"I very much doubt it. Try to think of it as a loss at bingo."

With a wail she burst into tears, for some reason

flapping her hand in front of her face like the flipper of a sea lion.

"They haven't heard the last of me. Forget about it? I don't think so. Someone's head'll roll over this."

"Why not have a cup of tea? Come on, Mrs Turnbull, you've been through an ordeal. A cup of tea from the café will do you good. Make a change from that machine stuff. Have something to eat as well."

Red-faced and howling, she let him take her arm. They were in the corridor on their way to the restaurant when a voice rang out in the entrance hall.

"Tom! Tom Chaudhuri! The very man I'm looking for."

Thirty-Seven

Ashok Sen Gupta came bustling along the corridor, a lock of hair that he wore over his premature bald spot fluttering like a black wing. He was tall and gaunt with eyes like black olives glistening in oil.

"I knew it could be no one else," he panted, showing uneven but very white teeth. "When they said an Inspector Chaudhuri was waiting, I knew it must be you. What can I do for you, Tom? Come along to my office and tell me all about it."

"I thought you worked in Birmingham." Chaudhuri allowed himself to be led away, leaving a disgusted James to cope with Mrs Turnbull.

"Got a transfer to Hammersmith last year."

"But you work here at The Churchill, too?"

"A few hours a week – private patients."

He preened. Same old Ashok. Even as a young boy he'd been a snob. His family kept a grubby corner shop in a Kilburn terrace, thought people with money were wiser and better than those without, and had a downstairs bathroom paved floor to ceiling in marble.

"How's your father keeping?" Ashok put an arm

round Chaudhuri's shoulders.

"Great. He's got a dog."

"Really? That'll give him an interest. Oh, but it's good to see you, Tom. You must come for a meal one night. Amita will be delighted. Here, take my card while I remember. We're in Pimlico, right next to the river. Fantastic place. I've got a view from my balcony straight into the MI6 building. Always makes me think of you."

"Of me? Why?"

"Oh, I don't know – similar line of work, I suppose – ferreting information out of people. Still footloose and fancy free, are you? It's about time we packed you off to Kolkota to find you a nice Bengali wife. Bet you could do with the dowry on a policeman's salary, eh? All right, I'm only joking, keep your hair on. At least you've got some to keep, you glamorous bugger. Here's my office. Now, you want to look at our records, am I right? Any particular time? Any particular person?"

"A woman of the name of Kelly Parker, for starters. I want to know if she was a surrogate mother for any of your patients...or is it clients? Better go back about seven years to begin with. She'd be about twenty at the time."

While Ashok unlocked a cabinet and busied himself with a box of compact discs

Chaudhuri sat on a corner of the desk and surveyed the room. Ultra sleek, it might never have been occupied until now. There was not even a pen to indicate anyone worked here. Ashok had always been neat to the point of priggishness, his schoolboy hair parted at the side and combed flat, his studiousness and ingratiating self-discipline sinister. He'd been a taleteller, shooting up his hand in class to split on someone. After all these years he still got on Chaudhuri's nerves.

"Get involved with this surrogacy lark, do you?"

"Lark? You sound like Joe Gargery in *Great Expectations.*"

"Racket, if you prefer."

"Oh, really, Tom. It's not a racket. It's perfectly legal."

"Not in most countries it's not."

"I know, but this country's different – got more sacred cows than India."

He laughed the way he used to laugh in class when someone made a mistake.

Chaudhuri found himself clenching his teeth.

"Causes quite a bit of confusion as far as I can make out – who's the rightful mother, and so on."

Ashok waved a long thin hand as if to swat away uninformed views and inserted a CD into the computer.

"There's no confusion. Obviously the woman who gives birth is the rightful mother unless she chooses to forego that right. After all, without her the child wouldn't be born at all. She's the vital receptacle."

"That's the criterion, is it? Apply the same rule to test tubes, do you?"

"Test tubes? What on earth are you talking about, Tom?"

"They're responsible for the birth of a child in IVF, aren't they? They're the vital receptacle. I don't hear anyone referring to them as the mother, though."

Ashok shook his head and concentrated on the computer screen. "You're being silly, Tom. And very arrogant over matters you know nothing about. Or has your grasp of science improved since we were at school?" He sniggered then held up a bony finger and waggled it. "We're dealing with human beings here."

Human beings? Humbug. Ashok had always treated others as inferiors. "You're also dealing with ethics. You're redefining the concept of motherhood. And a right bloody muddle you make of it. As if that weren't enough, you leave it to be sorted out by potentially the most unethical person of all – a woman who's prepared to sell her child."

Ashok frowned. The hair between his brows bristled as the skin creased.

"We have firm rules and laws which clients are made aware of before they embark on treatment."

"Inhuman rules – rules drawn up by those with so little understanding a robot would do a better job."

Being disagreed with made Ashok girlishly shrill. "As for selling, that's nonsense."

"No, you call it expenses to cover your own back. You make me sick. You break hearts with your firm laws and rules, but you've no regrets. You've made a packet and washed your hands by then. Tell me something – supposing you brought one of these babies into the world and neither woman wanted it, what would happen then? Suppose it was disabled or something and neither of them had bargained for that? Would *you* take it and look after it? I mean, someone, somewhere must take responsibility, surely? Or would the poor little thing go straight into care?"

Ashok flounced to the cabinet, brought out another CD and slammed the drawer shut.

"I'd love to discuss ethics with you, Tom." He made

it sound as if in doing so he would annihilate him. "But some other time. I'm afraid at the moment I'm in a bit of a rush. Now, let's see. Here she is. Kelly Parker, born twenty-third of May in South East London. She's the one you're interested in, is she?" To show he was unaffected by their disagreement, he reached out and clapped his hand on Chaudhuri's knee.

"What's she been up to?"

"Murder, amongst other things." Ashok's smile wavered.

"You're joking."

"No, I'm not. Have you got the details there of the people she was surrogate for?"

"Yes." He looked more unsettled than Chaudhuri had ever seen him. "Sit down and scroll through. I'll do you a copy of the disc when you're ready. In the meantime, I'll see if there's anything in the archive cabinet. We keep the less important documents in there, thank-you cards and photos of babies and things."

He unlocked a drawer and flicked through tightly packed folders, each with its hospital number printed on the corner.

"Yes, here's a photo. Two women and a man. Don't recognise them – before my time, I'm afraid. But it was obviously taken in the gardens out there. Any use to you?"

Chaudhuri turned from the screen to look at it. The three people seemed idyllically happy, like the best and closest of friends. The man was wearing a dinner suit. The woman, linking arms with Kelly, was in a lamé evening dress beneath a full length black coat with a hood. Raven's coat, black as a raven's back.

"Anyone familiar?" Ashok looked at the photograph over Chaudhuri's shoulder.

"Yes. This person here – that's Kelly Parker."

"Right. And she's the one you want for murder, is she?"

"My mate Trent would if she weren't already dead. But it's the other two I'm interested in. Don't look like murderers, do they? But one of them is." He felt a lump rise in his throat.

"Good God. Why?"

Chaudhuri looked into Ashok's lively, ruthless face. Unlike the people in the photo he had everything he wanted. He was a bastard yet things would always go well for him. For a second Chaudhuri wanted to hit him. He looked away.

"It's a bit complicated. I'll save it for another time." He stood up. "Ashok, you've been invaluable. I'll give you a ring as soon as I get back and explain."

"Back? Back from where?"

"The Isle of Wight. Got to catch the first available ferry."

Thirty-Eight

A mist had come down. On the Solent foghorns bellowed like sea monsters lost in a miasma of grief. James phoned Trent to tell him they were back then phoned the Painted Plough to rebook their rooms.

They drove across country down darkening lanes. Sometimes the mist lifted. Then as they turned a corner it would be hanging before them like a curtain of ectoplasm. Lights from ships far out at sea winked through the vapour.

On Westover Down Trent joined them. The mist was thinner here and floated in strips around the Longstone. A glow from one of the windows at Westdown Farm told them someone was at home. Peter Rogers answered their knock.

"What, still working, gentlemen? Come in. Dad's in the barn but he shouldn't be long. Have a drink? I'm sure you deserve one on a night like this."

They refused the drinks politely as they were shown to armchairs by their host who was now wearing a watchful expression. Once they'd sat down Chaudhuri spoke.

"What was the cause of your wife's death, Mr Rogers?"

"My wife?"

"Yes. What did she die of?"

"Why do you want to know?"

"I believe it may have a bearing on the death of Kelly Houghton. Or Kelly Parker, as she was known to you. How did your wife die?"

Peter looked at each of them in turn as if he doubted the reality of their presence. "She killed herself." He reached out for a chair and sat down.

"When did this happen?"

"Five years ago."

"I see…about the same time as your child died…the child for whom Kelly Parker was a surrogate mother."

His elbows resting on his knees, Peter covered his face. His hands muffled his voice.

"Alison – that's my wife – couldn't bear to live knowing what we'd done. But for us, Catherine need never have been born."

The three policemen remained silent. Peter moved his hands from his face.

"Catherine was the name we chose, though Kelly called her Latisha. She kept her, you see. It was her right. The surrogate has a six-week period after the birth in which she can decide whether to do so. And Kelly did. In the eyes of the law, she was the real mother."

He stared ahead of him as if looking into the eyes of the law with disbelief.

"What made you choose Kelly as a surrogate?"

He shrugged.

"What quality would you look for? The most basic

and superficial one – is she, like a stock animal, capable of carrying a healthy child to term. There's little point dwelling on her character because you can't get to know her in the time available. Like all irresponsible people, you simply hope for the best. You trust to the discretion of the organisation that recruited her; trust that she will, when the time comes, hand over to you the child that the law says is hers. So you see, there's dishonour on all sides. The only honourable thing would be to treat such a woman like the outcast she ought to be. To remain childless rather than risk a helpless human ending up in her care."

His face flushed red.

"Power-crazed fascists. They're self-sacrificing paragons if they give the child to a couple of strangers, and super-humanly maternal if they decide on a whim to keep it. Literally on a whim, the mood of the moment. Would you say such a woman was fit to be a mother? I say she's so unfit she should be sterilized. The law should punish her. And I who colluded in it should be punished. Corrupted and corrupting, I should be punished."

From the look of him, Chaudhuri thought him already punished beyond endurance. His shoulders shook. It appeared at first that he was crying. But he was laughing as though teetering on the edge of sanity.

"She's dead, isn't she? Kelly, I mean. Wiped off the face of the earth. If only it could have happened before she harmed my Alison. Why does God allow such rubbish to exist and let my Alison die?"

He got up and stood before the portrait of the young girl over the mantelpiece.

"Sometimes, after our daughter was born, Kelly would let us call at her flat in Woolwich to see her. She put a stop to the visits before long, but at first she enjoyed gloating. Alison put up with whatever she dished out. She always left money and presents. She even tried to be friendly with that Pakistani turd. He broke my baby's neck, do you know that? He broke her little neck and my Alison hanged herself. But a neo-Nazi killed him. That's justice. That gladdens my heart. First torture, then execution. That makes me want to dance for joy."

For a moment it seemed as if he would do just that. But the impulse was short-lived. He remained before the childhood portrait of his wife and stared at it with agonized longing.

"Did you kill Kelly, Mr Rogers?"

"Kill her?" He smiled in what might have been ecstasy. "Need you ask? Of course I killed her."

"Why did you wait so long?"

"Because I couldn't find her. I tried. I called at her flat several times. But no one would tell me where she was. She seemed to have vanished into thin air. And all the time she was here, literally in this house, without my realising it. Dad always gave her time off when he had anyone staying, so I never saw her. Then last week, Thursday it was, I went to Newport to get some seafood from the fishmonger's. Dad's fond of seafood. And it was then that I saw her. I looked across the road straight into her eyes. For a few moments I was happy again. That I would kill her was certain – where and when, the only questions. I decided on London as the safest bet. I killed them both, her and her kid." He straightened his shoulders. "You can arrest me now."

"How did you know she was going to London?"

"She told me."

"You spoke to her?"

"On the phone, yes. I found her number in Dad's book. I told him I'd seen her, you see, and described her and the kid with her. A kid in a wig. And from my description of the kid he realised I was talking about his cleaner. He was pole-axed, I can tell you, to realise she was the one who'd been surrogate for Alison."

The room with its log fire was warm. But Chaudhuri felt cold. He knew Peter had made no phone calls to Kelly.

"You must have had quite a chatty call if she told you she was going to London. Unusual in the circumstances. What exactly did she say?"

Peter scowled. "I can't remember. I don't want to remember. I don't want to think of her alive except for her last moments. I want to remember following her and killing her."

"Where did you kill her?"

"In the park."

"Which park?"

"The name of it, you mean? How should I know?" There was wildness in the way he flung up his arms. "What does it matter? It was somewhere in London. I just followed her and when we came to the park I killed her."

Chaudhuri contemplated him.

"I seem to remember Sergeant James mentioning to you yesterday that Kelly was murdered in a park. But if it was by you, I should have thought you'd have recognised it. I should have thought it would be engraved on your memory. How many times have you walked through Ravenscourt Park with your wife on your way to the Churchill clinic?"

Peter hesitated for no more than a second. "I noticed nothing but her face. And I smashed it. I smashed it."

"That's how you killed her?"

"Don't try to trick me. You know how I killed her."

"No, Peter. He knows how I killed her."

They turned to Alec Johnstone. At the sight of him Peter threw back his head and sobbed. Alec went to him and took him in his arms.

"You'll forgive him for lying. No doubt each one of you would do the same. I'd have come to you eventually, Inspector, and confessed. I meant to do it when you called yesterday. But at the last minute I lost my nerve. There now, Peter, don't cry anymore. I don't mind prison. If it were capital punishment, I wouldn't mind. It's all the same to me."

He rested Peter's head on his shoulder.

"All these months I'd no idea the woman responsible for so much tragedy in our family was working as my cleaner. I knew her as Kelly Houghton. It didn't occur to me that she was also Kelly Parker. But on Thursday Peter told me he'd seen her here on the island. And when he described Jade, I knew for certain who Kelly Houghton was."

He took Peter's hand and led him to the sofa.

"She'd told me she was going to London, though I already knew. She'd used my phone to set up the meeting and I overheard some of it. I wasn't eavesdropping. At the time I thought no more about it except that it was typical of her not to ask when she wanted to make a call, as if I might refuse. I never refused her anything. But she was both ungrateful and mistrustful. However, this is by the by. A few days after that call, she told me about her trip and asked if I would look after Jade. As I said yesterday, I declined. I didn't want the hateful child monopolising even a second of the time I should spend with Peter. I killed her without hesitation, you know. And the world will feel no loss."

He smiled at Chaudhuri.

"Anyway, as I say, I knew Kelly was going to London on Monday. It was the perfect place, the God-given place, to avenge my Alison's death. On Friday evening, while Peter was cooking the supper, I rang Kelly and told her I was travelling to London myself on Monday. I offered her a lift. Of course she jumped at the chance. To refresh my memory I asked her where in London she needed to be and what time she had to be there. She gave me all the details I needed. Mind you, when she said she was going to Ravenscourt Park hospital it didn't mean anything to me – I'd forgotten, if I'd ever known, that it was the clinic that treated Alison."

An idea occurred to him.

"Do you think…could Kelly have been on her way to do the same thing again? Do you think I might possibly have saved some poor couple from her? If I have, then God is merciful. I thank Him for that."

He closed his eyes as if praying. When he spoke again he was practical, almost chatty.

"Once I knew exactly where she was going, I got out

my London A-Z and studied the lie of the land. When I saw the park on the map, I decided to kill her there, if possible. Lots of murders happen in parks, don't they? With this plan in mind, I rang her again on Saturday night to say I couldn't take her to London after all. I told her my car had broken down. I was very apologetic. I even phoned early on Monday morning, ostensibly to apologise again, but really to make sure she was still going. She was. So, telling the most terrible lie to my son-in-law here about a dying friend," he patted Peter's hand, "I set off. I knew there was no danger of her seeing me on the journey, because I'd be travelling by car ferry from Yarmouth. But I took one of my daughter's coats with a hood, not only as a disguise and to protect my clothes, but as a talisman to keep me from flinching. You know the coat I mean, Peter – Alison was wearing it the night we went to that open-air concert at Appeldurcombe House – the last night she was happy. It's hung in the wardrobe ever since. Hung the way she hung from the tree."

He cried out: a sound of primeval agony torn from a throat unused to expressing emotion. Old wrinkled hands lying motionless on corduroy clad knees. Then silence for a moment and speech resumed; eerily matter of fact.

"When my grand-daughter Catherine was killed by Kelly's boyfriend, Peter brought Alison here. He hoped her old home might heal her. She'd become very ill in her mind, you see, and didn't know who we were. She thought we were all against her. In a way she was right. We were trying to deprive her of what she most desired and longed for – death. But she finally gave us the slip one afternoon and hanged herself in that wood up there. The tree grows out of the side of a bank and you can walk along its trunk like a bridge. I once had a go at building a house in it for her when she was little, but I couldn't make it safe, and by the time I admitted defeat she'd grown out of the idea. It was Naomi who found her hanging from it. There was a lot of talk – never to me, of course, though inevitably some of it reached me – about Naomi being negligent and not trying to get help. I'm afraid most people never forgave her. But I did. My daughter wanted to die. In that respect, Naomi showed Alison infinite mercy." He smiled.

"But to return to Kelly. When I finally got to London, it took me so long to find a parking space, and it was so far away from where I wanted to be that I had to run to make sure I'd be in time – very difficult in wellies. Towards the end I was exhausted. My arthritis is always worse in wet weather and the pain in my feet was so bad I could hardly put one in front of the other. I must have looked extremely odd, shuffling along in my dear daughter's coat, but no one notices in London, do they? They simply don't care. And soon it started to rain quite heavily, so I don't suppose I looked odd at all. When I reached the park, I was delighted to see some bushes right next to the gate. I knew that was the gate Kelly and Jade would use, being closest to the tube station. It was also close to a market garden but I reckoned he'd have very few customers on such a day. So feeling confident, I went behind the bushes and waited. Soon I heard their hateful, whining voices. On and on and on they came."

His face was a battleground of conflicting emotions.

"It will seem strange to you, Inspector, but killing them exhilarated me. My strength returned. My mind cleared. I put my bloody disguise into my bag, put on my cap and scarf and left with a spring in my step. As I passed the entrance to the market garden I noticed what I hadn't noticed before – the traffic whizzing by. A gate in the wall was open onto the street. That's the way I left.

"But the evil Kelly caused wasn't finished. I doubt if such evil could ever be finished. I'd planned my disguise with CCTV in mind. I knew no one would be able to make a positive identification from my camera image. But if they saw such a person getting into a particular car, then it would be the car registration that would give me away. So on the ferry home I was especially careful to look different from both disguises I'd worn in London. This time I wore my woolly bobble hat but without my overcoat. On board I stayed locked in the lavatory for the entire journey. I thought I was safe. And till almost the last minute I was. It was when I was disembarking that I was seen.

"I waited to merge with the crowd before going down to the car deck and as I prepared to drive off I adjusted the sun visor to obscure my face further. Then I got the feeling I was being watched. I looked around and saw Emily MacArthur staring at me."

Peter moaned and Alec grasped his hand.

"I don't know if she actually recognised me but she was looking at me as if she thought she ought to recognise me. We were never what you might call friends but she and her brother used to come to the farm for vegetables years ago. Anyway, I couldn't risk it.

I followed them home and killed them. I did it for you, Peter." He raised his hand to his lips. "I wish I hadn't done it. But I didn't want you to be alone. Catherine dead, Alison dead. Why should God try to take me from you as well? I had to be free for you."

He wept in the soundless way of men, eyes screwed up and his body shaking. Exhausted, he leaned back resting his head against the sofa for a while.

"Poor Peter, you were so hurt when I left you that Monday morning, even though I said my friend was dying. That was prophetic, wasn't it? But you didn't believe me, did you? Did you think it was an excuse because I was bored of your company? No, never, never bored. Never happier than when you're here."

He raised his head and looked at Chaudhuri quite severely.

"Peter knew nothing about the murders. I hid all the papers and made sure we did something else when the news was on. It wasn't until you called yesterday that he started to suspect."

He stood up.

"Right, Inspector, I'm ready to go. You'll find the bag with the coat and the knife in the far left-hand corner of the barn. The wellies are beside the bag. I love you, Peter. You'll take care of Shirley, won't you? I shan't say goodbye to her – better not."

Thirty Nine

It was one of those endless days on the Isle of Wight when it seems night will never come: when time, sick of dawning on a less perfect tomorrow, decides to stop and make a sparkling moment in an English evening last forever. From the police station forecourt Trent waved as Chaudhuri and James drove away.

Newport was still bustling. Chaudhuri craned his neck as they passed Abigail's hair salon. It was so resolutely closed it looked as if it would never open again. James cocked a thumb over his shoulder.

"That's Lugley Street back there, haunted by the Mauve Lady." For the past few days he'd had his nose in Gay Baldwin's *Ghosts of the Isle of Wight*. "And see that charity shop on the corner? That's where they used to have public executions. Burning alive, I shouldn't wonder," he added with what Chaudhuri considered unnecessary enthusiasm. "Drawing and quartering at least." (Least? What was *least* about it?) "And you see that lovely old building down there – that used to be the council offices. Terribly haunted, it is, *and* that hardware shop further along."

359

Chaudhuri rolled his eyes. "You should pair up with Dougie Benson. I thought you were an atheist. Aren't you supposed not to believe in anything?"

James shook his finger. "Correction, I don't believe in *religion*. I don't believe in *God*. That doesn't mean I don't believe in life after death."

"Christ, what a thought. That's the worst of all bloody worlds. No God, just life in all its sinfulness going on for eternity? And no hope of any intercession? What do you want to believe in a horrible thing like that for? I'd rather have annihilation than that."

James grinned. "You tell yourself that when the time comes."

They had reached Maryford, the sight of whose castle drew from James yet more ghostly anecdotes, when Chaudhuri noticed a woman coming out of the Co-Op. In a white trouser-suit and sunglasses, she looked so bright she seemed to shimmer.

"That's Verity Shaw. Pull up a minute, James, and I'll have a quick word."

As if Verity were a villain he was chasing, he leapt out of the car almost before it stopped.

"Evening, Ms Shaw. Beautiful one, isn't it?"

She wasn't the first person he'd accosted like this to shrink from him. "Oh, it's Inspector…I'm sorry, I can't remember how to pronounce your name."

"Chaudhuri as in *chow*. Though I like the way the French pronounce it best – *chaud*, meaning *warm*. Anyway, my sergeant and I are going back to the smoke. Thought I'd stop and say goodbye when I saw you."

"How extremely kind of you. I hope you have a pleasant journey."

She was as condescending as the lady of the manor and with her eyes shaded her smile looked artificial. He was disappointed. Then it dawned on him – she was embarrassed. Policemen, like doctors and dentists, aren't always the most welcome of companions. It's difficult to maintain a social front with someone who knows your nastiest secrets.

"With any luck, we'll avoid the worst of the traffic," he persisted. "And you're getting your shopping done, I see."

"Yes, just a few things I forgot this morning. I always forget something. But I'm afraid I'm in a bit of a rush. Ballet class as soon as I've been home with the shopping, then the dramatic society."

"Really? I bet you're their leading lady."

She laughed and took off her sunglasses. There was a faint greenish bruise over her left eye. "Actually, I've never been before. Tonight will be my first time."

"Ah. Exciting or nerve-wracking?"

"Both, I think." She put down her shopping bags. "Before I became an actress, I used to be rather dismissive of amateur dramatics. But when you realise it's the closest you're ever going to get to real thing, it begins to seem quite appealing."

She was as vivacious as usual, but there was a melancholy in her words that matched the evening and his mood. He decided she needed encouragement.

"I'm sure you'll enjoy it. They'll be honoured to have you. And you'll get your pick of the parts, no doubt."

"Oh, no." There was something like panic in her eyes. "No, I shan't be performing. I realise it must sound snobbish, but when you've been a professional it's too big a comedown to perform on an amateur stage. The two attitudes are so different, you see. There's no one as humble and as ready to learn as a professional actor. That probably surprises you, but it's true. It's amateurs who tend to be prima donnas and think they know everything. I've explained my feelings to Bob and he quite understands. No, I'll be directing. And since I've never done it before," she gave a self-deprecating smile, "there are no associations with the past to get maudlin about."

He could sense the resignation in her, as if she'd finally admitted the end of something.

"I don't think you're being maudlin at all. Just realistic. But when you say 'Bob', do you mean Bob Trent?"

She nodded.

"Really? He's a member of the dramatic society, is he?"

"Yes, didn't you know?"

"First I've heard of it."

"Oh, he's their leading light. And after meeting me the other day," this time she blushed, "it occurred to him that I may be willing to help them out. Apparently it's almost impossible to find a director these days. I said I'd certainly go and talk to them. He's going to introduce me to them this evening."

"Is he, indeed? Well, if you decide to take them on, I'm sure they'll consider themselves fortunate. What's the play?"

She raised her arched eyebrows and at that movement he thought what a beauty she must once have been.

"Ah, there's the rub! It's a dramatic adaptation of *Wuthering Heights*. A good one, I believe. Still, I loathe seeing novels turned into plays, don't you? Totally inappropriate. The music of Emily Bronte should be heard only in the head. The language of a play is so different from the language of a novel, you see, as she well knew. But I'll do my best. I've a feeling Bob will make an interesting Heathcliff."

He knew he mustn't laugh. "No one could doubt that Ms Shaw, with you to guide him. Well, good luck for tonight." He hesitated. "By the way, if you happen to come across Abigail Benson at any time, give her my regards, would you?"

"Abby? Why, of course I will Inspector. I'll be seeing her often if she agrees to be in charge of hair and make-up for the play. Her uncle might even help with props. She's moved in with him, you know. Her marriage is over, I gather. Yes, I'll certainly give her your regards."

"Thanks, and...er...you can just say I hope everything works out for her. I...well...she's lucky having such a good friend in you. Very lucky."

He held out his hand to her. He wanted to say more but the words refused to come.

"I'll tell her." She looked into his eyes and he fell half in love with her. "I shan't forget."

The church clock struck five.

"Goodness, Inspector, I must fly. My daughter's coming to the society with me so I'd better make sure she's started to get ready. She needs two hours just to do her hair. Have a pleasant journey. I hope we'll see you again some time, and in happier circumstances."

"I hope so too. Goodbye, Ms Shaw."

He watched her leave through the churchyard then returned to the car and James' astonished stare.

"Finished courting, have you? I must say she's a bit of a babe but you normally like them younger, don't you?"

"Oh, it's not me that's courting her. It's Trent."

"What?"

"Yes, the sly sod. And he never said a word. Well, he's been rumbled James, and I'll let him know it this very minute."

He took out his mobile with a flourish. But for once James had a killjoy look.

"I wouldn't tease him, Tom. You never know, he might be really serious about her. She looked a bit of all right from where I was. And Bob could do with a bit of company, couldn't he?"

With a sigh of resignation Chaudhuri put his phone back in his pocket. "You're absolutely right, James. *Let me not to the marriage of true minds admit impediments.*"

"What's that mean?"

"Dunno," he lied before laughing quietly.

"What's up?" James started the car.

"I'm imagining Trent on stage. That's something else he kept very quiet about. Remind me to book tickets for his opening night. No, you're not going to stop me there, James. I wouldn't miss his Heathcliff for the world."

"Heathcliff?"

"Heathcliff."

And that set them both off until James was sniggering so much he nearly missed the turning that led to the ferry and then home.

Lightning Source UK Ltd.
Milton Keynes UK
UKOW030622160912

199052UK00001B/2/P